THREAT

London 1961. In the dying days of the Macmillan government, George Preston is in control of crime in West London and Rina Walker is his favoured contract killer. When Rina is hired by Soho vice king Tony Farina to investigate the disappearance of girls from his clubs she discovers that they are being supplied to a member of the English aristocracy for the gratification of his macabre sexual tastes. Rina's pursuit of the missing girls becomes increasingly perilous as she grapples with interwoven layers of corruption and betrayal and makes her way, via the louche nightclubs of Berlin, towards a final confrontation with depravity.

THREAT

THREAT

by

Hugh Fraser

Magna Large Print Books
Long Preston, North Yorkshire,
BD23 4ND, England.

British Library Cataloguing in Publication Data.

A catalogue record of this book is
available from the British Library

ISBN   978-0-7505-4477-1

First published in Great Britain in 2016 by Urbane Publications Ltd.

Copyright © Hugh Fraser, 2016

Cover illustration © Brandon Shane Warren/Arcangel
by arrangement with Arcangel Images Ltd.

The moral right of Hugh Fraser to be identified as the author of this
work has been asserted in accordance with the Copyright, Designs
and Patents Act, 1988

Published in Large Print 2017 by arrangement with
Urbane Publications Ltd.

Magna Large Print is an imprint of Library Magna Books Ltd.

Printed and bound in Great Britain by
T.J. (International) Ltd., Cornwall, PL28 8RW

1

London 1961

I pull the van into a side street off Hoxton Square and park behind a coal lorry. I get into the back of the van, lift up my skirt, unclip my suspenders and slide one stocking down my leg. It gives off a crackle and a couple of sparks as I pull it past my toes and shake it out. I gather the sheer nylon into folds and pull it down over my head. I take a black bonnet out of a hat box, put it on, tie the ribbons under my chin and lower the veil. I undo the ropes holding the old bike against the inside of the van, and put my gun and silencer into the front basket under a folded scarf. Bending into my old lady's stoop, I open the back doors of the van, lower the bike onto the road and step down beside it. I lock the van, get on the bike and wobble off along Hoxton Street just as dawn begins to break. I got the bike from an old boy in Portobello Market for five bob and I'm finding out I paid too much for the old bone shaker.

I turn into the street I'm looking for and see the green door of the spieler about halfway along it. I ride past it to a phone box at the far end. I lean the bike against a wall and go into the phone box. I put a threepenny bit in the slot and dial the spieler. After a few rings a bloke answers. I tell him the filth are on their way and put the phone down. I screw the silencer onto the gun, hitch up my long skirt, mount the bike and wait by the kerb. Minutes later the door of the spieler opens and men start filing out. Some get into cars, others hurry along the street in both directions. I see the man I want in a group heading towards Hoxton Street and I pedal in pursuit. As I draw level with him a car comes alongside and blocks my view. I slow down and when it overtakes I get a clear sight of him. I take the gun out of the basket, put three shots into his back and he falls head first onto the pavement. The car stops and his mates scatter. I slip the gun back into the basket, pedal past the car and on round the corner. A bunch of men run past me up Hoxton Street without looking my way.

I cycle back to the van and stow the bike in the back. I get in, shut the doors, take off the stocking mask and my old spinster outfit and put on a pair of slacks and a sweater. As I sit in the driving seat and start the engine I can hear one of the new sirens whooping away on a police car that'll be on its way to clean up the scene.

It's gone six o'clock and the morning rush hour's building up by the time I get near to Harlesden. I stop just beyond the Mitre Bridge on Scrubs Lane, take the bike out of the back of the van and chuck it in the canal. I drive on and turn into the cobbled yard where my lock-up is, open up the doors and pull the van inside. I put my gun and silencer in the old safe under the workbench, stuff granny's clothes into a carrier bag, lock the garage doors and walk across the cobbles to the gate. I go down Scrubs Lane until I see a litter bin, stuff the carrier bag into it and hail a taxi coming the other way. I get in and hope the driver's not going to talk all the way to Maida Vale. Thankfully he's half asleep and I sit back and enjoy the clear peaceful feeling I always get after a job.

The cab turns into the service road in front of my building and I get out and pay the driver. I push open the glass front door. The night porter looks up from behind the mahogany desk in the corner of the foyer.

'Good morning miss.'

'Morning Dennis, still here?' I say, as I head for the lift.

'I'm off in ten minutes miss.'

Dennis is old and bald and quite sure I'm on the game, or otherwise up to no good, but he knows it would cost him his job to try and find out so he contents himself with clocking my body whenever I walk across the foyer. He's out of luck in the leg department this morning as I'm wearing trousers, but my sweater's quite tight and he's making the most of what's on offer. I press the call button and the lift announces itself with a distant clanking and then glides gently into view. Dennis appears beside me and pulls open the metal gate. I step in and give him a smile as I select the fifth floor. He shuts the gate and watches me as I rise out of reach.

The lift stops and a gent in a bowler hat and a pinstriped suit, carrying a briefcase and a rolled umbrella, opens the gate, bids me a tight-lipped good morning and steps aside to let me pass before he gets into the lift. I walk along the carpeted corridor towards my flat at the far end. I hesitate

11

as I reach Lizzie's door next to mine. I expect she's asleep or still at the club where she works, but I can't help knocking in case she's in. As I'm about to go to my place the door opens and she's there, looking beautiful in a baby doll nightie. Her deep blue eyes soften as she reaches for me, pulls me inside and shuts the door. I put my arms round her and kiss her. We hold each other for a moment and she says, 'Been working?'

'Just a bit.'

'Go all right?'

'Yeah.'

I slip my hands under her nightie and stroke her back. She sighs and I feel her relaxing into me. I say, 'Are you alone?'

'Not quite.'

'What?'

'Lordy's here.'

'Oh.'

'He won't be long.'

'Good.'

'Want to have a look?'

'Go on then.'

We walk along the corridor to her bedroom at the far end and go in. The room's dark and I reach for the light switch but Lizzie stops me and puts a finger to her lips. She crosses the room and opens a pair of curtains to reveal a large gilt-framed mirror and a view into the bedroom next door which is bathed in a soft red light. A white-haired old man is crawling slowly across the floor. He's naked except for a studded leather collar around his neck that is tethered to a leg of the bed. His back is criss-crossed with red weals. He strains against the collar in an effort to get to a dog bowl that is just beyond his reach. As he heaves desperately against his tether, Lizzie turns a dial on the wall next to the mirror and we are treated to the strangled whimperings of the Earl of Dunkaid, deputy leader of the House of Lords and owner of a large part of Scotland.

'Hang on a minute while I go and finish him off, we don't want him dying on us.'

She slips off her nightie to reveal a studded black leather bikini, pulls on a pair of black leather thigh boots, and goes to join His Lordship. Through the glass I see her enter the room. She picks a whip up off the bed and lays a few lashes across the old man's back, then she moves the dog bowl towards him with her foot. He lowers his face into the bowl and laps water from it. Lizzie kneels behind him, forces the handle of the whip into his anus and works it vigorously in and out.

The Earl of Dunkaid throws back his head and rolls his eyes as his shrivelled penis grows to the size of a small chipolata. Rasping moans of pleasure ooze from his contorted lips as he grips his manhood and works it frantically back and forth. As he approaches a climax Lizzie slips the dog bowl underneath him in time to catch the few pale droplets that flutter towards the carpet. As she moves the bowl towards his mouth I turn away from the mirror, pick up a copy of Woman's Realm from the bedside table, sit on the bed and start reading an article about Jackie Kennedy decorating the White House.

Lizzie comes in, puts on a silk dressing gown, sits beside me on the bed and pulls her boots off.

13

She puts her arm round me and says, 'It's ok, I've had a wash.'

I let the magazine drop and snuggle into her. We lie back on the bed and kiss and hold each other. As Lizzie's undoing my belt there's a knock at the door.

'Oh fuck,' she says.

The door opens slowly and the Earl's pale face appears.

'I'm terribly sorry to disturb you my dear but I'm afraid I've...'

Lizzie jumps off the bed, leaps to the door, flings it open, grabs him by the collar and snarls at him. 'Get the fuck out of here you snivelling little shitbag before I cut your fucking balls off!'

The Earl drops to his knees and whimpers. 'Yes, yes, yes, I'm sorry, I won't do it again, I'm sorry, I'm so sorry.'

'OUT!'

She hauls him out of the door and along the corridor, barking more abuse at him as he begs for forgiveness. I hear the front door open and slam shut. I'm laughing as Lizzie comes back in with a bottle of whisky and two glasses.

'Silly old thing,' she says.

'He's such a turn out.'

'The whole family's round the twist.'

'Is he ok with you?'

'He's all right.'

'Have you thought about putting the black on him?'

'Why should I when he keeps me and gives me anything I want.'

'As long as you keep knocking him about.'

14

'Simple as that.'

I finish my whisky and stroke her hair. 'Are you expecting anyone?'

She shakes her head, pulling me close for a kiss.

I wake up later, slip out of bed and leave Lizzie sleeping. I dress quietly, go to my flat along the corridor and let myself in. There's a letter on the mat. I pick it up, go into the kitchen and put the kettle on. I open the envelope and take out a card. It's an invitation to the opening of a club called the Rembrandt in Berkeley Square. It'll be a casino full of toffs, high-class pimps and easy girls. A few have opened in Mayfair and Knightsbridge since they legalised gambling last year. I chuck it on the table and make myself a cup of Nescafé. The kitchen door opens and my sister Georgie comes in. She goes to the bread bin, takes out a slice of bread and puts it in the toaster.

'You all right?' I ask.

She nods, picks her satchel up off the floor, takes out a book and opens it. As she sweeps her dark brown hair away from her face I see how lovely she's becoming as she grows up, not that she seems to care.

'What's that you're reading?' I ask.

'Jane Austen.'

'What one?'

'Pride and Prejudice.'

'Do you like it?'

'Yeah.'

I go to the dresser and write down the name of the book. When I was in Holloway on remand I learnt to read properly, which I'd never done at

school because of bunking off all the time. I've
been following what books Georgie's studying in
her English lessons at school. *Great Expectations*
was the last one and I really loved it.

'Do you want a cup of coffee?'

'No thanks.'

'You've got an exam today haven't you?'

'Yeah.'

'What subject?'

'Divinity.'

She's in the middle of her mock O levels. She's
only fourteen and the youngest in her class.

They normally take them at fifteen but her
teachers say she's exceptional. I know how hard
she's worked and I'm so proud of her.

'Do you want a lift to school?'

'No, I'm all right.'

'I'm going to Knightsbridge, I can drop you
off.'

'I want to do some work on the bus.'

She drinks some water from the tap. Her toast
pops up and she butters it, folds it over and holds
it between her teeth. She puts on her school
blazer, packs up her satchel and goes to the door.

'Have you got your dinner money?' I ask.

'Yeah. Bye.'

She's off down the corridor and out of the front
door.

I pick up my coffee cup, go to the window and
look at the gardens and the backs of the posh
houses up the hill on Hamilton Terrace. I'm remembering the night that bastard Johnny Preston
raped Georgie when she was nine, and the blood
spurting all over her when I slashed his throat for

him. Then our little brother Jack passing a few days after and I think it's no wonder she's quiet.

Jack died of the whooping cough in the hospital and I think she blames herself somehow, even though I've told her there was nothing she could have done for him. If anyone's to blame it's me for not taking him to the doctor sooner. I undo my belt buckle and press the point into the palm of my hand until the pain kills the memory.

The phone rings. I rinse the blood off my hand under the cold tap, go into the hall, pick up the receiver and wait. I hear the sound of money being put into a call box.

'Walmer Castle, one o'clock.'

I put the receiver down, head back into the kitchen, put my coffee cup in the sink and go through to my bedroom. The clock beside the bed says twenty to nine. I take off my sweater and slacks, open the wardrobe and take out a dark blue fitted dress with three-quarter sleeves. I put it on, step into a pair of black leather stiletto heels and select a grey Hermès handbag. I check the effect in the mirror, brush out my bobbed hair and put on light make-up.

I step out of the front door into the sunshine and walk round the corner into Hall Road. My Mini Cooper's parked on the other side of the road, facing towards Hamilton Terrace. I cross the road, get into the car, swing a U-turn back to the lights, turn left and join the traffic heading towards Marble Arch. I wind the window down, switch on the radio, and listen to some toff saying how brilliant it's all going to be with old Macmillan steering the country towards more and more prosperity, as if he's got the faintest idea of what life's like for most people. I twiddle the dial and Ray Charles tells him to *Hit the Road Jack*. An Austin Healey with the roof down pulls up next to me at the lights halfway down Park Lane. The driver's a good looking young bloke with hair down over his collar and his radio's tuned to the same station as mine and up loud. He's smiling at me, tapping the steering wheel and singing along with Ray. A cab driver on the other side of him shouts out, 'Turn that fucking row down!'

The young bloke gives him two fingers and turns it up even louder. The cabby gets out, runs round the front of the cab and punches the young bloke in the face. The young bloke grabs the windscreen and tries to pull himself out of his seat while the cabby keeps hitting him and forcing him back down. The lights have changed and horns are blaring behind us. I slip my shoes off, get out of the car, vault over the bonnet of the Healey, grab the cabby by the collar and crack his head against the roof of the cab. He goes down onto the road and the young bloke sinks back into his seat with his head rolling forward. I jump back over the bonnet, get into my car and roar away as the lights go red.

2

Tony Farina is a big man in a very expensive suit. He shakes my hand, waves me to a seat on a white leather sofa and pours coffee from a silver pot. He hands me a cup and sits on the matching sofa opposite. I can see the dome of Harrods through the tall window behind him. He looks at me for a moment before speaking.

'You look good Rina.'

I accept the compliment with a nod and wait. 'I am losing girls.'

'What do you mean?'

'From my clubs. Seven girls have disappeared in three months.'

Tony Farina and his brother Luca run most of the clip joints in Soho, as well as a lot of the regular prostitution going on there. They're well known for keeping order with an iron fist.

'Why are you telling me?'

'I want you to find out what's happening.'

'That's not what I do.'

'I know.'

'Then why are you asking me?'

'My people have tried and got nothing. You are not known and can go places a man can't.'

He's not used to being refused when he asks for something. He's put work my way, pays well and he's been discreet; but this is not the kind of game I want to get mixed up in as it involves too many people. I've always kept my head down and got work through third parties. I met him through Lizzie and he put a couple of hits my way. He's got a lot of police on his payroll and if I refuse him he could make things difficult.

'I'll have a look, but I can't say I'll get anything.'

'Good.'

'Is the law involved?'

'No.'

'Any bodies?'

'No.'

'Anything at all?'

'Nothing. I send boys to where they live but they find nothing but maybe a few clothes or something.'

He goes to a desk by the window, picks up a piece of paper and hands it to me.

'This is a list of the names of missing girls, where they worked and their home addresses. They are stupid. If they work only in my clubs the boys make them safe, but they try to be clever and meet punters outside for more money with no protection.'

He takes a fat wad of flyers out of a drawer and hands it to me. 'Expenses.'

I put the money and the list in my bag. 'There's one thing,' I say.

'Yes?'

'None of your lot must know I'm in this.' He thinks for a moment, nods.

'Ok.'

I get up and ask, 'Is your phone straight?'

He nods, gives me a card from his pocket, and shows me to the front door. It closes behind me as I walk across the parquet floor and call the lift.

I've got time to do a bit of shopping in Harrods before I need to be at the Walmer Castle. I wander through the perfume department thinking about dead brasses and wonder how many of the posh girls behind the counters are seeing to a gentleman's pleasure for a few quid on the side. I try a few perfumes and end up buying my usual Chanel and some mascara. I go up to ladies' fashions, try on a few things and come away with a black chiffon cocktail dress with a pleated skirt, and a beautiful dark blue and silver lurex evening dress by Dior that's all clingy and sophisticated. Then it's downstairs to ladies' shoes for a pair of Enrico Coveri stilettos in a dark purple. I count what's left of Tony's money, making it near to three hundred quid, and go downstairs to the bank in the basement. I pay it into a snide account I've got there, using a false passport that I carry for identification.

I drive to Notting Hill Gate and on down to Walmer Road. I park the car and put on an old coat that I keep in the boot so I don't look conspicuous in the pub. The man I'm meeting is sitting at the far end of the bar. He sees me, finishes his pint, slides his fat arse off the stool and follows me into the street. He walks past me and round the corner towards a white Jaguar parked in Artesian Road. He gets in and opens the passenger door. I get in beside him as he takes out a packet of cigarettes and belches beer fumes. He lights a fag.

'Nice job Rina,' he says.

'Where's the money?'

'He had it coming.'

'I don't want to know.'

'Took a right fuckin' liberty.'

'Just give me the money.'

'All in good time.'

'I want it now.'

'It's in the boot.'

'And I get out to get it and you drive off eh?'

'You know me better than that.'

'I know you're a conniving old bastard that would kill your granny for a fiver.'

He laughs.

'You're old Harry's girl all right.'

'Old Harry's girl wants her money.'

He heaves his bulk out of the car, goes to the boot, comes back with a brown envelope, and tosses it into my lap.

'One and a half large, I think we said?'

I take the notes out of the envelope, flick through them and put them in my bag. Bert Davis fancies himself as a dangerous villain but he's just an errand boy for George Preston, who is dangerous. Bert grew up with George and my dad in the Notting Hill slums. He hung onto George's coat tails while he built up a strong firm out of robbery and protection, becoming the most feared man in Notting Hill and Shepherd's Bush. George Preston's son Johnny was the one I killed when he tried to rape Georgie when she was little. Johnny's brother Dave chickened out of taking revenge and made me kill a face from a rival firm who he'd put it about was Johnny's killer. I did it and got grassed for it, but Dave took the rap in the end rather than lose face in front of his father. George knows everything, but he's let me get away with it rather than having it known that his oldest boy was a nonce and his youngest one a coward. Bert looks at me.

'You started a fashion last night.'

'What?'

'Some tom got done in Stepney.'

'Where did you hear that?'

'In the pub.'

'From who?'

'Just some geezer.'

He reaches for the door handle and says, 'You want a drink?'

'No, I've got to get back.'

'How's your Georgie, all right?'

'She's fine thanks.'

'See you then.'

'Yeah.'

I walk to my car wondering why an old sleazebag like Bert Davis is asking about Georgie. Bert follows me round the corner and slouches back into the pub. I sit in the car and have a look at the list of missing girls that Maltese Tony gave me. One of the girls, Mary Weedon, lived in Stepney and worked at a clip joint in Dean Street called the Heaven and Hell Club. If she was only killed last night, then it's a long shot that Tony would have known about it but I've got to start somewhere. I reckon I've got time to go to Stepney and be back in time to get Georgie's tea. I start the car and head along Westbourne Grove into town.

An hour later I've waded through the traffic into east London and I turn off Mile End Road and find the street I'm looking for. I park and walk between the rows of small terraced houses. I can see a mechanical digger knocking eight bells out of the far end of the terrace. They're probably demolishing the whole lot for slum clearance and building a block of new flats. I find the house I want and ring the bell. After a bit I hear someone coming down some stairs and a girl's voice.

'Who is it?'

'Mary Weedon?'

'She's not here.'

'Are you expecting her back?'

'No.'

'Where would I find her?'

'I don't know.'

I hear footsteps going upstairs. I say, 'I'm a friend of her mother's.'

The footsteps stop.

'I've got something from her mother for her.'

She comes downstairs and opens the door slowly. She's a thin, frail little thing of sixteen or seventeen with dark hair, haunted eyes and a pretty face, wearing a silk dressing gown and last night's make-up. She looks frightened. I smile and show her my handbag.

'Like I said, I've got something for her. Can I come in?'

She hesitates, then she nods and opens the door a bit wider. I go in and follow her up the stairs to a room with a threadbare sofa and an unmade single bed against the wall. Drab grey curtains are drawn across a small window. A TV set, with the sound off, is showing some kids' programme with puppets. She turns it off, opens the curtains and turns to me.

'Where's the body?' I ask.

'What?'

'I know she's dead so don't fuck about.'

'Who are you?'

'Never mind that. Tell me all you know, now!'

I take a blade out of my handbag and step towards her. She cowers against the wall and starts crying.

'I found her last night but that's all. I don't know anything!'

'Where was she?'

'In her bedroom next door. She was...'

'She was what?'

'Dead.'

She collapses onto the floor, tears pouring. I put the knife away and go to her. I help her up off the floor and put my arms round her.

'It's all right. I'm not going to hurt you. You've had a nasty shock, that's all.'

She leans against me and sobs. I stroke her tears away and she puts her arm round my shoulder. I help her to the sofa and sit beside her. I can see how terrified she is. I take her hand.

'What's your name?'

'Julie.'

'You're quite safe now Julie. Just tell me what happened and I'll leave you in peace.'

She looks at me. 'It was late. I was in bed.'

'And?'

'I heard Mary come back from the club and she was with someone.'

'Was that normal?'

'Most nights, yeah.'

'Go on.'

'I must have gone to sleep 'cos I suddenly heard her screaming and this thumping and banging.'

'What did you do?'

'I got out of bed and went on to the landing, and then the noise stopped. It was dead quiet and I was scared to go in so I went back in my room and hid under the bed. Then I heard her door open and someone going down the stairs and out the front door. I waited a bit and then I went into her room and found her.'

She starts weeping again. I put my arm round her. 'It's all right.'

She leans into me and rocks against me as she continues.

'She was on the floor, naked, and her neck was twisted round and her back was all bruised. I heard the front door opening and I ran into my room and hid under the bed again and he came upstairs. I could hear him in there moving about and that, until it was almost getting light outside and then I heard him on the landing dragging something along and down the stairs. I opened the door a crack and he's at the bottom of the stairs and he picks up this big plastic sack and he puts it over his shoulder and carries it out the front door. I waited for a bit and went into Mary's room and she was gone and I knew he'd taken her away.'

'What did he look like?'

'I only saw him from the back.'

'Tall or short?'

'Tall, I think.'

She's crying again and I put both arms round her. I'm stroking her hair and soothing her when

I hear the front door open and heavy footsteps on the stairs. The bedroom door opens and a short bald-headed man in a black overcoat walks in.

'What the fuck's this?'

Julie pulls away from me, wiping her eyes. 'We was just talking.'

He looks at me and says, 'Who's this?'

'Just a friend.'

'You ain't got no fucking friends and you should be out on that street girl.'

'I'm not well,' she says.

'I'll give you not well.'

He slaps her hard across the face and she falls off the sofa onto the floor. As he goes to hit her again I say, 'Leave her.'

He turns, and looks hard at me.

'Mind your fucking business and piss off before I chuck you down them stairs!'

'Fuck you!'

He lunges for my neck so I twist sideways and smash my elbow into the side of his head. As he staggers I punch him hard under the chin which snaps his head back and knocks him out. Julie screams as he lands heavily on the floor beside her. I feel the blade in my pocket and think about cutting him and although I'd like to there's probably no point.

Julie gets to her feet. 'Oh my Christ, he'll fucking kill me now!'

'Get some clothes on. You're coming with me.'

'What?'

'You can't stay here.'

'But...'

'It's all right. Get dressed.'

As she goes to the wardrobe and takes off her dressing gown I see how thin she is in her lacy bra and panties. I go onto the landing and have a look in Mary Weedon's room. There are a couple of old armchairs and a bed. I check the wardrobe and the chest of drawers and find them empty. Whoever cleaned up did a thorough job.

I go back into Julie's room and she's dressed in a tight black skirt, an off the shoulder sweater and high heels. She's holding her handbag.

'Ok, let's go,' I say.

She looks at the figure lying on the floor.

'What about Don?'

'Forget him.'

'But...'

'He'll come round in a bit. Come on.'

She takes a jacket from the wardrobe and puts it on. I take her hand, lead her downstairs and out of the front door. There's no one about in the street as we walk to my car and get in. As I drive back along Mile End Road I can feel her relaxing beside me.

'Where are we going?' she asks.

'Maida Vale.'

'What's there?'

'My flat.'

This seems to satisfy her and we drive in silence for a while, but I'm curious. 'Don's your pimp?'

She nods.

'He was lovely at first. Then he turned nasty.'

'That's what they do.'

'Are you...?'

'No.'

The traffic thickens as we reach Pentonville

Road. Julie is turned away from me, staring out of the side window.

'Where are you from?' I ask.

'Bromley.'

'What brought you into London?'

'I ran away.'

'How come?'

'They chucked me out.'

'Who did?'

'My mum and this bloke who moved in with us after my dad left.'

'Charming.'

'They was drinking and fighting all the time and when he started trying to do things to me I told my mum on him and she wouldn't believe me. She called me a slag and threw me out.'

'How old were you?'

'Fifteen.'

'Where did you go?'

'I stayed with my friend for a bit until I got caught thieving then I did a runner up to London.'

'Did you know anyone here?'

'No.'

'How did you get by?'

'I was dossing where I could and robbing shops and that, then I met Don.'

'Where?'

'Victoria Station. You could sleep in the waiting room there, unless the police came and threw you out. He bought me a meal and took me to his house and let me stay with him and he was really kind to me.'

'How long before he had you working?'

'A couple of months. He said he'd lost all his

money on a bet and there were blokes after him who'd kill him if he couldn't give them something and I had to help him out like he'd helped me.'

I turn right off Marylebone Road and drive round the edge of Regent's Park wondering why I didn't rid London of one more lowlife scumbag while I had the chance.

The setting sun's dropping behind the big white terraces on one side of us and there's people walking dogs and women pushing prams and push-chairs in the park. Julie is looking round her in awe.

'Imagine living in one of them houses, eh?'

'You'd get lost I reckon.'

'No one does live in them though do they, it's all museums and that ain't it?'

'People live in them all right.'

'Blimey.'

3

It's almost dark by the time we get to the flat. Dennis has just started his night shift and he looks up from behind his desk as we walk through the glass door and clocks the contents of Julie's tight skirt. He beams at us, wishes us a good evening and scurries across the foyer to call the lift. As it appears from the basement he pulls the iron gates open and ushers us in, almost sniffing Julie as she passes him. When I see that he's about to say something I drop half a crown in his hand and he thanks me ever so much and closes the gates on us.

We get out at the fifth floor and I can see Julie looking worried as we walk towards my door. I stop and put my hand on her arm.

'It's ok. It's just me and my sister. There's nothing to worry about.'

She nods and manages a smile. I open the door and see that Georgie's bedroom light is on. I lead Julie into the hall and turn on the light.

'Let's have a cup of tea, eh?'

I take her into the kitchen, hang up her jacket, sit her down at the table and put the kettle on. 'Back in a sec,' I say.

I pick up my handbag, go in the bathroom and use a nail file to unscrew one of the panels on the side of the bath. I put the money I got from Bert in with the rest of my petty cash and replace the panel, then I go and put my head round Georgie's door. She's at her desk with her school books, writing.

'You ok?' I ask.

'Yeah.'

'Exam go all right?'

'Yeah.'

'There's someone here.'

She looks up from her writing. 'Who is it?'

'A girl who's been chucked out of her flat. She might stay for a bit.'

'Ok.'

'Come and say hello?'

'In a bit. I need to finish this.'

She picks up her pen and starts writing again.

'I'll put the tea on,' I say.

I'm hoping she and Julie'll get on. Georgie doesn't have any friends that I know of. All she does is her school work and reading, and whilst I'm glad she's learning things and doing so well at school I wish I could see her having a bit of fun sometimes and coming out of herself. As I'm closing the door she says, 'The phone's been ringing.'

'All right,' I reply and go into the kitchen. The kettle's boiling, so I fill the teapot and light the gas under the frying pan.

'Fry-up all right?'

'Yeah, lovely,' says Julie.

'I didn't have time to shop today.'

While the fat's melting in the pan I pour a cup of tea and give it to her. I pull down the flap of the kitchen cabinet, lay out eggs, bacon and a tin of beans, and take half a loaf of bread out of the bread bin. Julie says, 'Can I do anything?'

'You can cut the bread if you like.'

I put the bread on the table with the bread knife and turn on the radio. Some old orchestra's playing some classical. Georgie must have had it on the Third Programme. I turn the dial and find Radio Luxembourg and we get The Shadows twanging away. I put the bacon and eggs in the pan and open the tin of beans. Julie finishes cutting the bread.

'This is a lovely flat.'

'Mm.'

I can sense her relaxing as she sips her tea and looks out of the window. She turns to me and says, 'I'll work for you, you know.'

'No you won't.'

'Isn't that what you want?'

'No.'

'Then why...?'

'There's knives and forks on the draining board.'

She goes and picks them up and puts them on the table. I go to her and take her hands in mine.

'I want nothing from you.'

I see tears welling up in her eyes and I put my arms round her and pat her back. There's a pop from the frying pan and I sit her down, turn off the gas, dish up the food, put the plates on the table and call Georgie. When she comes in, I say,

'Julie, this is my sister Georgie.'

Georgie looks warily at her for a moment and then nods a greeting as she sits at the table and puts an exercise book down beside her.

'Doing your homework?' Julie asks.

Georgie nods and butters a slice of bread.

'Georgie's taking her mock O levels,' I say.

Julie looks confused.

'They're like a practice for the real exams they take in the summer.'

'Oh.'

'Didn't you have them at your school?' asks Georgie.

'I don't know. I was gone before they had exams and that.'

I think Georgie wants to ask why but she sees Julie looking uncomfortable and decides not to. I say, 'Your family moved away didn't they?'

Julie nods and we eat in silence until I hear a knock at the front door. I go and answer it and Lizzie's there. We kiss and hold each other for a second then she says, 'Do you want to go to a club opening tonight?'

'That Rembrandt place in Berkeley Square?'

'Yeah.'

A night out with Lizzie is just what I feel like after today. Georgie's used to being on her own in the flat but there's Julie to think of.

'I'd like to but I'm not sure I can.'

'Why?'

'There's someone here.'

'Who?'

'A young brass I got out of a bit of bother earlier.'

'What's she doing here?'

'Nowhere else to go.'

'Give us a look then.'

I smile and open the kitchen door a bit.

'Mmm nice, looks clean. Bring her along if you like,' says Lizzie.

'Maybe. What time do you want to go?'

'About ten?'

'Ok.'

She pecks me on the cheek and leaves. When I go back into the kitchen the girls are sitting in silence. Georgie drinks the last of her tea, stands up from the table, puts her plate in the sink and walks past me.

'Working?'

'Yeah,' she says as she closes the door behind her. I sit at the table and take a last mouthful of bacon. Julie's looking down at her plate and I can tell she's uncomfortable.

'She's got a lot of work to do.'

Julie nods. She looks as if she's trying to say something but can't find the words.

'You all right?' I ask.

She looks at me and I can see tears in her eyes. 'I'm thinking about Don.'

'Well don't.'

'If you knew him...'

'I don't need to.'

'If he finds me he'll...'

She puts her head in her hands and starts crying. I put down my knife and fork, go round to the other side of the table and pull a chair up next to her. I look down at her bowed back and see how thin and delicate she looks. She's too young to be a street girl. If Don doesn't find her and beat her half to death, some other worm'll get hold of her and bleed the life out of her. I sit down and put my arm round her. She turns towards me and puts her head on my shoulder. I think for a minute then I make a decision. I pick up my handbag, go to the bathroom, close the door and unscrew one of the panels round the bath with a nail file. I take the bundle of notes I got from Bert Davies out of my handbag, count off two hundred quid and put it in my pocket. I wedge the rest of the money behind the bath and screw the side panel back on. I go back in the kitchen and take Julie's jacket off the back of the door.

'Put this on.'

'Eh?'

I hold her jacket out for her and she stands up and puts it on. I pick her handbag up off the floor where she's left it by her chair.

'Come on.'

'Where are we going?'

'You'll see.'

She lets me take her arm and I lead her out of

the flat and into the lift. When we get into the car I lock both doors and pull onto Maida Vale. I turn right off Edgware Road at the lights, left at the roundabout and pull into the Paddington Station slip road. I park the car by the entrance to the station, take the money out of my pocket and put it in her handbag. She looks at me in surprise.

'What are you doing?'

'I'm giving you two hundred to get out of London.'

'What?'

'It's that or end up dead.'

'But ... where do you want me to go?'

'Have you got any relations anywhere?'

'I don't know.'

'Well then you go wherever you fancy, where nobody knows you. Get yourself a place to live and a straight job and forget about whoring. Give yourself a chance of having a proper life.'

She's looking at me as if I'm talking Chinese then she opens her handbag, looks at the money, then at me again.

'You'd do that for me?'

'Yes.'

I can see she knows that I mean what I've said. She closes her handbag, and asks, 'Could I go somewhere by the sea?'

'Yes.'

She's quiet for a moment.

'I went with mum and dad once. We was on the beach. It was lovely.'

'Do you remember where it was?'

She shakes her head. 'I was only little. We went on the train.'

'Let's go and have a look.'

We walk into the station and along the platform to the booking hall. I look at the big clock and see that it's just after eight. We join a group of people staring up at the departures board. I ask her if she recognises any of the towns but she shakes her head. I see that there's a train to Brighton in five minutes and one to Bournemouth in ten. I've heard that Brighton's a tough old town so I ask a bloke next to me if Bournemouth is on the sea. He looks a bit surprised and then he tells me it is so I take Julie to the booking hall and buy her a one-way ticket and a platform ticket for me.

The train's waiting at the platform so we show our tickets at the barrier and walk along past the first class carriages. She gets on the train and I shut the door behind her. She turns, lets down the window and leans out. There are tears in her eyes. I hold her hand. 'When you get there, go straight to a hotel or a bed and breakfast for to-night and then you can sort yourself out some proper lodgings tomorrow.'

She nods, pulls me towards her and puts her arms round me. She holds on to me for a moment then she pulls back, and looks at me with her sad eyes.

'Why are you being kind to me?'

A whistle blows and there's a blast of steam from somewhere underneath us and we're all wrapped up in it, coughing and laughing as the train pulls away. I let go of her and watch her getting smaller and smaller until the train curves off on the track and she's gone.

I walk back along the platform towards the

barrier. I've no idea if I've done the right thing, but at least she's out of danger for now.

I can hear the phone ringing as I walk along the corridor to the flat. I open the door, drop my car keys on the hall table and pick up the receiver. It's Bert.

'Rina?'

'Yeah.'

'You need to watch your back.'

'Why?'

'Stepney.'

'What about it?'

'You give a bloke a kicking didn't you?'

'What if I did?'

'And had a young tom away?'

'So?'

'The geezer you slapped was one of Bielsky's and he's been asking around about a bit of blonde crumpet your age with a right hook.'

Feliks Bielsky is a slum landlord who owns large areas of Notting Hill. He lets houses and flats to whores, West Indians and Irish after he's forced out the white people by threatening to beat the shit out of them if they don't make way. He's a dangerous man with some heavy muscle. I check that Georgie's door's shut before replying.

'Does Bielsky know about it?'

'If he doesn't, he will.'

'Yeah. Cheers Bert.'

Soon after our Jack died one of Bielsky's enforcers tried to throw me, Georgie and my mum out of two ratty old rooms that we were renting off him in Notting Hill, but I done a jeweller's in

Hatton Garden and made enough to buy a flat in Portland Road off Bielsky and moved us there. I bought it through someone else because I didn't want anyone to know I had money at the time, as the police were sniffing round about the killing I'd done to keep Dave Preston from grassing me up for Johnny's murder. I met Bielsky then, but I doubt if he'll remember me five years later. He's got an office down Westbourne Grove and another one in Soho. The pimp isn't a problem but Bielsky could be.

My watch says it's nearly ten and if I'm going out with Lizzie I need to get dressed. I look in on Georgie and tell her I'm going out, then I go in my bedroom, open my wardrobe and wonder what I want to wear to the club. I take out the Dior evening dress that I bought earlier. I hold it against me, look in the mirror, and decide it's a bit formal. I look at a couple more things then I decide on a brocade sheath dress with low neckline in a deep red with the Coveri stilettos that I got today. I slip into a black bra, panties and suspender belt, and a pair of ultra-sheer nylons. I slip a blade into the suspender belt, and put on the dress and the shoes. Once I've done my hair and makeup, I say goodbye to Georgie, put on my black velvet coat and walk along the corridor to Lizzie's.

As I get near, her door opens and a really fat woman with a large head and a big mop of black hair comes out. She closes the door, gives me a sour look, pulls her coat round her and waddles off towards the lift as fast as she can. I knock on the door. Lizzie opens it and gives me a long look.

'You look beautiful my darling.'

She pulls me inside and into her arms. I melt into her and feel her warmth and softness and her sweet taste. She takes me to her bedroom and I sit on the bed while she changes into an off the shoulder chiffon dress with a flared skirt and a fresh pair of nylons. When she puts each leg up on the bed beside me to clip her stockings into her suspenders I just want to tumble her into bed and let the club open without us.

'Who was that who just left?' I ask.

'She's a Russian athlete.'

'You're joking.'

'No.'

'With all that weight?'

'It's muscle, silly. She's a shot-putter.'

'A what?'

'They heave this iron ball about.'

'What for?'

'The Olympics and that.'

'Fuck.'

'I know.'

'What does she...?'

'Don't ask.'

I reckon we're best in a taxi to Berkeley Square, in case the pimp who's after me knows my car and happens to be in the West End tonight, so I flag one down on Maida Vale. The driver's a shrivelled up old boy in a flat cap, smoking a fag. I tell him the address. He grunts, puts the flag down and we get in. As we pull away he angles his driving mirror so he can see up our skirts. Lizzie sees him do it, puts her arms round me and snogs me. The old boy swerves the cab and nearly hits a lamp post.

40

Lizzie leans forward and says, 'Do you want me to drive?'

The old boy chucks his fag out the window. 'Fucking three wheelers!'

Lizzie shuts the glass partition.

'What's he on about?' I ask.

'Three wheel trike – dyke.'

'Saucy old git.'

4

We round a corner and drive along the north side of Berkeley Square. The cab stops in front of the club and we get out and walk up the steps. The doorman tips his hat to Lizzie and shows us into the foyer. We walk under a big archway with a statue of some Roman bloke in a toga set into the wall above it. A couple of heavy looking types in evening suits clock us as we cross the marble floor.

One of them stops me and asks me how old I am. When I tell him I'm twenty he waves me on and we check our coats in at the cloakroom. We go up the wide curved staircase and I'm looking at the pictures of people from the olden days on the walls. There's one of a girl and a boy in a sailor's suit sitting on a bench beside a pond. The girl looks a bit like Julie, though I reckon her life was a bit different. We make our way through a babble of upper class voices, braying laughs and chirruping women wearing Norman Hartnell, towards a curved bar at the back. Men inspect us as we pass.

One of them catches Lizzie's eye, quickly turns his back, takes the arm of the woman he's with and moves swiftly towards a side room where people are playing cards. Lizzie laughs.

'Oops.'

We get to the bar and I order a whisky, and a gin and tonic for Lizzie. While the barman's pouring I notice George Preston with Bert and a few of his firm at the end of the bar. George is with a beautiful young redhead who he's ignoring completely while he listens to a grey haired old man with a plummy voice telling a story. The old boy delivers the punchline and gets his laugh from George and his minders. I turn away as George looks along the bar and we pick up our drinks and move off towards the main room. There's a kidney-shaped table in the middle with people seated at it playing cards and others standing behind them watching. As we move forward to watch the action I feel a hand on my arm and a voice says, 'I believe I owe you a drink.'

I turn and see the man with the Austin Healey who I stopped from taking a beating in Park Lane. His cheekbone is a bit swollen and I can see he's tried to cover up a black eye with powder.

'Don't worry about it,' I reply.

'Oh but I insist,' he says.

Lizzie turns and looks him up and down. He smiles at her.

'Your friend here saved me from getting bashed up by a very angry cabbie this morning.'

'She's stronger than she looks.'

'I'll say. May I buy you a bottle of champagne?'

'Why not?' says Lizzie, before I can speak.

The bloke calls a passing waiter and orders a bottle of Bollinger. He's tall and good looking, maybe thirty years old, thin and whippety with a strong jawline and a mop of black hair that falls over his forehead and nearly covers his deep blue eyes. He gestures towards the card table.

'Do you play Chemmy?'

'Not likely,' I say.

'Most sensible of you. Lord Kilgowan's down about thirty thousand and counting.'

He nods towards an old geezer with a moustache, sideburns and a red face who's at the table and looking glum with a pile of markers next to his cards.

'Do you play yourself?' I ask.

'Not since a chap at Oxford relieved me of my entire Michaelmas term's allowance in one evening.'

'Bad luck,' says Lizzie.

'Not sure it was entirely above board actually.'

'He's not here is he?'

'As a matter of fact he is. It's that ginger-haired chap over there.'

'Rina could duff him up for you.'

Our man has a good laugh, puts out his hand and says, 'I'm Nicholas Boulter by the way. Call me Nick.'

The champagne arrives as we're introducing ourselves and we move to a side table. While Nick is pouring, an argument starts at the card table between the dealer and one of the players. Nick looks over.

'Old Biffy Stratherne getting his knickers in a twist.'

Other players and spectators get involved and a woman in a black evening gown starts shouting and throws a drink in a bloke's face. Two minders appear and hustle her out. The player who started it throws down his cards and stomps off towards the bar. An elegant looking type who's been standing behind the dealer and watching the game steps forward, calms everyone down, apologises on behalf of the house and offers drinks all round. Waiters appear and take orders and the game goes on. A couple of girls who were on the edge of the ruck come over to our table. One of them puts her arm round Nick.

'What time are we leaving darling?'

Nick looks at his watch.

'Couple of hours or so?'

The girls nod and move off again. Nick looks at us and says, 'Would you excuse me for a moment?'

He walks over to the table and speaks into the ear of a player who's seated next to the dealer.

The man glances in our direction and says something to Nick, who joins us again.

'I know this is a bit out of the blue and we've only just met and all that, but I'm wondering if you two charming ladies might feel like a trip to the country?'

Lizzie looks at me and replies. 'Tell me more.'

'Well, you see that gent next to the dealer that I was just talking to?' We nod and he continues, 'That is Jonathan the Viscount Brigstock, who's got this country cottage in Hampshire called Ringwood Hall. He's having a few friends down for the weekend and he'd be absolutely delighted if you'd like to come along.'

Lizzie smiles at him and says, 'Why not?

She's clearly got her eye on drumming up more business among the gentry and I'm thinking that since I've just nicked one of Bielsky's girls and that bald-headed pimp is looking for me it might not be a bad idea to get out of town for a couple of days.

'Why not?' I say.

'Jolly good,' says Nick as the waiter arrives with the Bollinger. 'We can go in my car.'

'It'll be a bit of a squash in that two-seater of yours,' I say.

'I'm driving the Bentley tonight,' says Nick.

'Mmm, lovely,' says Lizzie as she raises her glass. 'Cheers Nick.'

As we clink glasses I see Bert Davis come in from the bar. He comes over, leans close to me and says, 'You're wanted.'

I excuse myself and follow him through the bar and along a corridor to a door at the far end. He opens the door, shows me in and closes it behind me. George Preston is sitting at a desk with a bottle of whisky and two glasses in front of him. He's over six foot with broad shoulders and a large head. He used to be a boxer and although he's not young he looks in good shape and quietly dangerous in his handmade suits. He gestures to me to sit and gives me a hard look.

'What the fuck are you doing?'

'What are you on about?'

'I've got enough aggravation with Bielsky and his fucking army already without you battering one of his ponces and nicking a tom.'

'I'll sort it.'

'Fucking right you will. The ponce is called Don Beale.'

'Yeah?'

'Kill him.'

'All right.'

'Before Feliks finds out and gives me a hard time about it.'

'Why would he?'

'He knows you're one of mine and he'll think I'm taking a liberty.'

Even though I've done a lot for George I'll never belong to him or his firm but this isn't the time to tell him.

'Where's the tom?' he says.

'Out of the way.'

'The ponce is in the Three Bells. Bert'll take you there.'

'Who's going to get rid?'

'Bert will. Do you need a tool?'

'No, I'm all right.'

He gets up and opens the door. Bert is waiting outside. He leads me through a door at the end of the corridor, down a narrow flight of stairs and through a door into the street. His white Jag is parked with two wheels on the pavement but he steers me towards a dark brown van that's parked beyond it, which he will have nicked for the job. He opens the door for me and I sit in the passenger seat.

We drive across Regent Street and into Soho. The Three Bells is in Poland Street and Bert parks the van round the corner in Noel Street. I tell him to wait and I walk to the pub and go in. The bar is crowded and it takes me a minute to spot Beale at a table in an alcove at the far end of the room. He's got his head down, talking to a man in a trilby hat and a dark grey overcoat. I go into the toilet, take off one of my stockings and put it in my pocket. I take out my knife, then I notice there's a good long chain hanging from the cistern. I stand on the toilet seat and prise the end of it off the cistern lever with my knife and pocket the chain.

I go back in the pub and move to a place near the door where he'll see me if he looks up. He stands, picks up the empty glasses off the table and clocks me. His face hardens and he puts the glasses down, says something to the other man and pushes through the crowd towards me. I slip out of the door and run to the corner of Noel Street. I take out my powder compact and open it. In the mirror I see him come out of the pub and look around. He sees me and comes after me. I walk round the corner and slip into a shop doorway. I pull the stocking over my head, take the chain out of my pocket and wind an end of it round each hand. As he passes me I step out, get the chain round his neck, pull it tight and drag him into the doorway. He struggles and kicks at me but I push him onto the floor and kneel on his back. I keep the chain just tight enough to strangle him without cutting his neck so I don't get blood on me. He struggles a bit until I feel him go weak and then he's gone. I stand up and see a young bloke and a girl watching from the other side of the road. I take my knife out, step out of the doorway onto the pavement and they see me and leg it round the corner. Bert gets out of the van, opens the back doors and we pick

Beale up and stuff him inside along with the chain. Bert shuts the doors and gets into the van. I take off the stocking and go to his window.

'You all right?'

He gives me a nod, fires up the engine, heads towards Berwick Street and turns south. I reckon Don Beale will be spending the night at the bottom of Shadwell Dock with a tyre lever in his pocket.

I walk round the corner and along Poland Street. Everything looks clear and bright and I look up at the sky and I feel light and relaxed as if I could float up above London. That song where they play among the stars echoes in my head, until the traffic on Oxford Street brings me back to earth and I hail a taxi.

The club's in full swing when I get back there. The mob in the bar are louder and drunker as I weave through them to the ladies' loo. I wash my hands and check my face and neck for any specks of blood. I go back to the bar and see George Preston at the far end with his minders. He looks at me as I walk past. I give him a nod to let him know the job's done and move towards the main room. The crowd round the card table has grown and there's a collective sigh as the house snares another loser. Tony Farina gets up from the game table. He sees me and makes a quick sign for me to phone him as he leaves. Lizzie's at a table with Nick and the two girls who spoke to him earlier. She sees me and comes over.

'What did Georgie Porgie want?'

'Nothing much.'

'You've been ages.'

'Had to sort something.'

'You all right?'

'Yeah.'

I don't tell Lizzie anything about my work if I can help it in case it makes trouble for her.

She slips her arm round me.

'What do you reckon to our Nicholas?'

'Posh pimp isn't he?'

'You fancy this country jaunt?'

'I haven't brought a toothbrush.'

'Just ask the butler darling.'

'Or knickers.'

'He'll lend you a pair of his.'

Nick sees us laughing and comes over. 'Shall we get going?'

'Could we stop by Maida Vale and pick up a couple of things?' says Lizzie.

'Certainly,' says Nick.

He beckons the other two girls and they follow us through the crowded bar, down the staircase and out through the front door. Nick leads us to a silver Bentley that's parked in the square and opens the back door for us. As we get in the smell of expensive leather wraps itself round me and I sink back into the soft seat and relax. While Nick is showing us the cocktail cabinet with its cut glass decanters something makes me look out of the back window of the car. The man in the trilby and dark grey overcoat that Don Beale was talking to in the pub is standing on the pavement outside the club and looking our way. As Nick gets into the driver's seat and starts the engine the man in the trilby crosses the road and gets into a small black car.

Lizzie pours whisky from the decanter, gives a glass to me and the girls and passes one to Nick in the front. Nick proposes a toast to a fun weekend and we clink and drink. He introduces us to the two girls as Jane and Poppy, turns on the radio and Elvis tells his little sister what not to do as he swerves onto Park Lane and accelerates towards Marble Arch. Poppy is blond and sassy in a gold dress with lots of bouncy curls and cleavage. Jane is dark haired, slim and beautiful with a quiet, watchful look about her. Poppy rummages in her handbag and produces a small bottle. She unscrews the cap, shakes some pills into her hand and offers them to us.

'Blues anyone?'

Lizzie takes a couple, swallows them with a slug of whisky.

'Cheers.'

When Jane and I decline Poppy says, 'I've got Mandrax for later.'

'I'm fine thanks,' I say.

Jane shakes her head and Poppy offers the blues to Nick, who palms a couple. She takes the rest herself, slithers over into the front seat, puts her arm round Nick and they have an animated discussion of who was responsible for various excitements and aggravations that happened at the club.

We drive up Edgware Road and Nick pulls the car into the service road in front of our building. The small black car noses into a parking space on the main road. I think about staying in London but decide that it'll be easier dealing with whoever is under that trilby out of town, where he won't have any backup. Lizzie and I go in and up to our floor. I unlock the door to my flat and go in. Georgie's asleep and I leave a note on the kitchen table with a fiver for food. She'll be fine on her own for a couple of days and will probably prefer it. I call Tony Farina's number and I'm about to hang up when he answers.

'What have you got?'

'Mary Weedon.'

'I know. Do you have anything?'

'Not yet.'

'Come and see me Monday.'

'Ok.'

I put the phone down, go to my bedroom, put some clothes and a few bits of make-up in a bag and get my fur coat out of the wardrobe. I take my little Smith and Wesson .38 revolver from the top shelf, check the safety and put it in the bottom of the bag with a spare clip. It's not too powerful but it's good for short range and it's a snub nose so it's easy to conceal. Being a revolver it doesn't leave any bullet casings behind like an automatic will. I slip my fur coat on, pick up my bag and wait for Lizzie in the corridor.

5

Nick swings the Bentley through the gates of Ringwood Hall and as we scrunch round the curves of the drive the headlights shine into the trees and give us glimpses of neat lawns and a rippling lake. There's enough moon for me to make out the house standing firmly at the head of the drive. The 'cottage' Nick told us about is the biggest house I've ever seen. It's like one of the pictures in Georgie's history books, with a massive grey stone front with three rows of tall windows, a square turret thing on each corner and battlements going along the top in between. I half expect someone to start shooting arrows at us when Poppy gives a whoop of delight at the sight of it. There are lights on in a couple of the downstairs rooms. Nick turns off the radio, stops the car by the front door, gets out and takes a bag out of the boot, then he opens the door for us. We get out of the car and Nick pulls on a big metal ring hanging by the door. A light comes on above the door and it's opened by a grey haired old boy in a black tail coat.

'Good evening sir.'

'Good evening Symmonds. I believe His Lordship is expecting me.'

'Indeed sir.'

Symmonds opens the door wide, takes Nick's bag from him and we step into the hall. It's about as big as two tennis courts with a marble floor and three big chandeliers that tinkle as Symmonds shuts the front door. The wide staircase leads up to a landing and then divides and curves off to left and right up to a gallery with another staircase leading off it. There are paintings of olden days' people in robes and big hats looking down on us as if they're not sure we should be there. Symmonds turns to Nick.

'If I may have your keys sir, I shall have your car

taken to the stables.'

Nick hands him the keys. Symmonds beckons to a nervous looking young girl in a cap and apron who's standing at the foot of the stairs with her hands clasped in front of her.

'Jones, please take the young ladies' luggage to the cloakroom.'

The girl nods and comes forward. We give her our coats and she picks up our bags and heads for a door at the back of the hall. Symmonds turns back to Nick.

'Perhaps you'd care to join His Lordship in the long gallery sir.'

'Splendid,' says Nick.

'I trust your usual room will be to your liking sir?'

'Absolutely.'

'With your permission sir, I shall inform you of these ladies' accommodations once I have made the necessary arrangements.'

'As you wish Symmonds.'

A door opens along the hall and a white haired old boy in a maroon smoking jacket appears and heads for the foot of the stairs. As he turns onto the bottom step, he looks over and says, 'Is that young Nicky Boulter I see?'

'Good evening My Lord,' says Nick.

The old chap comes over and holds out a withered hand to Nick. 'How are you dear boy?'

'Quite well, thank you sir.'

'Here for bit of a party with the lad, are you?'

'That's the general idea sir.'

The old fossil looks us over.

'Well, you've brought a fine pride of fillies with

you, eh what?'

'Won't you join us sir?' says Nick.

'I would dear boy but I've to be up at sparrow twitter and to the Atheneum for an emergency meeting with "you know who".'

'Ah. Tricky sir.'

'Damnably so.'

He turns and toddles off saying, 'Goodnight ladies, goodnight sweet ladies, goodnight,' in a fluty voice, as he climbs the stairs.

We follow the butler along the hall, past more paintings and bits of armour, and swords and the like. Poppy takes my arm and whispers, 'That was the Lord Marquess himself, no less.'

The butler stops in front of a door at the far end and knocks. I can just hear a voice above the music.

'Who is it?'

Symmonds opens the door a little. 'Mr Nicholas Boulter and friends sir.'

The door is wrenched open and the card-playing Viscount from the club who Nick told us about is swaying in the doorway. His shirt's off and he's got a bottle of champers in one hand and a tennis racquet in the other. He swipes Nick one with the racquet.

'Nickers, you old bastard!'

'Hello Johnny.'

'And lovely ladies! How bloody marvellous! Come and have a drink!'

We're ushered into the room and a tennis ball sails towards us and hits the half-naked Viscount on the head. He picks it up, whacks it back towards a tall thin geezer with ginger hair who we also saw playing cards at the club.

'Fuck off Benders, we've got company!'

The ginger one drops his racquet and lopes towards us.

'Ben Duckworth. How do you do?'

He gives us each a limp handshake and flops on a sofa next to an old boy who's passed out.

He waves a hand over the body.

'This is the Lord Marchmont. He's rather tired.'

Lord Marchmont replies with a long wet fart and Johnny and Ginger guffaw with laughter while Johnny sloshes champagne into glasses and hands them to us. Ginger gets to his feet and goes to a radiogram that's been pulled out from the wall. He lifts the lid, sorts through a pile of LPs and puts one on. It's Chubby Checker telling everyone to twist again and Ginger takes him at his word. Poppy downs her champagne in one and joins him and in a minute we're all at it, twisting away in a mass of arms and legs and whooping and swooping and I'm loving the feeling as I'm singing along and letting it all go. Then after a couple more tracks Nick puts on some Bossa Nova and goes to the sofa and rolls a joint. Ginger's holding Poppy close and feeling her up, and the Viscount's smooching and snogging Jane. Me and Lizzie are dancing and the joint's going round, and then there's another joint and then Poppy's handing out the Mandrax. There's more champagne and the Viscount's moving towards the door with Jane and Ginger and Poppy following, and Nick's taking me and Lizzie with them. We go across the hall with the music still thrumming, up the stairs and along a corridor into a bedroom with soft lights and a massive four-poster. We're on the bed and clothes are coming off and bodies are slithering and sliding until I don't know who's who and what's what and who cares anyway, and there's sighs and groans and it's going on for what seems like forever. Then there's cries and moans and it's slowing up and calming down until everything's quiet and still.

I open my eyes and I'm lying on the edge of the bed under an eiderdown with a leg round my waist and an arm across my neck. The bedside lights are still on and I can see Nick sitting in an armchair across the other side of the bedroom. He's awake and he's got all his clothes on and I remember that he's not been part of what's gone on. I gently move the arm off me, slide out of the leg's grip and look for my clothes among the various garments strewn around the bed. I find my bra and pants and suspenders and put them on. I pick up a random pair of nylons and hope they'll fit. I lift the edge of the eiderdown and see that my dress is underneath the Viscount who is snoring peacefully with his arm around Ginger's waist and his head between Poppy's thighs. I manage to pull the dress out from under them without waking anyone. As I'm putting it on Lizzie stirs. She slides off the bed, comes to me, puts her arm round me and whispers, 'You all right darling?'

'Mmm,' I say.

I help Lizzie find her clothes. When she's dressed Nick walks over to us. 'Let me show you to your room.'

We go into the corridor and he shuts the

bedroom door quietly behind us.

'What time is it?' asks Lizzie.

'Four-thirty,' says Nick.

'What time's breakfast?'

'Probably nine o'clock or so.'

'Lovely.'

As Nick leads us along the corridor a door opens and a young girl in a maid's uniform appears carrying a towel. She starts when she sees us and drops the towel. She picks it up again and a couple of pound notes flutter out onto the floor. She looks embarrassed as Nick picks them up and gives them to her.

'That's Lady Northrup's room isn't it?'

'Yes sir.'

'What were you doing in there?'

She turns red and says, 'Nothing sir.'

The door opens and a tall woman with a hooked nose and a lined face wearing a long nightdress and a hairnet says, 'What is all this noise?'

Nick turns to her.

'I beg your pardon your ladyship, I merely wondered what this girl was doing in your room.'

'None of your damned business!' snaps her ladyship.

'I do beg your pardon, I...'

She looks him up and down and then at me and Lizzie.

'It's Boulter isn't it?'

'It is.'

'Jonathan's friend.'

'Yes.'

She looks at me and Lizzie again.

'And why indeed are you roaming the corridors

with these women in the middle of the night?'

'We were just going to bed your ladyship.'

'I should think so too.'

'A late rubber, I'm afraid.'

She snorts at him, turns back into her room and shuts the door. The maid scurries off and we go on along the corridor. When we get to a door at the far end Nick stops and opens it for us.

'I'll arrange breakfast in your room for you and then I think perhaps we might make a move back to town. That was Jonathan's mother, Lady Northrup. I'm afraid she can be a little tricky on occasion.'

'Particularly when she's been caught at it with the servants,' says Lizzie.

'Quite,' says Nick as he turns and walks away.

We go into the room and close the door behind us. Lizzie turns on the light and I say, 'I didn't notice anyone using a rubber.'

We laugh and Lizzie takes her clothes off and gets into one of the two beds. The room's lovely with pale pink wallpaper, a big fireplace with china ornaments on the mantlepiece and arm-chairs in front of it. There's a table and chairs under the window and a washstand with our bags beside it. I go to the window and look out. There's a light in front of the stables where all the Rollers and Bentleys are parked and there's an old brick building next to it, like a warehouse or something that looks derelict with a couple of smashed windows and big double doors. Round the side of it is the small black car. I think about going down to have a look but I decide to leave it in case I run into someone. I get undressed, get into bed with

Lizzie and she wakes up, turns over and wraps her arms round me. We cuddle for a bit.

'Was that your first orgy?' she asks.

'Mmm.'

'Hard work ain't it.'

We have a giggle and then she strokes my hair as I drift off to sleep.

There's a knock on the door. I wake up and look around and nothing seems familiar and I don't know where I am and I'm panicking, then Lizzie sits up in bed and once I see her I'm all right. I lie back and relax while she gets out of bed, throws her dress on and goes to the door. She holds the handle and asks, 'Who is it?'

'Breakfast, madam,' says a voice.

Lizzie opens the door and there's the young maid from last night holding a big tray. Her face is pale and drawn under her white cap and she looks no more than fifteen. Lizzie opens the door wide and the maid comes in and puts the tray down on the table. There are two big silver domes on it and a coffee pot and cups and toast and fruit. The sight of it makes me realise I'm starving. The girl stands back for a moment then she bows her head and moves to the door.

'There's no need to bow to us love, we're just like you,' says Lizzie. The girl hesitates at the door then she turns and says, 'Last night...' She looks down at the floor.

'It's all right,' says Lizzie.

'You won't say anything...'

'Not a word.'

'Only she'd have me sacked if anyone knew.'

'You're quite safe love.'

'Thanks.'

She almost manages a smile and then she leaves.

I get out of bed and join Lizzie at the table. She picks up the coffee pot. 'Poor kid's scared half to death.'

We make short work of the scrambled eggs and bacon that's under the silver domes and then we linger over the toast and marmalade while talking in posh voices about whether we're going hunting or shooting or fishing today, and decide that we'll stop indoors and do our embroidery and make the under gardener give us a good seeing to in the potting shed after tea.

There's a knock at the door and the maid comes in with two jugs of hot water and puts them on the washstand. As she goes to leave Lizzie says, 'What's your name love?'

She stands for a moment with her hands folded in front of her looking embarrassed.

'Mary.'

'Come and have a cup of coffee with us Mary.'

'I can't.'

'Come on, no one'll know.'

'I'm not allowed.'

Lizzie stands up and says in a posh voice, 'I'm ordering you to sit down my girl!'

She looks scared for a second until Lizzie laughs and then she giggles and says, 'Very well, my lady.'

Lizzie offers her a seat and pours her a cup of coffee. 'I'm Lizzie and this is Rina.'

Mary still looks embarrassed as she sips her coffee.

'Where are you from love?' asks Lizzie
'Here.'
'You were born here?'
'My mother was a scullery maid.'
'Is she still here?' asks Lizzie.
'She died when I was born.'
'I'm sorry.'
We're quiet for a moment, then Lizzie asks, 'Did your dad work here too?'
Mary looks at the floor and says, 'I don't know.'
As Lizzie starts to speak Mary puts her cup down and stands up.
'I've got to go now.'
Mary slips out of the door and Lizzie closes it behind her and comes back to the table. I pour us another cup of coffee and say,
'I wonder who the father is.'
'Probably Jonathan, or some other rich cunt.'
We finish breakfast and while Lizzie's having a wash I look out of the window and see that the black car's gone from beside the derelict building. The sun's shining on the rolling parkland and I can see grooms leading horses across the yard and into a field behind the stables. In the distance there are sheep and cows grazing and a tractor ploughing a field. I feel the peace and wonder what it must be like to live in a place like this with all the servants and the grooms and never have any worries or strife or small black cars in your life. I pour warm water into the bowl on the washstand and feel the steam on my face and I want to hold the moment forever. There's a knock at the door and Nick appears.
'Ready to make a move?' he says.

I splash my face with water and dry it on the towel. We put on our coats and Nick picks up our bags and leads us along the corridor, through a door at the far end, down some narrow back stairs and into a dimly lit passageway. We pass a room where an old man and a young boy are bent over a bench brushing away at boots and shoes, and then the kitchen where a big woman with a red face is plucking the feathers off a dead bird on a table and a couple of younger women are peeling potatoes and lobbing them into a bucket on the floor. Next to that is a room where a girl with her back to us is bent over a big sink with dirty plates and dishes piled up beside it. We go through a door into the yard. A group of riders are mounting up in front of the stables and Nick greets a couple of them as we walk across the cobbles to the Bentley. I have a look around but there's still no sign of the black car. We get into the Bentley, Lizzie in the front with Nick, and me alone in the back.

The engine purrs, and we roll round to the front of the house and off down the drive.

6

When we get to Maida Vale Nick's all apologies for having to cut the weekend short and he asks us if he can take us to lunch at the Connaught to make up for it. Lizzie's keen to go but I say I've got to do something so he drops me at the flat and they go on together. They've been chatting away in the front of the car while I was dozing in the back and I expect they've found a few mutual interests.

I go in through the glass doors and notice that there's no one behind the porter's desk as I walk to the lift. I get out at my floor and the snooty city gent that lives next door comes out of his flat. As it's a Saturday he's wearing a tweed jacket, cravat and grey flannels instead of his pinstripe suit. He walks past me towards the lift and says, 'There was a deuce of a lot of banging about and shouting in your flat in the middle of the night.'

'What?' I say.

He presses the lift button and as the doors close he gives me a dirty look.

'Some people work you know.'

I get to my door, go to put the key in the lock but the door's open. I take my gun out of my handbag and push the door open slowly. The coat stand's lying on its side, the photograph of my mum and dad is smashed on the floor and I can see the kitchen's been wrecked. The table's upside down and the chairs are piled on top of it. I go into Georgie's room and find it empty and untouched. In my bedroom the wardrobe's been emptied, my clothes are all over the floor, the dressing table's on its side and the bed's been torn apart. I run into the living room looking for Georgie but she's not there. I go back into her room and try to think where she could be. I look at her school books on her desk. An exercise book she's been writing in is open and her pen's lying on it. I can see that she's stopped halfway through a sentence and I know she's been taken. I curse myself for leaving her when I knew I was followed from the club last

63

night and I ram the muzzle of the gun into the palm of my hand and screw it into the cut. The pain fills me up and when I see it bleeding I feel calm. I go to the bathroom, clean up my hand, and wash the blood off the gun. I take the screwdriver out of the cabinet and loosen one of the bath panels enough to check the money's still there. I go into the bedroom, take off my black dress, pull a pair of slacks and a sweater from the pile of clothes on the floor and put them on. I find a handbag, put my purse and gun in it and run to the lift. In the foyer, Reg the daytime porter is behind the desk.

'Was Dennis on duty last night?'

'Yes miss.'

'Is he in his flat in the basement?'

'He's in hospital.'

'How come?'

'There was some trouble and he got hit.'

'Where is he?'

'St Mary's.'

'What's his other name?'

'Baker.'

'Did you call the law?

'I was going to but Dennis said no.'

I dash out of the front doors and head for my car. A cab appears and I flag it down, stick a quid in the driver's hand and tell him to get to St Mary's Paddington as quick as he can. The Saturday traffic's light on Edgware Road and I'm soon at the main entrance on Praed Street. I go to the desk, ask for Dennis Baker and say he's my dad. The old biddy searches through her lists, finds where he is and tells me that he's in Witherow

64

Ward and how to get there. It's on the first floor in the main block and it's visiting time so I'm in luck. I hurry up the stairs and along the corridor until I see the ward sign. I go in and I can't see Dennis so I ask a nurse if he's there, and she looks in a book and points me to the far end of the ward. I spot him lying in the end bed with a bandage round his head and down over one eye. I go to his bedside, sit down, and he turns his head towards me. I can see the edge of a nasty black eye under the bandage. 'Are you all right Dennis?'

'I've been better miss.'

'What happened to you?'

'Two blokes come in and ask me what flat is yours. I don't like the look of them so I refuse to say and one of them knocks me out. Reg found me on the floor when he come in and he called the ambulance and they brought me here.'

'Are you going to be all right?'

'It's just a bump on the head and a shiner but they've kept me in 'cos they reckon my ticker's a bit dodgy and they want to do tests or some such.'

'What were the two blokes like?'

'One short with dark hair, and a tall one with a hat.'

'Trilby and a grey overcoat.'

'Yeah.'

I open my bag, count fifty quid off a wad that I keep sewn into the lining and put it into Dennis's hand. He looks at it with his good eye.

'What's this?'

'A bullseye for your trouble and for keeping it quiet. I'm sorry you got hurt.'

I shut my bag, head along the ward and out of

the door. They must have got hold of a list of residents after they smacked Dennis and found out which was my flat.

I get to Praed Street, hail a cab and tell him to take me to Ledbury Road. I'm hoping Bert will be in the Walmer Castle and that he knows something. If Don Beale was one of Bielsky's mob it could be that our man in the hat is one of his as well. The cab pulls up outside the pub. I give the cabby half a crown, walk into the public bar and I'm glad to see Bert sitting at a table at the back with a few of George's firm. I catch his eye and go outside. After a bit he comes out and we go to his Jag and get in.

'Georgie's been taken,' I tell him.

'Are you sure?'

'Of course I'm fucking sure.'

'Where from?'

'The flat.'

'When?'

'Last night.'

'Fuck.'

'Know anything about a tall bloke who wears a trilby and a grey coat?'

'Can't say I do.'

'He was in the Three Bells with that ponce I done last night.'

'Some of Bielsky's mob go in there.'

'No one saw me at it last night did they?'

'Only those kids across the road and they soon scarpered.'

'I'm going to see Bielsky.'

'Do you want a lift?'

'Is he still in Westbourne Grove?'

'He's let that gaff to a solicitor. He just uses Frith Street now.'

'You can drop me at my car if you like.'

'Where is it?'

'At the flat.'

Bert starts the car, drives towards Westbourne Park Road and over to Maida Vale. As I get out of the car he says, 'Watch yourself Reen.'

'I will. Cheers Bert.'

'She's a good girl, your Georgie.'

I drive down Edgware Road to Marble Arch and then left into Oxford Street. I turn off after Oxford Circus, park in Soho Square and walk down to the bottom of Frith Street where it meets Old Compton Street. Even though it's only early in the afternoon there are girls in short skirts and tight blouses standing in doorways ready to tempt punters into clip joints and strip clubs. I find the door I'm looking for next to a shop window full of mannequins in lacy underwear standing in front of shelves of sex magazines. I ring the bell and wait. A bloke in a black overcoat and a bowler hat lingers beside me but before I can tell him to get lost the door opens and a ratty looking old man stands peering at me through a pair of thick glasses. I tell him I want to see Bielsky and he looks me up and down and then stands aside as I walk past him and up the stairs. On the first landing I can hear a drummer and an electric guitar rocking away and then a whiney nasal voice starts singing some words I can't make out. The old goat coming up behind me moans and groans about 'that bleedin' racket' then he scampers past me and up to the next landing. He opens a door and shows me in.

'Wait here while I get him. Who shall I say?'

'Rina Walker.'

He heaves himself up another flight and I go into an office with a desk and a chair behind it and two chairs in front. There are pictures of pop singers on the wall, boys in suits with Brylcreemed quiffs in front of microphones, and a girl with a beehive in a white ball gown with three sharp dressed black men in a tight group behind her. The band downstairs finish the rocking number and then start up again with a slow one as the door opens and Feliks Bielsky comes in. He closes the door, goes behind the desk and offers his hand to me.

'Good day Miss Walker.'

I shake his hand and we sit. He's a little tub of a man with a bald head, a pale chubby face and glasses with thick black frames. He's wearing a grey suit with a striped tie and highly polished shoes, and he looks a good bit older and fatter than he did when I met him with Dave five years ago, although it looks like he doesn't remember it. He picks up a paperknife from the desk and weighs it in his hand. When it's clear he's not going to speak I say, 'You've got my sister.'

'You killed my employee.'

'I don't like men who beat up girls.'

'Beale is of no consequence but as you will understand I have to obtain satisfaction. You also have a girl who belongs to me I think.'

At least he's being straight with me.

'What do you want?' I ask.

He's silent for a bit then he puts the paperknife

on the desk.

'You return the girl and you take care of some-one for me.'

'Who?'

'He is Russian. Not known to you.'

'In London?'

'Yes.'

'I'll give you two grand for the girl and do your Russian for you but I want my sister now.'

'Four thousand and you get your sister.'

'Three.'

'Then you kill Russian.'

'Yes.'

He puts his hand out and we shake.

'Where is she?'

'Money here first.'

'If you've hurt her...'

'She is unharmed.'

'I'll be back in an hour.'

I'm down the stairs and walking up Frith Street and thanking my stars that I know where Georgie is. When I get hold of the bloke in the hat he's going to wish he'd never been born. I get to the car and step on it back to the flat. On the way I decide that Georgie's got to go to boarding school to get her away from this horrible life. I don't mind what happens to me but I can't risk her getting hurt. I tried to get her into a boarding school a couple of years ago but the headmistress said no. I'd dressed her up all posh and expensive to meet her but the stuck-up bitch wouldn't have her because of her accent. She looked down her nose at her and said, 'Not quite the kind of pupil we want I'm afraid. Perhaps a secondary modern school would be more suitable.' I told her she was at Holland Park Comprehensive and top of her form but the cow just sniffed and told her secretary to show us out.

Reg is at the desk when I get there and he asks about Dennis. I tell him he's going to be all right and slip him a score to keep quiet about what's gone on. I go up to the flat, into the bathroom and count up how much I've got stashed behind the bath. Even with the wedge I got from Bert I'm three hundred short. I've got plenty hidden somewhere else but I can't get at it until it's dark. I go and knock on Lizzie's door. She's back from her lunch with Nick and I tell her I need to borrow the three hundred but not why. She's fine with it and while I'm waiting for her to get the money Nick comes out of one of the bedrooms followed by a boy of about sixteen with a crewcut and a leather jacket. Nick looks embarrassed when he sees me. He says hello, opens the front door and the boy skips off down the corridor. Lizzie comes out of the kitchen and hands me an envelope.

Nick says, 'Well, I'd better be getting off. See you both around and about I expect.'

'See you Nick,' says Lizzie.

When the door closes I say, 'Who's the boy?'

'Some renter.'

'Why did he bring him here?'

'He can't have them at his place in daylight, there's a retired Colonel next door who's spying on him.'

'Why doesn't he tell him to get stuffed?'

'In case he tells the police he's a homo. Do you want a cup of tea?'

'I've got to go.'

'Ok love.'

'Do me a favour?'

'Of course.'

'Next time you see Lordy can you ask him if he can get Georgie into a good boarding school?'

'Yeah sure. He's coming tonight.'

'Thanks.'

We kiss and I beat it to the car.

I park in Frith Street and walk towards the corner of Old Compton Street. It's beginning to get dark and business is hotting up for the strip clubs and clip joints as punters grab a quick bit of tit and bum before catching the six-fifteen to Surbiton. I get to Bielsky's door and I'm let in by a big bloke with a mean look and a foreign accent. He takes me upstairs and opens the door to Bielsky's office. He's sitting at the desk and I put the money down in front of him. He counts it and puts it in a drawer then he gets up, walks round the desk and opens the door. The minder is waiting on the landing.

'He will take you to your sister now. Meet me at the Glendale tonight at nine o'clock.'

I walk to the door and close it again. I stand in front of him and look him in the eye.

'If you ever touch her again...'

'Of course.'

He waits a moment to show that he knows I mean it and then opens the door and nods to the minder who leads me down the stairs. We go a few yards along the street to where an even bigger bloke and a blonde girl in a flared skirt and a tight white sweater are standing each side of an open

71

door. I follow the minder inside and down some narrow steps into a basement room with a bar in one corner and plastic tables and chairs. There's smoochy music and pink lighting and men at a few of the tables sitting with girls in off the shoulder dresses or tight skirts and halter tops with a lot of make-up, all drinking what looks like champagne but probably isn't. The girls pick the punters up in the street, bring them to the club and push them to buy overpriced drinks on a promise of going in the back room and doing the business if they spend enough money. When they've cleaned the punters out the bouncers get rid of them. There's a couple of heavies at the bar in case a punter cuts up rough and an old bird with bleached hair pouring drinks.

I follow my man past the bar to a door at the back. He leads me through the door, down a dark corridor with crates of bottles stacked on each side, to a door at the far end. He unlocks it and when he opens it I can see Georgie sitting on a bed inside. Her head's down and she looks as if she's crying. I go to her and put my arms round her. She pulls away from me.

'I fucking hate you!'

'Have they hurt you?'

'Get me away from here!'

I take her by the wrist, push the minder out of the way and lead her along the corridor, through the club and up the stairs. She tries to pull away from me when we get to the street but I hold on to her and people are staring as I drag her towards the car.

7

She does her silent bit all the way back in the car and when we get home she goes into her room and slams the door. I phone a locksmith who I robbed a couple of safes with a few years back and tell him I want new locks, a spy hole and a steel security plate bolted to the back of the door and I need it now. He says he'll come round as soon as he can. I clean up the kitchen and straighten the furniture, then I put all my clothes back in the wardrobe, make the bed and get my dressing table back into some kind of order. As I'm finishing Georgie comes in and stands by the door. She doesn't speak so after a bit I say,

'I'm sorry Georgie.'

She comes to me and I put my arms round her, then we sit on the bed. 'Why did they take me to that place?'

I look at her sitting there beside me and I feel so bad for what's happened in her life. Her father shot dead, finding her mother after she killed herself with the drink, and her little brother who she loved dying of the whooping cough when he was only six.

'It's because of something I did.'

'What?'

'I can't tell you.'

'Why did you do it?'

'I had to.'

'Is it something from the old street and the horrible man?'

She means my killing of Johnny Preston when he was raping her.

'In a way,' I say.

'Can't we get away from that and start again?'

'It's not that easy.'

If I do a runner now Bielsky won't let it go, nor will Tony Farina, and I'll be looking over my shoulder wherever I am and waiting for a knock at the door. I've got no choice but to stay in the game and protect my reputation, and the truth is I like hurting bad men and the thrill of it and the money, and I love Lizzie, and I don't want to leave her and have some dull job somewhere and dull friends and Friday night in the pub. I feel terrible about what Georgie's been through, and I know that what I do puts her in danger, but all I can do is try to keep her out of it as best I can. I look at her frightened face.

'Would you like to go to a boarding school?'

'A what?'

'A school where you live when it's the term and just come home in the holidays.'

'Like that one we went to that time?'

'Yes.'

She thinks for a bit. 'Away from here?'

'Yes.'

'A long way?'

'If you want.'

'In the country?'

'Yes.'

'I'd like that.'

The doorbell rings. It's Gerry, the locksmith

74

and another bloke who's holding the steel plate.

I have a look at the new locks they've brought, offer them a cup of tea and leave them to get to work. I bring Georgie into the hall, show her what the men are doing and tell her that no one'll be able to get through that door again. Gerry says you'd need a Sherman Tank to break it down when they've finished with it and he gets a smile from Georgie. We go in the kitchen, I put the kettle on and she takes a book off the sideboard, sits at the table and opens it. I look over her shoulder and see that it's *Pride and Prejudice*. I remind myself to get my own copy. I look at her sitting reading and I hope I can get her into a boarding school and that maybe she'll be able to make some friends there.

'Did they hurt you when they came in here?' I ask.

'The short one tried to but I punched him in the throat like you showed me.'

'Good girl.'

'Then the one in the hat told him to leave me.'

She goes back to her reading then she looks up and says, 'Will you come and see me when I'm in the boarding school?'

'Of course I will.'

The kettle boils and I make the tea, give a cup to Georgie and take some to Gerry and his mate. Georgie seems settled with her book and so I go across the hall and knock on Lizzie's door. When she opens it I get a flash of her studded leather bikini under her floaty silk dressing gown and I know I'm in luck and His Lordship is with her. I go in and she closes the door and we have a cuddle and I enjoy the studs digging into me while I move my hands over her back and her thighs. There's moaning coming from along the hall.

'You want to see the old scamp about a school for Georgie don't you?'

'Not if you're in the middle of...'

'It's ok, I've just finished him. Go in the bedroom a tick while I get him dressed and I'll bring him in.'

She slips off her dressing gown and gives it to me. In the bedroom the curtains are drawn back from the mirror and it takes a minute before I spot His Lordship. He's under the bed, curled up in a ball inside a net that is stretched tight around his naked body. Lizzie enters, pulls him out from under the bed, unties the net and picks him up off the floor. While he stands trembling and biting his nails like a little boy she gathers his clothes up off the floor, throws them at him and tells him to get dressed. She picks up a whip, cracks it near his arse and shouts at him to get a move on because there's someone who wants to see him. This puts him in even more of a panic and he scrambles into his trousers and begs Lizzie to help him with his collar stud. She gets him dressed, ties his tie for him and calms him down a bit before she opens the door and ushers him into the hall. I close the curtains so he won't know I've been watching.

The smart older gentleman who enters the bedroom moments later looks relaxed and self-assured. He shakes my hand.

'Hello, I'm Gordon.'

Lizzie puts her arm through mine and says, 'This my friend Rina. She wants to ask you about boarding schools.'

His Lordship gives my body a quick shufti and says, 'How interesting; and what is your subject?'

I look at him a bit blank and he says, 'I assume you wish to teach?'

'I want to find somewhere for my younger sister to go.'

'Ah, I see.'

'She's fourteen.'

'Do you have anywhere in mind?'

'I tried Leavenden but the headmistress wouldn't have her.'

'Margot Rainsford?'

'That's her.'

'A pity, I believe it's excellent. Why wouldn't she take her?'

'Because she's not posh,' says Lizzie.

'Ah,' says Gordon.

'So we need you to oil the wheels.'

'I see.'

Lizzie goes to her dressing table, writes on a piece of paper, gives it to His Lordship and says, 'That's Rina's number. Get it sorted and phone her.'

Lordy puts the paper in his inside pocket and smiles at me.

'Your sister's name is...?'

'Georgina Walker.'

'How old did you say she is?'

'Fourteen.'

'I'll see what I can do.'

He shakes my hand, gives me a little bow and leaves. Lizzie goes with him and then comes back in the bedroom a few minutes later with a bunch of fivers in her hand. She puts them in her bag and says, 'I wonder what he's got on our Margot eh?'

'If she's anything like him I'm not sure I want her to go there.'

'She can fight her off with her hockey stick.'

There's a banging noise and the sound of a drill.

'What's occurring out there?' Lizzie asks.

'New locks.'

'You had trouble?'

'Nothing much. I'd better get back and see to it though.'

I put my arms round her, get the studs again and I want to stay but I can't because I've got to meet Bielsky. We kiss.

'Thanks Liz.'

'Look after yourself, eh?'

I go across to my flat and find that Gerry and his man have finished the job. They show me how they've fitted a metal strip down the door jamb, new locks and the steel plate with a spy hole. I can see that although a pro could still get through it he'd need to either blow it open or use a massive battering ram. I call Georgie, show her what Gerry's done and tell her to always look through the spy hole and see who it is before she opens up. She looks at me as if I'm stupid and slopes off to her bedroom.

The lads want sixty-five notes for the job. I remember that I've given all my cash to Bielsky and I've only got a few quid in my purse which I'll need for tonight. Gerry says he'll take a cheque as he's all legit now and he knows me so I give him one from Harrods Bank and sign it in the false name that I use for that account. I'll need to go up Kensal Green later and get some cash. Gerry gives me two sets of the new keys and they pack up and leave. I go into the kitchen and give a set to Georgie, then I put the frying pan on the stove, light the gas and look through the kitchen cabinet for something for our tea. I find some sausages that smell ok and some sliced bread. I put the sausages in the frying pan and open a tin of beans. The phone rings and I ask Georgie to put the beans on and watch the frying pan while I go in the hall and lift up the receiver. It's Tony Farina.

'I need to see you.'

'When?'

'My office, now.'

I reckon I've got time to see him and still meet Bielsky at nine. He sounds peeved.

'Half an hour.'

'Ok.'

I go back in the kitchen and tell Georgie I've got to go out. She's ok about it and I suggest she watches TV but she says she's going to read in bed. I wish I could think of someone she could stay with but there's no one. I've lost all my old friends since I came out of prison. I tell her I'll ask Lizzie to look in on her later and she nods while she stirs the baked beans. I take a sausage out of the pan, wrap a piece of bread round it and go into my bedroom and eat it while I look through my wardrobe. The Glendale is a cabaret club in Beak Street that has a band and dancing girls and I need to look a bit glittery to get in by myself. I pull out a peach chiffon dress with a fitted skirt and a cotton lace top that's got a low neckline. I hold it against me, look in the mirror and decide it'll do the job. I put on silk pants and a Triumph bra for maximum cleavage, clean stockings, four inch heels and freshen up my make-up and hair. I slip a blade into my suspender belt, go through to Georgie's room and ask her to zip up my dress. She seems quite happy in bed with her book and I say goodnight, slip on my fur jacket, sort out which keys close the new locks and head for the lift.

There's a new porter at the desk who'll be filling in for Dennis. He's young and well-built and he looks as if he can take care of himself. I say hello and ask his name. He tells me he's called Mike and opens the front door for me.

I drive to Knightsbridge, park in Hans Road and walk round the corner to Tony Farina's building. The doorman lets me in when I say my name and I take the lift to the sixth floor. A young Italian looking bloke answers the door, shows me into the hall, offers me a seat, knocks on the door of Tony's office and goes in. I sit in a leather armchair and look at a big colour photograph of a beautiful blue lake glistening in the sun on the wall opposite. I'm thinking how I'd like to be there and swim in the lake when the young bloke comes out of the office and holds the door open for me.

Tony is seated at his desk. He looks me up and down.

'Always the beautiful blonde.'

I ignore the remark and look him in the eye. He indicates a chair in front of the desk and offers me a drink from the decanter in front of him. I shake my head and sit down. 'What do you want Tony?'

'Another girl killed last night.'

'Where?'

'Dukes Meadows.'

He means the open ground by the river next to Chiswick Bridge. It's where toms from that part take men, known as Gobblers Gulch in the trade.

'What happened?'

'A man kills her with knife and puts her in boot of car.'

'Who saw it?'

'One of my girls, also in the Meadows. Too dark to see his face but Luca recognised a man who was in the club with her before and we know she used to meet tricks later.'

'Who is he?'

'Nazi bastard we know from prison camp.'

'Prison camp?'

'After death of Il Duce, Germans shipped me and Luca to camp in Bavaria, made us work with no food, beat us all the time. Luca nearly died. This bastard, Heinz, was one of the worst. We know he killed some prisoners.'

'Do you know where he is?'

'We have address.'

'How come?'

'Luca dipped his pocket.'

He passes a slip of paper across the desk to me. The name Heinz is written on it with an address in Catford.

'No second name?'

'Just Heinz. You just watch for now, see what you can find.'

I put the paper in my handbag and walk to the door then I turn and say, 'Did the girl say what

car it was?'
  'No.'
  'Ok,' I say.
  'Call me.'

I drive into Soho and leave the car round the
corner from the Glendale where I've got to meet
Bielsky. There are two bouncers in black suits
outside the club looking me up and down as I
approach, and it costs me half a quid to get past
them. I could have told them I was there to see
Bielsky but the fewer people who know that I'm
doing work for him the better. I walk past the
cloakroom and wait while the cigarette girl with
her tray and her fishnet tights comes up the stairs.
I go down into the club and the smell of booze and
fags hits me. It's dimly lit apart from small lamps
with red shades on the tables. The walls are a dark
purple with photos of film stars and singers hanging between big gilt-framed mirrors. There's a bar
at one end of the room and a bandstand at the
other, with a dance floor in front of it with tables
round it.
  As I walk towards the bar there's a drum roll,
the dance floor lights up and a line of showgirls
in skimpy feathery costumes and silver tights
appear from behind a screen and shimmy onto
the dance floor. The band go into an up-tempo
show tune and the girls prance about in some
kind of formation, waving their arms and kicking
their legs up to give the punters at the tables a
good view of what they've got. I order a whisky
and sit on a bar stool. The club belongs to Bielsky
and he's opened it to compete with the posh

clubs in Mayfair and Knightsbridge where they won't let him in because he's foreign and he's not a toff. The place is full, with hostesses sitting at the tables, drinking champagne and flirting with older men. I can see Poppy, the blond and busty one who came to the country with us, at the other end of the bar talking to a bouncer. She sees me and comes along the bar.

'Did you get back all right?'

'Nick brought us.'

'We had to come on the bleedin' train. I felt a right fool in me finery at ten o'clock in the morning.'

'How come you had to leave?'

'Search me. One minute we're in the bath with the Viscount and then that butler comes in, whispers something in his ear and the Viscount jumps out of the bath, says he's sorry but the hunt's leaving, wraps a towel round himself and legs it back to his room. Then this maid brings our clothes in and the butler tells us to get dressed, takes us out the back door, puts us in a car and we get dumped at the station.'

'Charming.'

'What happened to you?'

Before I can tell her a bouncer appears beside me. 'He's waiting for you.'

I follow him past the tables, round the dance floor and through a padded door behind the bandstand into a small lounge with a couple of plush sofas and a small bar in the corner. Bielsky is sitting at the far end of the room talking to an older woman in a black sequinned dress. He dismisses the bouncer and signals for me to join them.

'Rina, this is Madame Greta, she looks after the girls here. Greta this is Rina who is going to carry out the business for us.'

Greta looks me up and down, gives me a friendly smile and I shake her bony hand. She looks elegant with her black dress, a necklace of pearls and shiny grey hair. Although her face is lined and wrinkled there's a knowing glint in her eye behind the mascara. I'd normally refuse to discuss a job in front of anyone else but I have the feeling that this lady's all right.

'Greta will show you the man I wish you to deal with and give you what details we have,' says Bielsky.

'When do you want it done?' I ask.

'You have forty-eight hours.'

He gives me a hard look and goes back into the club.

8

Greta's eyes soften as she looks at me and they remind me of my mum's eyes before the drink got hold of her. After a bit she smiles.

'How old are you Rina?'

I never tell anyone anything about myself when I'm working but before I know it I've told her that I'm twenty. She looks surprised for a moment.

'You are sure you want to do what Feliks is asking?'

'It's ok,' I say.

'There are other ways to repay him for a girl like you.' And I don't need her to tell me what they are.

'It's ok.'

'You are sure?'

'Just tell me where I can find this Russian.'

She stands up and says, 'Come.'

She picks up her stick and as she walks I can see how hunched over she is. She leads me into a small office, pulls back a curtain on the wall and I can see into the club through a glass panel. She looks round the club and says, 'He is not here yet. Usually he comes at this time.'

'Every night?'

'When he is in London, yes.'

'What's his name?'

'Pavel Budanov.'

'Where does he stay?'

'Dorchester Hotel. When he comes you can take him to a table perhaps?'

'No.'

'But you want to meet him, no?

'I just need to see him.'

'Ok.'

'Is there a back way out of here?'

'Yes.'

While we wait for the Russian to come in, I ask, 'How do you know Feliks?'

'From prison camp in Russia, in the war.'

She looks sad and troubled. I feel bad that I've asked and I look away but she puts her hand on my arm.

'There is Budanov. Going to the bar now.'

A man in a brown suit with a round face and

receding hair makes his way through the crowd around the bar and speaks to one of the barmen. When he turns round and looks round the club I've seen enough.

'I'll be off then,' I say.

'I show you the way.'

We go back through the lounge and into the dancers' dressing room beyond it. Greta points to an exit door with a metal bar across it at the back of the room, then she holds her hand against my cheek and says, 'Goodbye Rina. You be careful now.'

'I'll be all right,' I say.

She puts her hand on my arm. 'Maybe you come and see me again?'

'Maybe I will.'

I can feel her watching me as I brush past the feathers and fringes of the costumes hanging on the wall. There's something strange about her and even though we've hardly spoken I know I do want to see her again but I'm not sure why. I push the door open and step into the alleyway at the back of the club. It's gone midnight and I decide to have a look at the Dorchester before I go up Kensal Green to get some cash. I get to the car and drive across Regent Street, through Mayfair, turn into Park Lane, drive past the Dorchester and turn left into a narrow street that runs alongside the hotel. I can see what looks like a tradesman's entrance a bit further up and I park opposite and wait. I'm thinking about Greta and what she must have been through in her life when I get lucky and two maids come out and walk along the street laughing about something. One of them's got her coat undone and I can see her black dress and white apron underneath. I get out of the car and walk round to the main entrance.

A doorman in a uniform with lots of gold braid opens the door for me. I walk over to the desk and a girl in a black suit, with her hair in a dark brown bob, gives me a snooty look so I veer towards an older bloke who's sitting at the other end of the desk and looking bored. I tell him I'm here to see Mr Budanov. He gives me a look that tells me he thinks I'm a tom and dials a three-figure number on the phone in front of him. I lean forward so that I can see the phone below the counter, clock the number he dials as 427 and wait for him to tell me Budanov's not answering. When he does I thank him and walk back to the main door. As I go through, the doorman with the gold braid tries to speak to me. Doormen at the posh hotels always expect a little earner off the working girls but I ignore him and head to the car.

I drive north up Edgware Road, turn into Harrow Road and drive up to Kensal Green Cemetery. I park a bit beyond the gates and wait for an old drunk to weave his way past. Once he's out of sight I change my stilettos for a pair of plimsolls that I keep in the boot, climb up some ivy that's clinging to the brick wall of the cemetery and drop down on the other side among the gravestones. The moon's providing enough light to see my way and I walk among the headstones to our Jack's grave. I stand beside it and remember the brave little kid he was and how I loved him. I start crying and then I grind my fist against a tree trunk for the unfairness of him being taken.

87

Once I've calmed down I walk on to a big family monument at the far end of the cemetery. I kneel down at one end of it, push my fingers through a hole at the corner of one of the stone slabs until I get a grip of it, then I pull it towards me and lay it down on the grass. I push an old canvas bag out of the way, reach in and drag out the ammunition box that I keep in there. I open it up, take out a sheaf of fivers and two bundles of fifties. I put the fifties in each pocket, roll up the fivers and push them down my bra. As I'm closing the box and telling myself I really must count up the rest of the money that's in there, I hear a noise somewhere behind me.

I look round slowly and see nothing. I pull the canvas bag towards me as quietly as I can, slide open the zip and put my hand in. As my fingers touch the Smith and Wesson a great weight lands on my back and there are hands round my neck. I swing both elbows back, shove one foot against the grave, heave myself backwards and crush whoever it is against something solid. I pull his hands off my throat and roll away but he scrambles after me, grabs my ankle, throws himself on top of me and goes for my throat again. I bring my knee up hard between his legs. As he cries out he pulls his head back. I try to jab a finger in his eye but I miss and my nail just grazes his temple. I swing a short punch at his head, roll out from under him, stand up and kick him under the chin as he tries to get up. He staggers back but doesn't go down. He pulls a gun out of his belt so I dive at him, and knock him backwards onto a marble slab. I take hold of his head, smash it down on the stone and break his skull.

I didn't intend to kill him until I found out who he was but it's too late now. His face is thin and gaunt, with a hook nose and a small moustache above a pair of thin lips. He's bald with a scraggy fringe of hair round the back of his head and he looks a bit too old for the rough stuff. I search his pockets and find a wallet with a few quid in it but nothing to say who he is. I pocket his car key and drag his body off the marble slab. I take a small shovel out of the holdall and have a look at the headstones nearby. There's one where the engraving's so worn that I can't read the name but I can just see that the date is 1840 and I reckon whoever it is might like a bit of company after all that time.

An hour later I'm knackered and wishing I'd worn a flared skirt but I reckon I've dug down far enough so I drag him over, push him into the hole, chuck his gun in after him and cover him with earth and leaves. I go back to my hiding place, put the shovel back in the canvas bag, push it in beside the ammunition box and lift the stone slab back into place. I make my way back to the wall, climb up it and have a look over. I can see an old Ford Consul parked over the road. The dead bloke's car key has a Ford tag on it and I know I've got to get rid of his motor. I look at my watch and see that it's gone three o'clock. I get over the wall, go to the car, unlock it and get in. I search the car but find nothing but an empty fag packet and a beer can. I turn the key and press the starter. The engine fires up first time and I turn round and head back down Harrow Road, along Ladbroke Grove and up Westbourne Park Road. I park beside the Royal

Oak and walk past the El Rio club. A black guy in a dark blue zoot suit, holding a tambourine, asks me if I want to score. I shake my head and go down some basement steps by the corner of Chepstow Road. I knock on the door and wait until a small panel slides open and a voice asks what I want. I say my name and who I want to see and the panel shuts. A minute later it opens again, and Tommy Gaynor's squinty eyes appear.

'All right girl?'

'I need you to off a motor.'

'Bring it round the yard tomorrow.'

'Now.'

'I'm in the middle of a game.'

'I'll give you a ton.'

'Hang on.'

He goes inside and the door closes. I take two fifties off one of the wads in my pocket and wait. A couple of minutes later Tommy appears and I follow his broad back up the stairs. When we get to the car I unlock the driver's door.

'You're driving.'

He gets in. I sit in the passenger seat and give him the money.

'Drop me on Harrow Road by the cemetery, take this one to the yard and make sure it's well hidden.'

'Got it.'

'When can you crush it?'

'Tomorrow.'

As I drive home I'm wondering if the man I've killed is just any old rapist who's seen me going over the wall and fancied his chances, or if he could be the one who's been doing Tony's girls.

Mary Weedon and the girl in Dukes Meadows were killed and then taken away in a car and he had the chance to shoot me but didn't. I reckon my man either wanted to fuck me or capture me, and if it was capture I've no idea who he was or why.

I park in Hall Road, walk round the corner and let myself in at the front door of the flats. Reg is asleep behind the desk and he doesn't wake when the lift creaks down to collect me. I walk past Lizzie's and think about knocking on her door in case she's free. I always want to be with her when I've done a bit of work but my watch says four o'clock in the morning and I decide to be good and get some sleep. I find my keys and open up my new locks. I go in, lock the door behind me and feel glad for the protection of the thick steel plate. I look in on Georgie and see that she's sleeping. Her bedside light is still on and her book is open on the nightstand. I pick it up and see that it's still *Pride and Prejudice*. I read the first few lines and smile. I wonder what Jane Austen would make of some of the single men with a good fortune that I could introduce her to. I take the book with me into the bathroom. I unscrew the panel and put the two bundles of fifties and the roll of fivers behind the bath, then I turn on the taps, pour in some bubble bath and read on while the water's running. I slip off my clothes, sink beneath the bubbles and let the warmth ease the tension from my body. I lie in luxury for a bit and then I wash the graveyard dirt off me, get out, dry myself and slide into bed with Jane. By the time Mrs Bennet has given up trying to bully her husband into paying Mr Bingley a visit, I'm asleep.

Georgie's shaking me.

'I'm late for school and I can't find my book!'

I reach for it under the blankets and give it to her.

'I'm sorry, I didn't know you'd need it.'

'It's English Lit exam today, of course I need it.'

She goes into the kitchen and I get out of bed, grab my dressing gown and follow her. 'Do you want some breakfast?'

'I haven't got time.'

'Shall I make you a sandwich?'

She takes an apple from the bowl on the table, puts it in her satchel along with her book and says, 'I've got to go.'

'It's your last exam today isn't it?'

'Yeah.'

'Good luck.'

'Ta.'

She closes the door behind her and I can hear her cursing at the front door as she fumbles with her new keys. I go and show her which one's which and she unlocks the door and runs off to the lift. I watch her until the gates close and give her a wave. Lizzie's door opens and the Russian athlete appears and lopes off towards the lift. Lizzie's standing in the doorway looking a bit bedraggled. She sees me, comes across the hall and I take her hand and lead her into the bedroom.

9

It's gone ten o'clock by the time I get to Harlesden. It's a grey, rainy day and the car slides a bit on the cobbles as I stop outside my lock-up. I undo the padlock, go in and draw the bolts across on the inside. I check the tyres on the van then change the plates. I look in the wardrobe, sort through the clothes on the rail until I find my waitress outfit with the white apron and cuffs, take it out and hold it up against me while I look in the mirror on the back of the wardrobe door. I decide it's close enough to the uniform the maid coming out of the Dorchester had on so I reckon it'll do. I'm wondering if they wear a cap when they're working. I rummage through a basket of odds and ends and find one. I pick a pair of flat-heeled black slip-ons, put them in a bag with the uniform and put the bag in the back of the van. I open the doors, drive the van out onto the yard, pull my car inside, shut the doors and lock up.

Half an hour later I'm lucky with a parking space round the corner from Deanery Street which is where the side entrance to the Dorchester is. I park the van, walk to a phone box and dial the hotel number. A woman picks up and I ask for Mr Budanov in room 427. After a few rings a bloke answers with a foreign sounding grunt. I put the phone down, get back to the van, change into the maid's uniform and put the cap in the pocket. As

I'm walking towards the side entrance of the hotel a van pulls up outside and the driver and his mate open the back doors, take a box each out of the back and carry them into the hotel. They stop just inside the door and talk to a man in uniform sitting at a small desk. While he's reaching for a clipboard hanging on the wall I slip in behind the driver's back and walk down a corridor that leads off to the right. There's a bloke in a chef's white jacket pushing a trolley along in front of me and I can see the entrance to a kitchen up ahead and waiters and waitresses coming and going with trays. I turn left into another corridor before I get to the kitchen, and a couple of maids come round a corner giggling and laughing and push past without looking at me. They're both wearing caps so I take mine out and put it on then I turn and walk in the direction they came from and see a flight of stairs and a lift in front of me. I get to the stairs just as the lift door opens and an older woman in a black suit and a man in a tailcoat get out. There's a maid carrying a tray behind them and I run up the stairs and get round the corner before they can see me.

I'm guessing Budanov's room will be on the fourth floor so I climb seven more flights and go through the door that's opposite the lift. The carpet's thick and soft under my feet in the corridor, the walls are a warm peachy kind of colour with lights that shine upwards and there's soft music playing. I stand back as a grey haired man in a dark blue suit and a woman in a long fur coat and a hat with a veil come out of a room and walk past me talking in foreign. I look at the numbers and I can see that I'm on the right floor and my man's room should be along to my left somewhere. A maid comes round the corner pushing a trolley with piles of sheets and towels on it. We nod at each other as she stops outside a room, knocks on the door and waits. When she unlocks the door and goes in I lift a couple of fresh towels off her trolley, put them over my arm and nip round the corner. When I hear her move off with her trolley I find room 427 and knock on the door.

For a moment I think he's not there and it's all over but then a gruff voice says, 'Who is it?'

'Can I change your towels please sir,' I say.

I hear some grunting and then footsteps. The key turns, the door opens and Budanov's standing there in a white dressing gown with Dorchester written on the pocket. His round face is red and puffy, his eyes are bloodshot, what's left of his hair is sticking up in tufts and even at a distance I can smell his foul breath. I wait a second while he clocks my body, then I give him a smile and say, 'I'm sorry if I'm disturbing you, sir.'

He stands aside and says, 'Not at all, please to come.'

I brush against him ever so slightly as I walk slowly past him. There are two doors leading off the bedroom and luckily one of them is open and I can see it's the bathroom. I go in and put the new towels on the rail. Budanov follows me, leans on the door frame and watches me as I bend down and pick up the dirty towels off the floor. As I'm folding them I see him go to the bedside table and pick up a wallet. When I come out of the bathroom he's standing at the end of the bed with his dressing gown hanging open and a twenty quid note in his hand.

I smile, put the towels on a chair, walk towards him and take the twenty out of his hand. He pulls me into him but I push him gently away, gesture to him to stay where he is then I back away, lean against the wall, open my legs and slowly lift up my skirt. When it reaches my waist his face turns from pink to purple and he walks towards me with his arms outstretched and his cock sticking out like the beak off some giant bird. He leans his sweaty body against me, claws at my pants and tries to get himself inside me. I stroke my hands round his neck until I feel his Adam's apple then I put both my thumbs just under it and press hard. His eyes bulge and he struggles and kicks as I force him onto the floor, kneel on his chest and keep pressing. When he goes limp I wait a bit, then I check his pulse and make sure he's gone. I pull my skirt down and go to the door. The key's still in the keyhole so I lock it. I go and kneel down beside the body and check that I haven't left any marks on his neck, then I pull him up onto the bed, put his arm over my shoulder, pick him up in a fireman's lift and sit him on the windowsill with his back against the glass. The room's at the front and I can see the Park Lane traffic flowing along down below. I swing open the window, lift him up by his ankles and push him out.

I hear a woman's scream and a screech of car tyres as I'm unlocking the door. I wipe the door handle with my apron and check the corridor. It's clear so I walk to the corner and look for the chambermaid's trolley. It's parked further along but the girl's inside the room and I make it to the stairs before she comes out. At the bottom of the stairs I can see people hurrying along the passage to see what's happening in the street and I walk along among them and out of the door. I walk slowly to the van, get in the back and change into my stretch pants and sweater. Sirens are wailing as I start the van and drive through Mayfair. I stop by a litter bin in Berkeley Square and dump the maid's uniform, then I turn left up Regent Street and back to Harlesden with the radio up loud and I'm feeling great, singing along with Little Eva and doing the locomotion.

I pull up in Golborne Road by Portobello Market and go to a second-hand bookstall that I know and buy myself a copy of *Pride and Prejudice*. I go on down the market and buy eggs, milk, and some sausages and potatoes for Georgie's tea. On the way back up to Golborne I buy some apples and oranges from an old bloke's barrow that I used to nick from when I was a kid. He's a nice old geezer and he asks me for a date and we have a laugh while he's weighing out the fruit.

When I get back to the flat I let myself in and run a bath. I still can't get used to the luxury of having a soak when I feel like it. The public baths in Silchester Road we had to go to when I was younger were freezing cold in the winter and I always had to take Georgie and Jack with me and see to them because mum would be drunk. Some of the people who worked there were horrible to you because they knew you were poor and you might have the scabies or something.

I turn off the taps and pour in a good dollop of bath oil.

I take off my clothes, slide into the water and melt into the warm scent of roses. I close my eyes and soon I'm seeing rolling fields in the sunshine, lying in long grass among lovely flowers and feeling a soft breeze on my arms and legs. There's just me and the sky and little clouds chasing each other and playing games and I feel wonderful, and it's going on forever. Then I'm floating up and over the fields and the towns and the sea and swooping down under the waves and...

I sit up and spit out a mouthful of water. Someone's knocking at the door. I've fallen asleep and nearly drowned myself, silly cow. I take a second to calm down. I haven't had a call from the desk so it's probably Lizzie and she might want to join me in the bath.

'Is that you Liz?'

'It's Nick Boulter. I wonder if I might have a word?'

I can hardly tell him to piss off now so I say, 'Hang on a minute Nick.'

I get out of the bath, towel myself, put on my dressing gown, trying not to think about Budanov in his, with his beak. I open the door and he's standing there with half a smile on his face and a briefcase in his hand. 'Oh, I'm awfully sorry, I seem to have disturbed you...'

'That's ok. Do you want to come in?'

'Thank you.'

I show him into the lounge, point at the sideboard and say, 'Pour yourself a drink if you want. I'll be back in a tick.'

'Thank you.'

I go back into the bathroom and put my clothes on. When I get back he's standing by the fireplace looking a bit lost with a glass of whisky in his hand.

'This is a pleasant flat. Have you lived here long?' he asks.

'Couple of years.'

I go to the sideboard and pick up the whisky bottle. 'Top you up?'

'Thank you.'

I pour myself a whisky, refill his glass and say, 'Sit down Nick.'

He sits in the armchair beside the fire and I sit opposite him. We both take a drink. He's looking anywhere but at me and just as I'm thinking he's never going to tell me what's on his mind, he says, 'Some people I work with are interested in you.'

A tingle of alarm runs up my spine. I look at him and say nothing. He takes another drink.

'The way you dealt with Budanov this morning was impressive, to say the least.'

I try to look confused.

'Buda what?'

'The police can book it as a suicide by a visiting Russian businessman and nobody's any the wiser. Case closed.'

'I'm sorry Nick, I don't know what you're on about.'

'I am on terms with Feliks Bielsky.'

He's looking at me now all right. I hold his look.

'Who the fuck are you?'

'I'm with Military Intelligence.'

'You're what?'

'MI6 to be precise.'

'You're a spy?'

'Not exactly.'

'Then what?'

'There's no need to be alarmed.'

'Who says I'm alarmed?'

'I'm sorry. I appreciate that very little frightens you.'

I sit back in my chair. 'Tell me who you are and what you want.'

'I have been with MI6 since I left Cambridge and I run various agents both here and in Europe. I and my superiors sometimes have occasion to kill enemies of this country who would seek to do us harm and who operate with such ingenuity as to remain outside the reach of the law. You have come to our notice as one who is skilled and effective in that field and we would like to offer you employment.'

'And how exactly did I come to your notice?'

'After you were kind enough to intercede in that little skirmish with the cab driver in Park Lane I took the liberty of monitoring your activities.'

'You had me followed.'

'Yes.'

This is a nightmare. I've always been dead careful to stay unknown and off the books and here I am with the fucking government all over me. I try to sound casual.

'The bloke in the trilby with the black car.'

'Collins.'

'He was one of the two who took Georgie.'

'We wanted to see how you'd deal with Budanov so we sent him along to make sure your sister was treated gently.'

'Did you put the bloke in the cemetery after me?'

'In the nature of a preliminary audition.'

I don't know what he's on about but I get the general idea.

'Who was he?'

'A traitor who was a little too clever for us. Responsible for the recent death of two of our agents at the hands of the Russians. Believe me the country's a good deal safer with him buried in Kensal Green Cemetery.'

'Good job he didn't kill me then.'

'We told him to bring you in for questioning.'

He's got me. He's shown that he can get Georgie any time he wants and he's got me bang to rights for murder. I'm fucked. To buy a bit of time I ask, 'What was the casino and the country house all about?'

He smiles. 'Ah, yes. It was helpful to see you mixing easily with those of another class. Social inhibition can be a drawback in our work.'

I control the urge to smash my glass in his face. 'Where's Bielsky in this?'

'When the Russian army invaded Poland in thirty-nine, Feliks was captured, imprisoned in Talitsy work camp in Russia and interrogated. He managed to convince them that he was a committed communist, which was just as well since they executed anyone who they thought was anti-Soviet. He spoke good German so they sent him to Berlin as a spy. At the end of the war he escaped to Moscow and lived there for a couple of years. When the cold war started they sent him to spy for them in London and we caught him and turned him.'

Nick gets to his feet and puts his glass on the mantlepiece. 'I'd like you to meet my boss.'

'Have I got a choice?'

He laughs. 'Not really.'

I swallow the rest of my whisky and lead him to the front door. He puts his hat on and says, 'Shall I send a car for you in an hour?'

'If you want.'

I go to open the door but he puts a hand on my arm.

'Won't you be happier knowing that you're serving your country?'

'I'm not sure it's that simple.'

'There won't be any need for you to curtail your other activities.'

I open the door for him.

'Goodbye Rina,' he says, as he walks towards the lift.

I go back into the lounge, pour myself a whisky, sit down on the sofa and take a long drink.

My life's like a lobster pot; dead easy to get into but fucking difficult to get out of.

10

I'm sitting at the kitchen table with my third glass of whisky, dipping into a packet of crisps and staring out of the window. I'm thinking that maybe one source of work's much like another when all's said and done, and working for toffs might even be better than working for villains. If MI6 want to do me up they'll probably just put me away, but if a London firm want rid of me I'm dead. A bird wheels around in the sky above Hamilton Terrace. I wish I could glide about over the city like him and then out over the fields and the rivers and the sea. Georgie told me that some birds fly thousands of miles over continents to follow the warm sunshine and have their babies.

The phone rings and it's the porter telling me there's a car waiting for me. I look at what I'm wearing and tell him I'll be five minutes. I go in the bedroom, change into my black Emilio Pucci suit and a pair of mid-heeled court shoes. I put on make-up, brush my hair, pick up my handbag and push my flick knife into the opening that I've made on the strap. I check myself in the mirror and go downstairs to the foyer. I can see a grey Humber Hawk out front and the driver's standing beside it smoking a fag. Reg is at the desk and I go over.

'Any news on Dennis?'

'He's coming out tomorrow.'

'Is he coming back to work?'

'End of the week, I think.'

Reg opens the glass door for me and I put a two bob bit in his hand.

'Cheers miss,' he says and goes back to his desk.

The driver sees me, chucks away his fag and opens the car door for me. I get into the back seat. The man next to me turns, raises his black trilby and offers me his hand.

'I'm David Collins.'

'And if you go near my sister again I'll cut your face off.'

He puts his hand in the pocket of his raincoat. 'I was merely ensuring that she was unhurt.'

'Fuck you.'

He sniffs, turns and looks out of the window. I notice the driver taking a quick look at me in the mirror with a slight smile on his face.

We drive down to Hyde Park Corner, past Buckingham Palace, along the Mall, turn right along the side of St James's Park and on past the tube station. The car stops on a corner, beside a sign saying Caxton Street. Collins turns to me and points through the windscreen.

'Walk along there and you'll see St Ermin's Hotel on your left. Take the lift to the fifth floor, go to room 272 and knock on the door.'

I ignore him, get out of the car and walk past blocks of mansion flats on each side of the street. I turn left and see the entrance to the hotel at the end of a short road. I walk between two matching statues of a white lion with a bad haircut holding a shield with curly edges. I pass under a metal archway, up some stone steps and through the front door. The entrance hall is really big and swanky with pillars and crystal chandeliers and a white stone stairway in the middle which divides halfway up and leads onto curving balconies. I spot a sign for the lift at the far side of the hall and walk across the marble floor and round the side of the stairway. I look into the bar, where a couple of groups of men in suits are talking, and find the lift tucked away next to a barber's shop. I step in and ask for the fifth floor. The attendant closes the gates, turns the brass handle and the lift rises.

I find the room and knock. Nick opens the door and shows me into a bedroom with a leather topped desk at the foot of the bed and a sofa and a couple of armchairs in front of it. There are men's coats and hats and a couple of briefcases on the bed. A distinguished looking man in a dark suit and a blue striped tie with grey hair, bushy eyebrows and a full moustache under a beaky nose is sitting at the desk. He stands up and walks towards me. Nick says, 'May I introduce Sir Robert Monkton. Sir Robert, this is Rina Walker.'

I notice that Nick's wearing the same blue striped tie. I shake hands with Sir Robert and he smiles and says, 'Welcome Miss Walker. Thank you so much for coming. What will you have to drink?'

Nick moves to a table by the window. 'Whisky for you Rina, if I'm not mistaken?'

'Yeah, thanks,' I say and I notice Sir Robert wincing slightly as he hears me speak. He goes back behind the desk and says, 'I'll have one too Nicholas. Do sit down Miss Walker.'

'Call me Rina.'

'Very well.'

Nick gives us drinks and sits on the sofa. I sink into one of the armchairs and take a sip of a very good whisky. Sir Robert looks at me for a moment before speaking.

'I won't beat about the bush Rina. We've looked into your background and what little we've been able to find out about you indicates that you have a considerable talent for operating in such a way as to leave very little, if any, trace of your presence behind you. This, as you can probably imagine, is

105

a valuable asset for anyone involved in the field of military intelligence and we would like to know if you would be interested in working with us.'

'You've got me for a murder so we both know I can't say no.'

He hesitates a moment and I think I see a slight smile as he flicks a look at Nick.

'In order to bring charges we would have to reveal the identity of a man who doesn't officially exist.'

'You've lost me.'

'The long and the short of it is, we would lose control of a valuable network of agents in the process of attempting to prosecute you and it simply would not be a price worth paying.'

'So I could get up and walk out of here?'

'You could…'

'But you'd stay on me and get me clean for the next one.'

'Quite possibly.'

'I told you she was quick,' says Nick.

'I only wish some of our more educated colleagues could demonstrate such perspicacity,' says Sir Robert.

I want to ask him to write down whatever it is he thinks I've demonstrated so I can look it up later but instead I say,

'You want me to kill people.'

'Precisely.'

'What's the money?'

Sir Robert looks annoyed for a moment but I'm getting a bit fed up with all this upper class tom-foolery and I want to get home and get Georgie's tea. Sir Robert sits back in his chair.

'Untraceable cash payments, the size of which will depend upon locations, circumstances, nature of target and any other considerations.'

'A grand minimum.'

He thinks for a minute, gives a look at Nick and says, 'I think we'd find that acceptable.'

'Plus expenses.'

He seems to find this amusing. 'Fair enough,' he says.

'There's another thing,' I say.

'Yes?'

'I deal with you and Nick only. No one else knows my name or anything about me and nothing gets written down or recorded anywhere.'

'That we can guarantee. You should also know that should you be captured, arrested or otherwise detained either within or beyond British Territory we will deny any knowledge of you. You will be entirely on your own. Do you understand?'

'I understand.'

Sir Robert gets up, walks round the desk and shakes my hand.

'Welcome aboard.'

As Sir Robert walks back to his desk Nick goes to him and whispers something. Sir Robert says, 'Ah yes, indeed. Thank you Nicholas, I was forgetting.' He turns to me.

'I gather you'd like your younger sister to board at Leavenden School.'

'Er, yes I would,' I say, wondering how Lordy can be tied up with all this malarky.

'A place has been arranged for her which she can take up as soon as you wish. I believe you've already met the headmistress and so perhaps you would care to telephone the registrar and tell her when your sister will be arriving.'

He hands me a piece of paper with a name and a telephone number on it.

'The fees for the year will be taken care of.'

'Well, that's...'

'Goodbye Miss Walker.'

Sir Robert goes back to his desk, Nick opens the door for me and we walk down the corridor. As we reach the lift I decide to play it safe.

'I'll take the stairs.'

Nick smiles.

'You're right to be discreet but there's no need for that here.'

I think of those suited gents in the bar downstairs and turn and walk away. He puts his hand on my arm. 'Wait a second.'

I turn to face him and he says, 'We need to talk about how we communicate.'

'You know the Warrington pub in Maida Vale?' I ask.

'Yes.'

'Saloon bar, near closing time, when it's crowded.'

'Good.'

'You know my car?'

'Yes.'

'Tape a message under the front wheel arch on the driver's side when you need to see me.'

'Ok.'

'No phones.'

'Right.'

'And not a word of this to Lizzie.'

'Of course.'

He smiles and says, 'I knew you'd be good at this.'

I walk across the foyer and out through the glass doors. There's a fine drizzle of rain and I turn my face up to it and feel it nice and cool on my skin. When I get to Caxton Street I can see the Humber with Collins in the back seat parked along to the right, so I turn left and walk fast towards Buckingham Gate. As I get to the corner a cab comes along and I hail it and jump in. As it pulls away I look out of the back window but there's no sign of the Humber.

It's gone four o'clock when I get back to the flat. I push the heavy door open and the smell of bacon reminds me how hungry I am. I go in the kitchen and Georgie's sitting at the table eating a sandwich. She looks up.

'I finished my mock exams today.'

'Go well?'

'I reckon.'

'That's great.'

She looks happier than I've seen her in a long time. 'Is that enough for your tea?'

She holds up her sandwich and says, 'I'll have another one, if you're making.'

The frying pan's still warm so I light the gas and put in two rashers of bacon for her and two for me.

'There's tea in the pot,' says Georgie.

I pour myself a cup, put the bread board on the table, sit down and cut four slices. Georgie's looking out of the window and I think how long it is since I've seen her at this table without her nose in a book. When the bacon's done I make two sandwiches and give one to her.

'You remember that boarding school we went to see down in Kent a while back?'

'That massive country house with the lake and the woods and that?'

'That's the one.'

'It was amazing.'

'You can go there if you like.'

'You said they wouldn't have me.'

'That was only because they didn't have a place for you but someone's dropped out and they can take you now.'

'Now?'

'If you want.'

She looks down at the floor for a moment and then she stands up and looks out of the window again. I can see she's not sure what to do.

'Do you want to think about it for a bit?'

After a moment she turns back from the window and says, 'No. I want to go.'

'Now?'

'Yes.'

'You sure?'

'Yes.'

I look at her standing at the window and think how well she's done with her schoolwork and how I'll miss her and worry that she's all right among all those posh girls and the teachers and whether she's getting a hard time from them and how I won't be there to protect her. She turns to me.

'Will I still take my proper O levels this year if I go now?'

'Shall I phone them and find out?'

'Yes.'

I take the piece of paper that Sir Robert gave me out of my handbag and unfold it. The registrar's name is Dorothea Simpkins. I pick up my teacup, go to the phone table in the hall and dial the number. After a few rings a crisp woman's voice answers.

'Leavenden School for girls.'

I clear my throat and say, 'Can I speak to Miss Simpkins please?'

'Who's calling?'

'My name's Catherine Walker.'

'One moment please.'

I take a sip of tea and then a voice says, 'Dorothea Simpkins.'

'Sir Robert Monkton told me to phone you about my sister Georgina.'

'Sir Robert Monkton?'

'Yes.'

After a pause, she says, 'Would you hold the line for a moment please.'

I sip tea. Georgie's still staring out of the kitchen window. I close the door gently. After a minute or two Miss Simpkins says, 'Yes Miss Walker, we will be pleased to receive Georgina as a pupil. When would you like her to come?'

'As soon as she can.'

'If you would like her to begin immediately she could join us on Monday, one week from today, at the end of the half-term holiday. Girls will arrive on the Sunday evening prior, by the four-fifteen from Victoria arriving at Leavenden Halt at ten minutes past five, if that would be convenient for you.'

'It would.'

'Very well. I shall send you the school uniform list, and other information as to what she will require by the last post today. Winter and summer school uniform and sports clothing and equipment can be obtained from Perry Uniforms in Knightsbridge, where you will need to book an appointment. Ballet uniform is available at the Royal Academy of Dance shop in Battersea Square.'

'Ok.'

'I shall send you details of which boarding house she will be in, which form and all relevant information.'

'She's just done her mock O levels and she wants to know if she'll be able to take the real ones in the summer.'

'We're told she's only fourteen years old.'

'She's fifteen next month.'

'In that case, provided her mock results are satisfactory, I see no reason why not.'

'Ok, thanks.'

'As it happens we have another girl of the same age joining us at the same time. Her family are in the diplomatic service and I shall endeavour to put she and Georgina in the same boarding house so that they won't be the only new girls.'

'Ok, thanks.'

'Please telephone me if you need any further information.'

'I will.'

'Goodbye Miss Walker.'

I put the phone down, go back in the kitchen and tell Georgie that it's all on for her to go next Sunday.

'Ok,' she says, as she spreads jam on a piece of bread and takes a bite. I can tell she's nervous about going but being Georgie I know she won't let on.

'We've got to get your uniform and sports stuff from a shop in Knightsbridge. I'll make an appointment for us to go down there as soon as I get the list of what you'll need from the school.'

'Ok.'

'They do ballet at the school as well.'

She stops chewing for a moment and looks at me. 'Will I have to do it?'

'Don't you want to?'

'I dunno.'

'You've got the legs for it.'

'Have I?'

'You might as well give it a go.'

'I suppose.'

As I'm about to pour myself another cup of tea, there's a sharp knock on the door. I go through to the hall and I can see Lizzie through the spy hole in her fur coat. I open up and her look tells me something's wrong.

'Come,' she says.

'What's up,' I say, as she opens the door to her flat.

'It's Lordy.'

'What?'

'He's fucking dead.'

11

The bedroom looks empty when I walk in but when I turn round to speak to Lizzie I see him hanging from a hook on the back of the door. There's a leather strap round his neck and he's naked except for a nappy. His face is purple, his eyes are wide open and his tongue is hanging out of his gaping mouth. Lizzie comes and stands beside me. I put my arm round her and I can feel her trembling. She grips my arm.

'What am I going to do?'

'It's ok, we can handle it.'

'How?'

'We get him out of here.'

'How the fuck do we do that?'

'I can make a phone call.'

'Do it.'

'It'll cost.'

'How much?'

'About a monkey.'

'Do it. I just want him gone.'

I go to the telephone in the hall and call Bert's number but there's no reply. He's probably in the pub by now, so I look in Lizzie's phone directory for the number of the Walmer Castle. After a few rings a bloke answers and I ask if Bert's there. The bloke tells me to hang on and after a bit Bert asks who it is. I tell him the score, knock him down to four hundred quid and he says he'll be over in an hour. I go back into the bedroom and tell Lizzie it's on.

'Thank fuck for that. Let's get out of here and have a drink.'

We go through to her bedroom and she pours two large whiskies and gives one to me. We sit on the bed.

'So what happened?' I ask.

'It was one of his nappy days. I'd finished him and put him to bed and read him a story. He dropped off, as he normally does and I went in the living room for a drink. After I'd been in there for a bit I heard the front door shut and I thought he must have got dressed and gone so I went back in and then I found him.'

'Someone got in.'

'Must have.'

'Is the lock forced?'

'No.'

'You need to change it.'

'Of course.'

'I'll give you the locksmith's number. Does anyone else have a key?'

'Not likely.'

'Do you lock it when you've got business?'

'Of course I do.'

'Who knows he came here?'

'No one that I know of.'

'How did you meet him?'

'Through a pimp.'

'Is he about?'

'He's dead.'

'How come?'

'Got called up, went in the army and got killed

115

by the Mau Mau in Kenya.'

'Bad luck.'

'Not really, he was a right cunt.'

'Did Nick ever see Lordy here?'

'No.'

'You sure?'

'Yeah. Why?'

'Just thinking.'

Lizzie stands up and says, 'I need another drink.'

'We should get him ready for the undertakers.'

We go back into the bedroom. Lizzie unpins his nappy and we lift his naked body off the back of the door and lay him on the bed. I unwind the leather strap from round his neck and close his eyes and his mouth. I get a wet cloth from the kitchen and wipe the drool off his chin. His pinstripe suit is hanging on the coat stand in the corner. When we finally get his trousers, shirt, waistcoat, jacket and shoes on him he looks a bit more like a deceased peer of the realm and a bit less like an old pervert.

We go into Lizzie's bedroom while we wait for Bert. Lizzie takes off her fur coat and her leather bikini and puts on a pair of jeans and a cashmere sweater. She pours us another drink and we sit on the bed. She looks sad for a moment.

'Who'd want to kill a nice old boy like that?'

I'm wondering the same thing but I don't want to tell Lizzie what I'm thinking as it could put her in danger. I put my arm round her and I can see tears in her eyes as she says, 'He was always so kind and polite.'

I settle her back against the silk pillows, nestle in

next to her and we sip our drinks. After a bit I put the glasses on the bedside table, turn towards her and lightly brush my fingers over the back of her hand, along her wrist, up her arm and delicately stroke her neck. I feel her relaxing and I close my eyes, drift away from thinking about possible connections between Lordy and Nick and the secret service toffs' club, and slide my arms round the one person who can take me home. As our lips touch, the phone rings on the bedside table. Lizzie reaches across me and picks it up. She listens, then says, 'Fridge?' Another silence, then she says, 'I haven't ordered any fridge.'

I grab the phone from her, cover the mouth-piece and say, 'It'll be them, for the body.'

I uncover the phone, think of Dorothea Simpkins and say, 'That's all right porter, this is her flatmate. I'm expecting a delivery of a refrigerator. Kindly send them up.'

Lizzie laughs and says, 'Get you, Miss Poshpants!'

I reach for my jacket and say, 'Best if you leave this to me, ok?'

'Are you sure?'

'Yeah. Have you got the money?'

'It's in the kitchen.'

'Go and get it, leave it on the table, and then hide yourself in here.'

'Four hundred wasn't it?'

'That's it.'

Lizzie slips on a pair of mules, fetches the money from the kitchen and gives it to me. We sit on the bed and wait. She bows her head and I can tell she's upset by what's happened. I put my arm round her and settle her head on my shoulder.

There's a knock at the front door and I go along the corridor and open it. Bert and a ratty little mate of his called Bunny are standing there with a large white fridge on a porter's trolley. Bert says, 'Been busy again Reen?'

I step aside and they wheel the fridge past me and park it inside the door. I lead them to the bedroom and show them the body. Bert takes a look at it, notices a whip sticking out from under the bed, looks at me and says, 'This isn't your gaff is it?'

'Are you going to do this or not?' I say.

'All right, keep your hair on,' says Bert.

Bunny goes to the foot of the bed, takes hold of Lordy's ankles and Bert grabs his shoulders. As they lift him off the bed the foul smell coming from his pinstripes makes me wish we'd left his nappy on. They carry him into the corridor. I open the door of the fridge and they stuff the body in and close it up while I go and get the money from the kitchen. When I get back they're unfolding a green canvas sheet and putting it over the fridge. I give Bert the money.

'Where's he going?'

Bert counts the notes, puts them in his pocket. 'Crusher.'

I open the door for them and Bunny wheels the trolley towards the lift. Bert lingers a moment and I know he wants to find out what's gone on but he's too much of an old pro to ask.

'See you Bert,' I say, as I close the door.

I go into the bedroom. Lizzie's sitting on the bed with a glass in her hand. 'Everything okay?'

she says.

'All gone.'

'Thanks doll.'

'No bother.'

As I sit down beside her the phone rings. Lizzie picks up the receiver and says, 'Cunningham 4619.' After a moment she shakes her head. 'I can't do anything today I'm afraid. Can you come tomorrow?'

She agrees to a time tomorrow afternoon and puts the phone down. 'I can't work today.'

'I think you could do with a rest.'

I fluff up her pillows, take her glass and put it on the bedside table.

'Mmmm,' she says, as she settles back onto the bed and closes her eyes. I sit beside her and put my hand on hers. When her breathing slows and I know she's asleep, I kiss her lightly on the cheek and close the door quietly as I leave.

I let myself into the flat and look in on Georgie. She's lying on her bed with a big book. I sit down beside her and ask her what she's reading. She shows me it's the encyclopaedia.

'I've looked up Leavenden School. It was started in nineteen-twenty by three ladies and it was turned into a military hospital for soldiers and that in the war and it's got a swimming pool and a Norwegian princess has been there.'

'A swimming pool will be nice.'

'And the girls sleep in different houses and go to lessons in the main school.'

'Are you looking forward to going?'

'I think so. What's lacrosse?'

'I think it's like tennis.'

'Oh.'

Georgie goes on reading and I look at the row of Encyclopaedia Britannicas on the shelf and remember when my mate Sammy nicked a set years ago from a big house in Holland Park that we screwed together, reckoning they were some rare books that would be worth a few bob. When he couldn't sell them he hid them in Georgie's bedroom and she wouldn't let me get rid of them until I agreed to buy her new ones.

The phone rings in the hall and I leave Georgie reading and go and answer it. It's Tony Farina.

'Why no word from you?'

'I had to take care of a couple of things.'

'You need to get on it.'

His tone of voice tells me I'd better do as he says. 'Ok,' I say.

'Let me know.'

I hear the dial tone and put the phone down. I look at my watch and see that it's gone ten o'clock. I open Georgie's door.

'I've got to go out for a bit.'

She looks up from the encyclopaedia, 'When are we going to get my uniform and that?'

'As soon as we get the list from the school. Maybe tomorrow?'

'Ok.'

I go and find my handbag and take out the piece of paper that Tony gave me with Heinz's address on it. It's in Catford, which is quite a schlep, but I may as well start by having a sniff round his gaff before I start asking questions in the clubs. All I really want to do is go to bed and read about Elizabeth and Mr Darcy but Tony's got a lot of weight behind him and I can't afford to piss him off. I change out of my skirt and jacket and put on black ski pants, a T-shirt, my old leather biker's jacket and a pair of ankle boots with a solid toe. I put a torch, my gun and a leather wallet where I keep my lock picks, in my handbag. I find the locksmith's number, write it on a piece of paper and put it in my pocket. I tell Georgie I might be late and lock up behind me as I leave. On the way past Lizzie's I slip the locksmith's number under the door.

I check under the wheel arch of the car but there's nothing from Nick. I get in, find my A–Z and look up Pelinore Road in Catford. I drive to Marble Arch, down Park Lane and past Buckingham Palace then I'm over Westminster Bridge and on the Old Kent Road to Catford with Gene Vincent coming and going on Radio Luxembourg. When I reach Catford High Street I pull over and check the map again. I drive on and find the street I want on an estate of white prefabs; boxy little one storey houses that they made the German prisoners build after the war for all the people who were homeless after the Blitz. I drive along the street until I spot number twenty-three and park round the corner.

There's no light in the windows and the street's quiet so I open my handbag, put the gun in my belt and the wallet and torch in my jacket pockets. I get out of the car, put the bag in the boot and walk towards the house. Light from a TV flickers against the net curtains of the prefab next door and I hear someone laughing as I pass. I put one

121

hand on my gun, open the flimsy wooden gate of number twenty-three, walk up the path and round the side of the house. There are no lights on at the back so I move round to the front door, ring the bell and step back to the side of the house.

There's no response so I go round the back again and inspect the windows. The frames are metal and they're all shut tight with curtains closed behind them. The back door has an old mortice deadlock so I kneel down, open up the wallet and take out a cut down key and a wire pick. I put the key in the lock, slide the pick in above it, feel around for the levers and lift them one by one with the pick. When I've got all five, I turn the key and open the lock. I put the key and the pick back in the wallet, put it in my pocket and switch on the torch.

I turn the handle and try to open the door. It moves a bit and then sticks against something. I put my shoulder to it and force it open a bit more. I turn on the torch, aim it through the gap to try and see what's blocking the door. There's a head with long dark hair on the floor. I push the door open a bit wider, squeeze through and shine the torch on the body of a young girl. She's naked and has had her throat cut. She's small, almost like a doll that's been left out once a child has finished playing with it. Her skin looks too white against the dark lino, like it's been bleached. She's staring at the ceiling with that shocked, vacant look they get. An insect crawls out of her pubic hair and scurries off across her thigh.

I shut the back door and shine the torch round the kitchen. There's a cooker, a sink full of dirty dishes, a table and two chairs. A bin in the corner is overflowing with screwed up fish and chip paper, and there's a rotten smell that's coming from more than the dead girl on the floor.

I go through the hall and into the living room. There's a sofa and an armchair and a radio in the corner. There are some books on a low table in front of the sofa. I pick one up and look at the foreign title that I suppose is German. I go into the bedroom and shine the torch over an unmade bed. There's a suitcase and some rolled up sheets of polythene on top of the wardrobe. I open the doors and find a sawn-off shotgun, a box of cartridges and a coil of rope behind the hanging clothes. The other bedroom's empty so I go back into the kitchen and the foul stench. I search the cupboards but they're empty apart from a couple of tins of beans.

I lock the back door with the pick and the cut down key I used to open it and put the dead girl back in the same position against the door. I'm turning to leave by the front door when I notice a cupboard under the sink that I didn't check. When I open the doors the stench hits me full in the face. It's another young girl and she's been dead a long time. She's in a sitting position with her knees drawn up as if she's hiding in there. The head's missing and there's mould growing on her skin. Her neck's been stitched together but blood's oozed through the join onto her shoulders and chest. I'm feeling sick and I stand up and retch over the sink but nothing comes up. I need fresh air so I close the cupboard and make for the door. As I pass the cooker I notice a large

123

pan on the top. I look inside it and stop. The blue eyes staring up at me from under the water look alive for a moment in the light of the torch. The sides of the pan are warm to the touch and there are flakes of skin floating on the surface of the water. As I stifle another wave of nausea I hear a car draw up outside.

Although I'd like to welcome this man home and put a stop to his funny little ways for good, I remember that Tony's only told me to have a look for now so I cross to a window, open it and climb through. As I'm shutting it behind me I hear the front door open. I drop onto the path and crouch down as the kitchen light goes on. I hear the door shutting, then footsteps and the sound of something being dragged across the floor. Rather than risk a peep round the curtain I back off across the lawn and stand behind a shed where I can see the kitchen windows. When the kitchen light goes off I creep round the side of the house and across the front garden, jump the fence and make it to my car.

I can't see the house from the car so I open the door, slip the handbrake and push it round the corner to a position where I get a good view of the front door. I get my handbag out of the boot and get into the car. As I'm trying to find a hanky to blow that horrible stink out of my nose the front door of the prefab opens and a tall bald-headed man walks up the front path carrying something wrapped in plastic over his shoulder. He walks to a grey van and opens the back doors. As he lowers the load into the van a naked foot pokes out of the plastic wrapping. He pushes the body along the floor of the van, and closes the doors. He gets into the driver's seat, starts the engine and pulls away. I wait until he's near the end of the road, then I follow him.

12

The grey van snakes round the bends on a twisty country lane. The moon's bright, which is just as well as I'm driving without lights most of the time so he can't see me. I'm keeping well back but I'm afraid he'll turn off when he's out of sight round one of these bends and I'll lose him. We've driven west out of London and along the A4 but since we've turned off it I've lost any sense of where we're headed.

When we come to a straight stretch of road with an old stone wall on one side I see the van slowing down so I pull back. It stops in front of some wooden gates set into the wall and our man gets out and opens them. He drives the van through the gates and closes them. I pull up close to the stone wall, get out of the car, climb onto the roof and look over the top. In the moonlight I can see the van going along a narrow drive, through tall trees, towards a big dark building with battlements. When I see the lake off to the side of the house I know it's Ringwood Hall.

I climb down and get back in the car. If this German bastard is knocking off girls and delivering them to the gentry I want to know why and

I'm sure Tony Farina will too. I start the car, drive up the lane until I see a cart track that leads into the woods. I bump the car along it, until I reckon it's out of sight, then I turn it round so that it's facing the lane. My watch says it's almost three o'clock. I walk back towards the gates and climb up a tall tree by the roadside to where I've got a good view over the wall to the back of the house and find myself a solid branch to sit on.

Various indignant birds flap away, squawking at me for waking them up in the middle of the night. I can see the back of the van sticking out from behind the brick building that I saw from the bedroom window, when me and Lizzie were here before, but there's no sign of Heinz or anyone else.

I listen to the wind in the trees and the odd scuttling sound of some creature on the lookout for its dinner, and I think of that pale body on the floor with the life drained out of it. I wonder what hopes she had and what makes a man so cold that he could kill a beautiful little thing like her. When I remember the one under the sink I rub the inside of my wrist against the bark of the tree until there's blood.

I'm counting the battlements outlined by the moonlight to stop myself falling asleep when I hear the van start up. It comes down the drive towards me and I'm able to get a look at Heinz as he gets out and opens the gates. He's well over six foot, with a big bald head on a pair of broad shoulders and he looks solid and in good shape. I grip the gun in my belt and wish I could drop him now before he carves up any more. He pulls the van into the lane, closes the gates and drives off the way he came. I climb down out of the tree and let myself in through the gates. I take a detour through the trees towards the brick building and circle round the back of it to where I can see into the yard in front of the stables. It seems quiet so I go round the building again and find a small back door. The mortice is old and stiff but with a bit of fiddling I get it to turn, ease the door open and lock it again behind me.

There's moonlight shining through the windows and I can see a row of cars down the length of each wall. They're all old grand tourers with the hoods down. I shine the torch over the one nearest me and see that she's a real beauty in a dark red colour with a silver bird flying off the bonnet and Hispano Suiza written across the radiator. There's a blue overall hanging over the driver's door and a toolbox on the floor. I want to have a good look at all of them but I remind myself what I'm here for and walk along the side wall behind the cars. At the far end, in the corner near the main doors I find a trapdoor set into the floor and another mortice. I pick the lock, lift the trap and see a spiral staircase leading down into darkness below.

I stop and listen and then I step in and close the trap above me. With the torch in my mouth I twist the key and the pick around until I finally lock the mortice then I put my hand on the wall and move slowly down the steps. When I get to the bottom I'm at the end of a narrow passage with doors off it that looks like it runs the length of the building. I try the handle of the first door and it turns. I open it and shine the torch onto a heavy velvet curtain. I find a light switch beside the door. I turn it on, open the velvet curtain and see a long narrow room with a black and white tiled floor.

There's an old-fashioned wooden piano type of thing against the left hand wall at the far end of the room with a chair in front of it. The lid's open and there's a painting of a landscape on it. There's a cello leaning against it with the bow in between the strings, and on the far wall, a big painting in a gold frame of two old-fashioned men and a woman playing a lute. One of the men is feeling the woman up and the other man's having a go at him and pointing to his hand as if he wants money. The room looks ghostly and strange in the torchlight but I've an odd feeling that it's somehow familiar to me. As I'm closing the door I notice a pile of clothes in the corner. I lift up a blue and brown silk dress with white lace sleeves and a brown wig with a hairnet with white bits sewn into it. I put the clothes back and turn off the light.

I go along to the next door, open it and shine the torch round. The room's empty except for a bed with a dark red velvet cover and a light blue pillow. There are dark red drapes hanging behind the bed and the dead girl from the kitchen in Catford is lying on it. She's naked with her arms folded behind her head. Her hair is pulled back from her face, her eyes are open and her eyebrows and her eyelashes have been darkened with make-up. Her knees are drawn up a bit, her lower half is turned away slightly and she looks as though she's stretching herself after she's woken up. There's a lamp on a stand beside the door. When I find the switch and turn it on, a warm red light touches her curves and she almost seems to come alive.

There's a noise above me. I snap off the light and freeze in the doorway. I can hear the trap-door being unlocked, then there's light at the foot of the stairs and footsteps. I slip into the room, close the door and roll under the bed.

There are more footsteps then the door opens. The light goes on and I hear a voice I recognise.

'I hope this will be to Your Lordship's liking.'

It's the old butler who let us in before. There's a silence and then another male voice,

'The lady is good Symmonds, but the arms aren't quite right.'

'I beg your pardon My Lord.'

'They should be slightly higher.'

I stop breathing as he approaches the bed. 'Like so... Do you see?'

'Indeed My Lord.'

'And the knees ... thus.'

'I must apologise My Lord.'

'No matter. You may leave me.'

'Thank you My Lord.'

'I shall knock in the usual way.'

'Very good My Lord.'

The door opens and then the Lord says, 'One moment Symmonds.'

There's a silence. I can see his feet stepping back from the bed and I breathe again.

'She's too small for the Vermeer and probably too old.'

'Very good My Lord.'

'She might do for the Renoir.'

'Rest after the Bath perhaps?'

'Possibly.'

'Would you wish her to be embalmed My Lord?'

'I think she'd appreciate it.'

'Very good My Lord.'

'Thank you Symmonds.'

The door shuts and he starts breathing heavily as he approaches the bed. The wooden frame sags on one side as he sits on it and I shift slightly to avoid it. He stands up again and I can see his feet pacing back and forth in front of the door and his breathing's getting louder and he starts making a strange kind of moaning sound as he walks faster and faster. His jacket lands in the corner of the room and then he's kicking his shoes off and then his socks and then his trousers come off.

His shirt and tie land next to them on the floor and he's moaning and groaning louder and louder until all his clothes are off and he's pacing faster and faster. He dives at the bed and lands full length and it's all I can do not to cry out as the bed frame digs into me. There's a moment of stillness with just the sound of his breathing and then he starts moaning again and bucking up and down on the poor dead girl and calling her a whore and a dirty little tart and all that stuff that they do and I'm being pummelled half to death with each thrust.

He finally gets to where he's going and after he's lain quiet for a bit he gets up off the bed and puts his clothes on. I'm hoping he'll be going and I can find a way out of here but he comes to the bed again and crouches down beside it with his knees next to my face. He's silent for a bit and then I can hear him mumbling something above me which I can't make out. He's sounding tearful and I catch the word mummy a couple of times, then his voice tails off and he stands up and walks to the door, opens it, turns back towards the bed for a moment before turning off the light and closing the door behind him.

I roll out from under the bed, feel my way to the door and put my ear against it. I hear a bang that sounds like the trap shutting. I listen for a bit longer and when I hear nothing I turn on the light and look at the dead girl. She's in the same position she was in when I first saw her with her arms stretched above her head and her knees pulled up and over to the side. In spite of the rosy glow of the light her skin is blotchy now with blue and white patches. Her mouth is open and her eyes have started to bulge. I go to her and close her mouth and her eyelids. I put my hand on her arm and feel how cold she is.

I turn the light off, move along the passage and up the stairs. I turn the lock, raise the trap very slowly until I can see that the coast is clear, and then I'm out and moving past the grand motors towards the back door. I do the lock, walk to the corner of the building and see if there's anyone about in the yard between the outbuildings and the house. It's daylight now and a door to the stables opens and a young lad with a mop of red hair walks across to the house and taps on one of the windows. After a second the window opens and a girl in a maid's uniform leans out and gives him a kiss. The boy says something and they laugh then the girl disappears for a moment and then

131

she's there again and giving him a slice of bread and jam. He kisses her again, she shuts the window and he trots off back to the stables chewing on his breakfast.

I go round the back of the brick building and it looks clear all the way to the gates. I set off through the woods, keeping away from the track. The birds are singing away and flying from tree to tree above me. I'm nearly at the gates and passing a big old oak tree when a man steps out from behind the trunk and stops a few feet in front of me. He's got a red weatherbeaten face under a wide-brimmed hat. He's wearing a long brown coat and he's pointing a shotgun at my head. He stares me in the eye.

'I seen you come in.' When I don't speak he takes a step towards me and says, 'I know what you done an'all.'

His eyes narrow and he puts the barrels of the gun right up to my face. I move my hand very slowly towards the gun in my belt. Just as my fingers touch the grip he says, 'I ain't going to kill you but they will if they catch you.'

He lowers the gun slowly and I let my hand drop to my side. He takes a step back and looks me up and down. He's half smiling when he says, 'You best not come round here again.'

He turns and walks towards the gates and I follow a few paces behind him. He opens them for me and I go through and onto the lane. I hear a solid thud as they shut behind me.

13

I park in Hall Road, walk round the corner and
in through the glass doors. Reg is at the desk and
I ask for news of Dennis. He tells me he'll be
back at the beginning of next week and goes on
studying his *Racing Times*.

I go up in the lift, let myself into the flat, knock
on Georgie's door and poke my head round. She's
lying on her bed reading with one arm behind her
head and I see the image of the dead girl on the
bed for a moment until I dig my nails into my
wrist and drive it away.

Georgie looks up from her book.
'I didn't know you'd be gone all night.'
'Something came up.'
'Ok.'
'You all right?'
'Just reading.'
'Do you want a cup of tea?'
'Yeah. I'll come through in a minute.'

I go into the kitchen and put the kettle on. I
open the cabinet, cut a couple of slices of bread,
make myself a jam sandwich and remind myself
that I must get some shopping done today. Lizzie
told me there's one of those new Sainsbury's
shops opened in Kensington High Street that sell
all sorts of food and I want to get down there and
have a look. While I'm filling the teapot I hear the
letter box snap shut and I put the kettle down and

go into the hall. There are two letters on the floor. One's the gas bill and the other has a crest on it with some foreign words underneath it. I open it and see that it's the list from the school of what Georgie needs for her uniform and her sports clothes. It's much longer than I was expecting, with a coat and a cloak and different skirts and dresses that we can get from this Perry's Uniforms place in Knightsbridge. There's another list of dance clothes as well from another shop. It says she's to be in Richmond House, and there's a plan of the school that shows where it is and a list of the names of the housemistress and the matron and that. It says she's in the fifth form and that her form mistress is a Miss Weston. I take it into the kitchen and I'm reading through it when Georgie comes in. She looks at the envelope on the table and asks, 'Is that the clothes list?'

'Yes,' I say and hand it to her.

She looks it up and down and says, 'Blimey.' She turns to the second page. 'What are bloomers?'

'Big knickers.'

'What do I need them for?'

'Nice and warm in the winter.'

'What's a straw boater when it's at home?'

'It's a hat, silly. Henley Regatta and all that.'

'When are we going to the shop?'

'This afternoon if you like.'

'Ok.'

I see that the phone number for Perry's Uniforms is on the clothes list. It's a Knightsbridge number that's easy to remember so I leave her reading the list while I go to the phone in the hall and dial it. A woman answers and when I explain that we want the uniform for Leavenden she says we can come in at three o'clock. I tell Georgie what time we're going, then I close the kitchen door and dial Tony Farina's number. When he answers I say, 'I need to see you.'

'Can you come now?'

'Half an hour.'

I go into my room and take off my clothes. All I want to do is get into bed and sleep but the vision of that dead girl all got up for His Lordship's pleasure keeps me on my feet. I put on clean underwear and nylons, a black skirt and jacket with a silk blouse and a pair of black heels. In the bathroom I splash my face with cold water and put on mascara and lipstick. Georgie's back in her room reading. I tell her I'll be back in time for lunch and head for the lift.

Two men in dark suits come out of Tony's office and one of them nods at me as they pass. I know I've seen him somewhere but I don't know where so I give him a quick smile and go on looking at the picture of the beautiful lake and wishing I was there. Tony opens his office door.

'Rina. Sorry for keep you waiting. Please to come.'

I follow him into the office and sit in front of his desk. He goes to the cocktail cabinet and picks up a bottle.

'For you?'

'Not now thanks.'

He pours himself a drink, sits behind his desk and says, 'Heinz.'

'He's killing your girls, taking them to the

country for an old creeper to dress them up and fuck them cold.'

Tony swallows a mouthful of his drink and puts the glass down. 'Who's the creeper?'

I'm going to kill the German anyway and I may as well get Tony to pay me for it but I reckon it's safer to keep him in the dark about whatever else I've lifted the lid on down at the old country seat.

'Just some old fossil,' I say.

'Where's the house?'

'Somewhere out west in the sticks.'

'You don't have the address?'

'It was dark and I was keeping my head down.'

He gets up, refills his glass and stands looking out of the window. I reckon he knows I'm not giving him everything but there's not a lot he can do.

'Ok. Enough with the girls anyway. You take care of Heinz for me?'

'It'll be two large. One now and one when I've done him.'

'How soon?'

'Soon as I find him.'

He comes and sits behind his desk, opens a drawer, takes out a bundle of fifties, counts off twenty and hands them to me. I fold them and put them in my bag. As I move to the door he says, 'You keep in touch.'

On the way back to the flat I stop on Edgware Road and buy a couple of meat pies from a baker's shop. It's gone half past ten by the time I get home. I tell Georgie we'll go shopping after lunch and to wake me up at one o'clock. I put the pies in the kitchen and the money behind the bath then I go into my bedroom, take my clothes off and slip between the sheets.

I'm in the red room again and the dead girl's lying on the bed. She's bruised black and blue all over and her skin's peeling off her legs and her arms. I turn and try to open the door but it's locked.

My hand goes to my pocket for my lock pick but I look down and I'm naked as well. I rattle the door and try to pull it open but I can't shift it. I look round and the girl's opening her eyes, getting up off the bed and coming towards me. There's blood dripping off the ends of her fingers as she walks. Her eyes are black and wide open and she's staring at me and grinning with bright red lips stretched over gleaming white teeth. As she comes near me I open my mouth to scream but I can't make a sound. She reaches out for me but I slip past her, run through a gap in the red drapes and I'm in a field in moonlight and I'm trying to run but my legs are like lead and I can hardly get one in front of the other. I struggle forwards over the wet grass and my legs are getting heavier and heavier and I can hear the girl laughing behind me and she's getting closer. I feel her clawing at my shoulders and I'm using all my strength to keep going and all at once there's a big broad tree in front of me and the man with the shotgun is there. The girl screams and I stop in front of him. The girl's standing beside me and the man's giving me that slight smile and looking me slowly up and down. When he looks at the girl she lowers her head and starts trembling. He puts his hand under her chin, lifts her face up and looks into her eyes. She turns slowly and walks away from us and after a few steps she fades into darkness. I look back towards the man but he's gone and the tree is moving and changing shape. The wood is becoming smooth and flat and shiny and then I recognise my wardrobe and Georgie's knocking on the door.

I tell her to turn the oven on and I get out of bed, go to the bathroom and splash cold water on my face to shoo the dream away. I put on the black suit I was wearing earlier and go through to the kitchen. I put the pies in the oven and open a tin of beans to have with them. I put the beans in a pan on the stove, light the gas, stir them with a wooden spoon and hope I'm not going to dream about what was in the last saucepan I looked in. When it's ready I call Georgie and we eat at the kitchen table. She's asking me questions about the school and that and I can tell she's worried about going but I'm glad to see that she's excited. I really hope she's going to be happy there. I know she'll do well with the work, as she always has, but I'm hoping she'll make some friends and start enjoying life.

I wash up the plates and Georgie dries them. I pick up the list from the table and we put our coats on, go down in the lift and walk over to where the car's parked in Hall Road. I check under the wheel arch and find a message from Nick to meet in the Warrington at ten o'clock tonight. I screw up the paper and put it in my pocket then I drive us to Knightsbridge. Georgie finds the Third Programme on the radio and we listen to an orchestra playing. It finishes when we get to Hyde Park Corner and while they're clapping the announcer says it's from the Wigmore

Hall and the soloist is a woman called Jacqueline du Pré. Georgie says she's brilliant because she's only sixteen and she's a prodigy. I don't know what a prodigy is but I don't let on.

I park the car in Beauchamp Place and we walk past the expensive clothes and jewellery shops. Perry Uniforms is near the corner of Old Brompton Road next to a hairdresser's. As I open the door a tall woman and a little girl are on their way out with a young bloke with very blond hair, who looks like a shop assistant, following behind them carrying two big carrier bags and a hat box. We stand back to let them pass and the woman nods to us as they head for a Bentley parked at the kerb. The chauffeur sees them and scoots round the back of the car to open the door for them. When they're seated inside he opens the boot and helps the assistant put the bags in. The assistant waits until they drive off and then he opens the door to the shop, ushers us inside, stands to attention, flicks his hair back and says, 'Can I help you madam?'

'I made an appointment for three o'clock. We want a uniform for my sister who's going to Leavenden School,' I say, indicating Georgie.

He looks doubtful for a second as he registers my accent so I take the list out of my pocket and say, 'She's going to be in Richmond House.'

He clears his throat and says, 'Certainly madam. Allow me to fetch someone for you.'

He minces off to the back of the shop swinging his bum and comes back with an older woman with grey lacquered hair, wire rimmed glasses and a disapproving look on her face. Our man puts his hand on his hip and says, 'This is Miss Stewart. She'll be looking after you.'

By the look of Miss Stewart I think I'd rather have blondie looking after us but I tell her our names and she spares us a tight smile. I show her the list and she asks us to follow her upstairs.

We walk past rows of clothes rails to a fitting room at the far end of the shop. Miss Stewart shows us in and writes down Georgie's name and takes her measurements, then she tells us she'll be back in a moment and disappears. The room's got mirrors all round and Georgie can see herself from angles she's never seen before. While I sit down she turns around and looks at herself and then she puts her arms out and then up over her head, then she stands on one leg and slides her other foot up to her knee and I can tell she's thinking about the ballet lessons she'll be having and I'm hoping it's all going to be all right for her.

Miss Stewart comes back in with an armful of clothes, followed by a girl carrying more.

They hang up various coats and dresses and lay out blouses and skirts and underwear and stockings and shoes on various chairs. Georgie's asked to take her clothes off and try things on. They begin with the underwear, including the bloomers and work their way to the skirts and blouses and coats. The things that fit go on one pile and the things that don't on another while the girl is sent off to get replacements. Georgie puts on a uniform of a grey pleated skirt with a white Clydella blouse and I show her how to tie the house tie that goes with it. She tries on a dark blue blazer that Miss Stewart says is for weekdays and then a crêpe dress that's for Sundays and evenings. Georgie says the crêpe dress is scratchy and uncomfortable and I can see she doesn't like it, but I tell her it suits her and she does look really good in it. Then there's the straw boater and a blue woollen cloak with a hood that's also for Sundays. It looks like it's from the olden days but Georgie seems to like it and she swirls it round herself and looks at it in the mirror. Miss Stewart takes a note of her being in Richmond House so that they can put the right colours on the hat band of the boater and then she disappears and comes back with singlets and shorts and plimsolls and white socks for sports.

When Georgie's been fitted with all the sports clothes Miss Stewart asks me if I want name tapes put in the clothes. I say that I do and she says she'll send some extra ones to the school for the clothes Georgie's travelling in and that she's to give them to the matron to have them sewn in. She leaves us again and comes back with a strange looking wooden thing that looks like a fishing net.

She says it's a lacrosse stick and tells Georgie to try it. Georgie looks confused and Miss Stewart, looking even more irritated than she has so far, tells her to pick it up and see if it's too heavy.

Georgie swings it about a bit and says it's all right and Miss Stewart puts it on the pile, then she has a look at the list and tells us that will be all.

I look at the amount of gear we're buying and realise that I'll never get it all in the back of the Mini. I ask her if they can deliver and she tells me that they can send everything to the school if we wish but that we will require a trunk. I ask her where we can get one and she says they have a luggage department in the basement. She tells the girl to make a list of all the clothes we're buying, and leads us out of the fitting room and down the stairs. She asks us if we'd like to take one outfit with us now for Georgie to travel to school in and I say we would. She tells us to go to the basement and select a trunk and then to return to the ground floor so that she can prepare the account.

As we get to the bottom of the stairs the young bloke with the blond hair appears and says, 'Did you get everything you need?'

'I think so,' I say.

'So now you need a nice big trunk to stow it all in, eh?' He winks at Georgie, turns on his heel and says, 'This way ladies.'

He leads us past rows of suitcases to the back of the shop to where there's a line of cabin trunks standing against the wall. He stops in front of a metal one, pats it on the top and says, 'This is a Mossman in stucco aluminium. Nice and roomy with good chunky brass clasps and locks so you don't rip your nails apart trying to open it, quite light too for the size and it comes in silver like this or a nice azure blue like the one over there in the corner.' He swivels away from the Mossman, sits on the one next to it, crosses his legs and says, 'Then you've got your Antler. More traditional but hard wearing in a brown Rexine fibre with wooden bracing. All a bit dowdy for my liking but it takes all sorts.'

As he moves on to his next exhibit and puts his arm round it I look at my watch and realise we'd better be getting on if we're going to get to the ballet shop before closing time. As he opens his mouth to speak I point at the Mossman and say, 'We'll take that one thanks.'

He looks a bit crestfallen for a second then he sniffs, looks at Georgie and says, 'Do you like the silver or the blue young lady?'

'The blue, thanks,' says Georgie.

'Good taste as well as good looks, eh?'

Georgie looks embarrassed but I can tell she likes the compliment. As we move to the stairs I remember another thing that was on the list. I turn to the assistant and say, 'We'll need a tuck box as well.'

'Of course you will. They're just over here,' he says.

He leads past more suitcases and shows us a row of wooden boxes with metal corners standing on a shelf at the far end of the room. They all look the same so he shows us the inside of one and finds a small padlock to go with it. I tell him we'll have it and I decide to take it with us in the car so I can put some treats in it for her before she goes.

Miss Stewart looks a bit taken aback when I put three hundred and twenty notes on her desk after she's handed me the bill. She gets all flustered when she can't find change and she has to go into the back office to get it. I tell her that Georgie's going to Leavenden on the four-fifteen from Victoria next Sunday and she makes a note of it and tells me the trunk will be put on the same train.

I put the tuck box and the bag with her travelling clothes on the back seat of the car and it's over the river to the Royal Academy of Dance shop in

Battersea Square for the ballet clothes. The girl serving us is really nice and not all that posh and Georgie seems to enjoy trying on the leotard and the little skirt and the ballet shoes. We buy what she needs and I take Georgie for a cream tea at Lyons Corner House at Marble Arch on the way home.

14

The Warrington's well crowded and noisy when I get there just after ten and I press through the crush to the bar and wait to get served. A gent in a striped suit sitting on a bar stool offers to buy me a drink and I tell him I'm waiting for someone. When he starts slobbering and telling me how ravishing and gorgeous I am I remember why I don't go to pubs any more and move away from him along the bar. I buy a large whisky and head for the back of the room where there's a bit of breathing space. A couple get up from a small table and I sit down and put my handbag on the other seat. I'm beginning to wonder where Nick is when I see him come in. He looks around until he sees me then he gets a drink from the bar, makes his way over, turns the chair so that it's facing away from me and sits. He opens a copy of The Times and starts reading. Without looking at me he says, 'You were at Ringwood.'

'I thought I could do what I wanted.'

'As long as it doesn't affect company business.'

'If the company's in that kind of business, I'm out.'

'It's complicated.'

'How?'

'It's a question of the greater good.'

'A greater good than young girls getting slaughtered?'

'There are some situations that we can't control as we'd wish.'

'Oh yeah?'

'There is a man at Ringwood who is in a position to compromise a vital aspect of the security of this country. If he were to do so, the consequences would be catastrophic.'

'And he will if the company stops supplying him with dead women to fuck?'

'I can assure you that we have no involvement in his private activities.'

'Apart from protecting him.'

He turns the page of his paper and flicks it with his wrists as if he's telling it to behave. After a bit he says, 'This is not a situation you should be involved in.'

'It's a bit late for that.'

He folds up his paper, turns round, looks me in the eye.

'If you honour your contract with Farina I shall name you as the murderer and place absolute proof of your culpability before the police.'

His tone is hard and I can see he means it. The amiable posh boy has turned into someone to be reckoned with. I'm wondering how he can know about the contract to kill Heinz.

'All that aside, I expect you know about the un-

145

fortunate death of a certain titled party at your neighbour's flat?'

'What about it?'

'We know who did it and we want you to deal with her.'

'Her?'

'Yes.'

'Why don't you place absolute proof of her culpability before the police?'

He opens the paper, folds it back, puts it on the table in front of me and I'm looking at a photograph of the Earl of Dunkaid in his ermine robes. Nick points to the last paragraph of the obituary and I read that he died peacefully at his estate in Banffshire and left a wife and four children. Nick folds the paper.

'We see no need to cause the family any embarrassment.'

'Or the government either.'

'Quite.'

The noise in the pub is getting louder as the bell for last orders rings and I suddenly feel tired. I want to go home and get some sleep so that I can try to figure out what to do about this whole mess with a clear head. Nick tells me to wait for a bit and then follow him to his two-seater which is parked round the corner in Randolph Avenue. He puts his glass down and leaves. I finish my drink and pick up the paper he's left on the table. As I stand up to leave I catch sight of the lecherous old fart from the bar stool weaving his way towards me through the crowd. He's well pissed now and he sways against me and starts mumbling about what a shapely young lovely I am, or some such nonsense. When he tries to put his arm round me I stomp a stiletto heel hard on his foot. He shrieks with pain and drops his drink. I shove him onto the chair I've just left, slip off through the crowd and out the door.

I go round the corner and I can see Nick sitting in his Austin Healey. I get in beside him and he opens a file, hands me a photograph and I recognise the Russian athlete that I've seen leaving Lizzie's. It makes sense that she did it, as she's a regular and it would have been easy enough for her to take an impression of Lizzie's key and get a copy. Nick closes the file before speaking.

'Olga Petrova. Member of the Russian shot-putting team at the Rome Olympics last year. She came last in the event and watched her old rival Tamara Press win it hands down. Olga was vilified and humiliated in the Russian newspapers. She said she'd been bullied by the coach who was having an affair with Tamara and claimed that he gave her a sedative before the event but no one believed her and she was thrown out of the team. We got to her while she was feeling angry at the motherland, offered her some cash and she defected and agreed to work for us. She's been listening to Russian radio transmissions that we've intercepted and sending false messages to Russian agents that we've got the frequencies for. However, we've reason to believe she's become a double agent, and that she discovered that Dunkaid was about to expose a Soviet agent within MI6 and killed him. The Russians are currently very keen to get hold of technical information about our nuclear submarines. We're sending her to Berlin with some fake documents containing information of that kind to pass to one of the GRU agents that she's been sending false information to. She'll also be given access to documents of the same sort, that she believes are genuine, just before she leaves. We shall tell her that you have recently been recruited as an agent and that she's to show you how it works in Berlin. You're to stay with her and see which ones she passes to the GRU. If it's what she thinks is the genuine information, it will prove that she's working for the other side and you're to kill her while she's on German soil.'

'I've never worked abroad.'

'This is where you start.'

'How would I know what's genuine and what's fake?'

'You will be briefed.'

'What if I refuse?

'You can't.'

I know he's right. If they don't put me in for the Russian at the Dorchester or the man in the cemetery they'll fit me up for something else.

He reaches into his inside pocket and takes out a sheaf of notes. Hands them to me and says, 'Your first payment.'

I put the notes in my bag. Before I can speak he says, 'As things stand you are leaving next Wednesday but that could change. Meet me on Monday evening at ten o'clock at the Glendale for your full briefing. I shall give you detailed instructions then.' He reaches across me, opens the door and says, 'Goodbye Rina.'

I get out of the car and walk back to the flat.

When I come out of the lift I see Gerry and his

mate working on Lizzie's door. They tell me Lizzie's at home and I call her name as I go in and walk along the hall. She opens the living room door and we have a cuddle. She goes to the drinks cabinet, shows me the whisky bottle and I give her the nod and sit on the sofa. She pours two glasses and comes and sits beside me. I open the paper, show her Lordy's obituary and point to where it says he died peacefully at home.

'Thank fuck for that,' she says.

'You're in the clear.'

'Are your fridge men kosher?'

'As good as it gets.'

'The family must have found out he was up to his tricks and glossed it.'

'Can't say I blame them.'

Lizzie smiles and starts reading the obituary again. I lean back on the sofa, sip my whisky, close my eyes and I'm wondering if I should tell her that one of her customers is a spy and a murderer, when she closes the paper.

'Yeah, that makes sense.'

'What does?'

'He was a member of the Joint Intelligence Committee.'

'What's that?' I say, even though I know what it is.

'Spying and that.'

'How come it makes sense?'

'I had a look in his briefcase once and he had a plan of a Russian submarine in there and diagrams and a map of some Russian port and I guessed he was in MI5 or something. Do you reckon that was why he was killed?'

'I know it was.'

'How come?'

'Pour us another drink and I'll tell you.'

Twenty minutes and two drinks later I've told Lizzie about Nick being a spymaster and what Heinz is doing to Tony's girls. I tell her what I've seen at Ringwood, and talk about Tony wanting me to kill Heinz, and Nick saying he'll grass me if I do, and that I've to go to Berlin and kill Olga if she's working for the Russians. By the time I've finished her eyes are wide and she's leaning back on the sofa.

'I knew you were a bit lively but fucking hell!'

'I had it under control until Nick turned up.'

'What are you going to do?'

'Go to Berlin, I suppose.'

'And leave Heinz killing our girls?'

'I'll sort him out first.'

'And get grassed?'

'I'll think of something.'

I suddenly feel tired. I snuggle up close to Lizzie and lean my head on her shoulder. She puts her drink down, stands up and leads me through to the bedroom.

By the time I've got dressed and left Lizzie sleeping I've had an idea. I take the new keys out of Lizzie's handbag, lock her door behind me and put the keys through the letter box. I go across the way to my place, check that Georgie's sleeping and change into slacks, leather jacket and a pair of black ankle boots. I put my revolver in my belt, lock up, take the lift down to the foyer and walk quietly past Mike who's sleeping behind the desk.

The clock on the wall above him tells me it's one o'clock. I walk to the car and check under the wheel arch in case there's been a change of plan since I left Nick, but no such luck. I start the engine and turn on the radio but Radio Luxembourg's finished for the night. I twiddle the knob and get the faint sound of Elvis asking me if I'm lonesome tonight. The song finishes and a foreign voice says I'm listening to Radio Veronica, broadcasting from a boat in the North Sea off the coast of Holland. I turn the volume up to full whack as Del Shannon starts rocking with Runaway.

I drive up Maida Vale onto Kilburn High Road. There's an Austin Cambridge behind me and he's a bit too far back for my liking. I turn left, make a couple more turns, get back on the High Road and the Austin's still behind me. I turn into Willesden Lane at the lights and he's still there as I get into Brondesbury Park. I'm on a straight stretch and there's nothing else on the road so I put my foot down hard then pull the wheel over and jam the handbrake on. The Mini spins round on its front wheel and stops. I shove it into first gear, stamp on the accelerator and shoot past the Austin, going back the way I came. I hear his brakes squealing as I throw the car round a left turn, then a right, then another left. I brake sharpish and park in a backstreet. Ten minutes later there's no sign of him and I drive back through Brondesbury Park to Harlesden and park the Mini beside the lock-up.

I go inside, change the plates on the van, open an old skip where I keep some of my working clothes and pull out a pair of dark blue overalls, a leather belt and an old corduroy cap. I put on the overalls and the belt and find a pair of hobnail boots among the shoes at the bottom of the wardrobe. I wipe off my make-up, put my hair up, hold it in place with kirby grips and pull the cap on. There's still a bit of blond hair showing at the back so I find an old donkey jacket, put it on and turn the collar up. I take a pair of wire rimmed National Health glasses from a box of odds and ends and put them on too. I look in the mirror on the inside of the wardrobe door and reckon I've made a passable sex change. I open the safe, take out a knife, lock picks, a torch and a roll of gaffer tape and put them in my pockets. I put my gun in the belt of the overalls then I back the van out of the lock-up, drive the Mini inside and lock the doors.

On the way to Catford I make a couple of detours round the back streets and a few fast turns to make sure I'm not being followed. An hour later I get to the prefab estate and drive slowly past Heinz's place. There are no lights on so I park the van a couple of streets away and walk back to the house. A cat scampers across the road, stops on the pavement, arches its back, studies me for a moment and then darts off into a front garden. I get to Heinz's prefab, step over the front gate and move slowly up the path. The front window on the left, which I remember is the bedroom, is open a little bit and as I get near it I can hear someone snoring. I take off the glasses and move round to the back door. I turn on the torch and hold it in my mouth while I pick the lock. This time there's no dead girl lying against the door as I creep into the kitchen. It smells like the

152

body's still under the sink but I open the cupboard door to check. She's seated in the same position but her hands have been cut off. There's polythene wrapped over the stumps and there are rubber bands round her wrists to hold it in place. As I'm closing the cupboard door I hear footsteps in the hall.

The light goes on and Heinz is standing in the doorway pointing a shotgun at me. He's even broader and taller than he looked before. His great big head is a nasty red colour and his squinty eyes are hard as steel. He raises the gun to his shoulder, pulls back both hammers and I see his fingers tighten on the triggers. Just as I'm thinking it's all over he lowers the gun, looks me slowly up and down and his mouth twists into a smile. He walks over to me, takes my cap off, leans in close and sniffs my hair. He says something in German, lays the gun on the draining board and shoves me up against the stove. He leans his weight against me, puts one hand over my mouth, forces my head back and brings the other hand up between my legs, still mumbling in German. I feel a sharp pain in my neck. I reach behind me, grab hold of a frying pan, swing it at his head and catch him a lucky one on the temple. As he staggers sideways I snatch the shotgun but he recovers and wrenches it out of my hands. He drops the gun, pulls me to him so my back's against his chest, puts an arm round my neck and locks it tight. I struggle for bit then I slowly let myself go limp.

When he thinks I'm gone and starts to release his grip I reach down, grab hold of his balls and twist. As he screams and doubles over I swivel round and knee him in the face. He hits the floor, rolls over, shakes his head and tries to get up. I pick up the shotgun, swing the stock at his big ugly head and knock him cold.

I lean on the sink while I get my breath back, then I switch off the light, open the back door and listen in case the noise has woken up any nosy neighbours. All seems quiet so I take hold of Heinz's feet and drag him into the bedroom.

I try to heave him up onto the bed but he's too much of a dead weight. I go to the wardrobe, open the door and feel around beneath the clothes for the coil of rope that was in there before. I find it, take it out and put it on the floor beside the bed. I look down at the great bald head on the floor. His face is already swollen from where I've hit him with the shotgun, and with his half grown beard he looks like the squashed carcass of some animal that's been run over. I poke the barrel of my gun into his ribs to make sure he's out cold, then I peel a length of tape off the roll in my pocket and stick it across his mouth. I push him next to the bed, take out my blade and cut three lengths of rope off the coil on the floor. I roll him over onto his stomach and tie his wrists together behind his back, then I push him up against the bed, wind a length of rope round his neck and tie it to one end of the iron bed frame. I tie his ankles together and bind them to the frame at the other end. As I'm tying off the last knot I hear the front door opening.

I move to the wardrobe, take the key out of the lock and get inside. I hear footsteps in the hall and then the bedroom door opens. I put my eye to the keyhole and see the outline of a short man

154

crossing to the bed and bending over the body. He pulls at the ropes, pokes Heinz in the chest, then he straightens up, takes out a gun, and comes towards the wardrobe. As the keyhole goes dark I kick open the door and punch him in the face. He staggers back and goes down on one knee. I grab his wrist, wrench the gun out of his hand, swing it at his head and knock him onto his back. As I'm mounting his chest he brings both knees up, shoves me over his head and I land against the wall. He launches himself at me but I squirm out of his reach and he hits the floor. While he scrambles to his feet I get behind him and crack him on the back of his head with the butt of the gun. He lands on the floor with a thump and he's out.

I turn him over, switch on the torch and have a look at his face. He's got ginger hair and a scar on one cheek. I don't recognise him. I don't want to kill him in case it gets me into even more bother so I pocket his gun, take hold of his ankles and drag him to the kitchen. I open the back door and it seems quiet outside, so I go into the garden and find a hole in the hedge that leads into another garden that looks like a rubbish tip. The prefab that it belongs to has its windows smashed and the back door's hanging off. I go back into the kitchen and lift my man onto a chair. I bend down, take hold of his wrist, heave him onto my shoulder, carry him across the lawn and through the hole in the hedge. I walk a few steps into the overgrown garden and dump him between a couple of rusty old dustbins. He starts to come round, so I duck back through the hedge, crouch down and watch

155

him stand up slowly and shake his head. He looks around and takes a couple of steps towards the hedge, then he stops and searches his pockets for his gun. When he can't find it he turns, limps up the garden and disappears round the side of the house. I wait a bit to make sure he's gone then I go into the house and check that Heinz is still tied to the bed frame and out cold. I go into the kitchen, find an old towel and wipe the shotgun, the frying pan, and the handle of the back door clean of prints. In the bedroom I wipe Ginger's gun and put it on Heinz's bed-side table then I pick up the phone and dial 999. A woman who sounds like she's just woken up asks me which service I require and I tell her the police. When a copper answers I put on a frightened voice, give him Heinz's address, pant a bit and say there's a girl's dead body in the kitchen. I wipe the phone, replace the receiver, and leave by the front door.

There's a prefab further along the road with a cement mixer and a pile of sand in the front garden and a tarpaulin over the flat roof. I go round the back of it and make sure there's no one inside, then I climb up onto the roof and get under the tarpaulin. I crawl to the front of the roof, lift the edge of the tarpaulin, and I've got a good view of Heinz's place.

Ten minutes later I'm hearing sirens and two police cars and a van pull up outside the house.

The coppers get out and stand by the front gate while an inspector tells them something and then one lot go to the front door and the rest go round the back. When the group at the front get nothing from a knock on the door they break it open, pull out their truncheons and file inside. The lights go on in all the rooms and a few in the prefabs on each side and opposite as the neighbours wake up with the noise and get interested in what's going on. A man comes out of the house next door and a copper on the pavement tells him to go back inside. A woman in a pink dressing gown and curlers leans out of a window of the next house along to try and see what's happening. Two coppers hurry out of the front door, fetch a stretcher and blankets out of the van and take them back inside. I'm hoping they'll come out with Heinz lying on the stretcher but when they do come out there's only a mound on the middle of the stretcher, covered in a white plastic sheet which I'll bet is what's left of the poor girl's body.

Half an hour later the van and one of the cars take off with most of the coppers. There's been no sign of Heinz and I know that the ginger haired bloke must have come back and got him away somehow. He won't be coming back to Catford and I should have killed him when I had the chance. I crawl out from under the tarpaulin and drop down off the roof into the back garden of the prefab. I put the glasses back on, pull my cap down and walk to the van. Driving back to Harlesden I'm wondering if the ginger bloke was one of Nick's mob who was watching Heinz's place in case I turned up.

It's light by the time I get to the lock-up. I open up, drive the Mini out and the van in, get changed and head home. When I go through the doors to the building and across the foyer Mike looks up from behind the desk. I say good morning to him and head for the lift.

I let myself into the flat, look in on Georgie and see that she's still asleep. I go into my bedroom, take my clothes off and get into bed. I reach for *Pride and Prejudice* from the bedside table and half a page later, I'm asleep.

15

The phone's ringing. I turn over and pull the pillow over my head. It rings and rings and finally I get out of bed, go into the hall and answer it, but I'm too late. I go back in the bedroom and put on a dressing gown. My watch says it's eleven o'clock.

I go into the kitchen and put the kettle on. There's a note from Georgie on the kitchen table saying she's at the Science Museum and she'll be back later. She's probably at one of those lectures that she goes to there. I make myself a cup of Nescafé and a piece of toast and marmalade and sit at the kitchen table. I look out of the window at the breeze wafting the leaves of the trees and it makes me want to get out of town into the country. I'd like to go somewhere with Lizzie, like the time we went to Clacton and stayed in a hotel and lay on the beach all day in the sun. Once Georgie's away at school I suppose I'll be able to go on trips and that. I decide that maybe I'll take Lizzie to Harvey Nichols, spend a few quid and then have a posh lunch. I finish my coffee, go into the bedroom and put on fresh underwear, stockings and a pale blue shift dress. I put on make-up at the dressing table, brush my hair and then I go and knock on Lizzie's door.

She opens up, puts a finger to her lips and beckons me inside. She points down the corridor, puts her mouth next to my ear and whispers, 'Olga's here.'

I go to leave but she puts an arm round me. 'If you're going after her you might want to see something.'

She takes me to her bedroom and opens the curtain that covers the two-way mirror. Olga is sitting on the bed fully clothed with her handbag on her knee as if she's waiting for something or someone. She's about as broad as she's tall and her muscled arms and thighs bulge against the serge of the black suit she's wearing. Her black hair is piled up on top of her pale pudding face, held captive by a grey hairnet and run through with hairpins. Lizzie takes her dress off, puts on a white coat, goes to the door and says, 'Watch and learn.'

I sit on the bed and through the mirror I see Lizzie enter the other bedroom. Olga stands up, opens her handbag and gives a small blue plastic box to Lizzie. Then she unbuttons her jacket, takes it off and lays it on the bed. She takes the rest of her clothes off and I can feel my toast and coffee rising from my stomach as she uncovers one lumpy great muscle after another and then the biggest arse I've ever seen with patches of matted black hair growing out of the crevice and spreading across the cheeks. Lizzie puts on a pair of rubber gloves, like doctors have, takes a plastic

159

sheet out of the wardrobe and spreads it out on the carpet. She takes a silk scarf from the clothes rail, ties it round Olga's eyes, leads her to the middle of the sheet and lays her down on her back. Lizzie opens the wardrobe again and takes a bag of Saxa salt off the shelf, opens it and walks round the sheet pouring the contents onto the edge of it until she's made a circle of salt around Olga. She puts the empty bag down, picks up the blue plastic box, steps over the salt circle and kneels down beside Olga. She strokes a hand over her flat breasts and then across the ridges of muscle on her stomach and on along her massive thighs to her knees. On the return journey the hand lingers between her legs and I turn away as Olga gives out a moan. When I look again Lizzie's opening the plastic box and putting something small and black on Olga's stomach. When it moves I can see it's a cockroach.

Another one tips out of the box, and there are spiders and ants and insects I haven't seen since I was a kid in the slums crawling all over her stomach and her tits and between her legs. She's writhing and moaning and rubbing herself and Lizzie's standing over her with a foot on her neck, half strangling her. The ants are biting her and there are trickles of blood and she's moaning and groaning and roaring towards a climax and I'm thinking if she gets any louder they'll hear her in Moscow. After some more heaving and wailing she gives an almighty bellow and flails her arms and legs about; then it's all over and her legs thump down on the sheet and she's done.

Lizzie smiles at me through the glass. She waits

while Olga's breathing's slows down and then she sweeps the bugs off her body onto the sheet with her gloved hands and pulls some out from between her legs. She helps Olga up, dusts her down and moves her onto the carpet, then she rolls the plastic sheet up into a ball, trapping the creepy crawlies inside it and stamps on a couple that get away. Olga takes her blindfold off and starts putting her clothes on while Lizzie takes her white coat and gloves off. When Olga's dressed she opens her handbag, gives Lizzie some folded notes and puts the empty plastic box in her bag. Lizzie picks up the bundled sheet, opens the door and follows Olga into the corridor. When I hear the front door close I go to the door and I can see Lizzie in the kitchen putting the sheet and her rubber gloves in a metal bin and closing the lid. She washes her hands at the sink then she sees me.

'At least she didn't bring snails this time.'

'What does she do with them?'

'Let's just say you wouldn't want to eat them after.'

'I never want to eat again.'

Lizzie puts her arm round me, rubs my stomach, and walks me towards her bedroom. 'Let's try and get your appetite back shall we?'

An hour later we're soaking in bubble bath and deciding whether it's going to be Harvey Nichols or Harrods for a late lunch and a bit of shopping. We reckon we'll drive down to Knightsbridge and see how we feel when we get there. As we're drying each other with her big fluffy pink towels the phone rings. Lizzie pads down the hall and

161

answers it. She listens, then she gives me a sad look as she says, 'Ok Nick. I'll be here.'

She puts the phone down and says, 'He's bringing some kid round in half an hour.'

'Another time then,' I say.

'I suppose I should keep him sweet.'

'I reckon.'

'Zoot Money's at the Flamingo tonight if you fancy it.'

'I'll say.'

'Pick you up about nine?'

'Lovely.'

I go back to my place and change into ski pants, a roll neck sweater and a light jacket. I've decided I'll drive up to Hampstead Heath, have a good long walk and then buy something nice for me and Georgie to have for our tea.

The sun's shining in a clear sky as I walk to the car. I check under the wheel arch and there's a piece of paper with: 54 Broadway SW1, 4pm written on it. My watch says it's almost three so a walk on the Heath's out. I decide to have a coffee at that new French café in Clifton Road while Nick's getting his end away, and then go and meet him at the address he's given me.

I walk to the café, drink two cups of strong coffee and have a read of a *Daily Mail* that someone's left behind. It's full of a lot of blather about Britain applying to join the Common Market and hardly any interesting scandals or gossip. I pay the waitress, walk to the car, dig out my A–Z and find Broadway. It's in St James's, not far from the hotel that I met Nick and his boss in.

I drive across the park towards Hyde Park

162

Corner. There are people walking dogs in the spring sunshine and kids playing football and mothers and nannies pushing prams. I wonder if they'll ever know about the knavery that Nick and his lot get up to in the name of keeping them safe. I go down Constitution Hill and turn left off Buckingham Gate. I'm a bit early so I park the car off the main drag and walk along to Broadway.

Number fifty-four is a big tall grey building with a plaque by the front door that says it's the Minimax Fire Extinguisher Company. Just as I'm thinking I must have got the wrong number the front door opens and two men in suits and bowler hats come out. As the door swings shut I catch a glimpse of Nick inside, sitting on a bench beside the porter's desk reading a paper. I pull the door open and walk in. Nick sees me and stands up. He puts the paper on a table, says something to the bloke behind the desk and walks towards the back of the building. I follow him and when he reaches a pair of double doors he holds one open for me and we go down a flight of stairs and along a dingy corridor with cream coloured walls that could do with a lick of paint. He stops at a brown door, opens it and shows me into an office with a desk, a couple of upright chairs, a filing cabinet and a hatstand. He waves me to one of the chairs, walks behind the desk, picks up a photograph and passes it to me.

'Do you know this man?'

It's me in the donkey jacket and cap. It must have been taken last night in Catford which means that Nick's lot were watching and Ginger's

163

one of them, but I'm relieved that he can't have got a look at my face when we were fighting. The photo's a yellowy green kind of colour and a bit blurred. It looks like it's been taken with one of those new night vision cameras. They've caught me walking under a street lamp and the light's catching the frame of my glasses but my face is just a smudge. While I'm looking at it Nick says, 'An associate of yours?'

'Why would he be?' I say.

'He tried to get our German friend arrested.'

'Oh yeah?'

'And failed.'

I hand the photograph back to him. 'Never seen him before.'

He gives me a long look then a tight smile. He opens a file on the desk, puts the photograph into it and places the file in a drawer. He takes out a bottle of whisky and two glasses.

'Drink?'

'Why not?'

He pours two stiff ones and hands one to me.

'I understand your sister is going to Leavenden tomorrow.'

'That's right.'

'So you'll be free to travel to Berlin the next day.'

'I thought you said Wednesday.'

'We've had to make it Monday. The Berlin contact is being recalled to Moscow unexpectedly.'

I take a drink and wonder where they get such good whisky.

'You have no passport?' Nick asks.

'I've never been abroad.'

'There's very little record of you anywhere in

fact, apart from an acquittal of a murder charge. No birth certificate, medical records, tax...'

'That's how I like it.'

'So you won't object to our giving you a passport in a false name to support your cover.'

'No.'

Nick picks up the phone, dials a number and says, 'Lumley please.'

Moments later there's a knock at the door and a little whippety man with white hair and bushy eyebrows hurries in carrying a camera on a tripod. He puts it down, spreads the legs of the tripod, takes a bag off his shoulder, steps towards me and thrusts his hand out. I put my hand in his and he shakes it hard. 'Good afternoon to you. No names, no pack drill, eh what?'

He gives me a grin, nips back behind the tripod, puts his head under a cloth on the back of the camera.

'Jolly good, yes. Take a step forward would you my dear?'

I move forward and he comes out from under the cloth, rummages in his bag, takes out a flash thingy and plugs it into an electric socket above the skirting board behind him. He holds the flash up with one hand and puts his head under the cloth again. He reaches his other hand round to the front of the camera and turns a dial back and forth a couple of times.

'Watch the birdy!'

The flash goes off and he's straight out from under his cloth and the flash is unplugged and back in the bag and the tripod's legs are snapped together, the bag's on his shoulder and he stands to attention. He turns to Nick.

'Celia Bryant-Wilkinson, Buckinghamshire or Caroline Ward, Essex?'

'Caroline Ward, I think,' says Nick.

'Very good. Sometime after tiffin?'

'That'll do nicely.'

'Toodaloo.'

He gives me a little bow, opens the door and skips out into the corridor.

I can't help laughing when he's gone and I say, 'He doesn't muck about does he?'

'He does tend to behave as if he's pursued by a bear.'

'I'll say.'

'He does fine work though. One of the best we've got.'

Nick reaches into another drawer, takes out a book and some bank notes. 'Deutschmarks and a German phrasebook that you may find useful, although Berlin is crawling with foreigners so don't be concerned about not speaking the language.'

He stands up, comes round the desk and gives them to me. I put them in my bag and he opens the door.

'The Glendale at nine tomorrow night. You'll receive a full briefing and meet your travelling companion.'

I walk along the dimly lit corridor wondering what this full briefing will be all about. I don't trust Nick and his posh friends and I'm hoping I'm not getting into something I can't handle. As I'm nearly at the stairs a door opens and a tall, grey haired woman in a grey wool suit with glasses on a chain and a briefcase in her hand comes out, glances at me and heads for the stairs. As she puts her foot on the first step she stops, turns, looks at me again and smiles. She stands back from the stairs and motions me to go up ahead of her. I hesitate for a second then I go up the stairs. I can feel her eyes on me as she follows just a bit too close behind me. At the top of the stairs I go through the double doors and head for the exit. As I'm passing the desk she catches up with me. Her hand lightly brushes my arm.

'Are you new here?'

'Just visiting,' I say,

'Anyone I know?'

'I don't think so.'

She opens the front door for me.

'Would you care for a drink after a long day?'

'Not now thanks,' I say as I walk away, wondering at the cheek of the old bird.

I stop at the baker's in Edgware Road, just as he's closing, and pick up a couple of pies and sausage rolls and a loaf of bread. I get tins of beans and carrots from a grocer's a few doors away and a couple of Mars bars for pudding. I buy some different sweets and bars of chocolate to put in Georgie's tuck box. I'm wishing I'd got a chicken or something for our dinner tomorrow before she goes off to school, but the butchers are all shut now, so it'll have to be whatever I can find, or scrounge off Lizzie.

When I get back to the flat Georgie's in her room reading and she tells me the phone's been ringing. I go into the kitchen and turn on the oven. I find potatoes in the kitchen cabinet, put

167

them in the sink and start peeling them. Georgie comes in, yawns and says, 'Are you taking me to the station tomorrow?'

'Of course I am,' I say.

'What time?'

'The train's at four o'clock, so we should get going just after three.'

She sits at the table and says, 'Can I take some books?'

'I'm sure you can.'

She comes and leans on the cabinet beside me and I can tell she's worried about going. 'How was the Science Museum?' I ask.

'Ok.'

'Was it one of those lectures?'

'Yeah.'

'What about?'

'Entomology?'

'What's that then?'

'Insects.'

My stomach turns over and I drop a potato as I think of Olga and her little friends on the floor at Lizzie's.

Georgie looks at me.

'You all right?'

I nod, pick up the potato and start peeling.

'Fine thanks. Do you want to open that tin of carrots for us?'

As she picks up the tin opener the phone rings. I dry my hands, go into the hall and pick up the receiver. Tony Farina says, 'You have something to tell me?'

'Not yet.'

'When?'

'When I can.'

'You call me.'

'Yeah.'

The line goes dead. I'm wondering how long I'll be away in Berlin and if I can string Tony along until I can see a way to get rid of Heinz without Nick catching on, and what he'll do to me if he finds out I'm playing him. Behind the smooth manners and the sharp suits, the Farinas are brutal bastards and I don't need them as enemies.

I go back in the kitchen, finish the potatoes, put them on to boil and put the pies in the oven. Georgie's put the carrots in a pan and she's sitting at the table reading a book. I want to talk to her about school because I'm worried how she'll get on with those posh girls and if they'll give her a bad time because of where she's from. I sit down opposite her but then I think that anything I say might only make her more frightened of going and I really want her to be well away from my doings and the people I work with. I reach for my copy of *Pride and Prejudice* off the sideboard and open it at the bookmark. I read for a couple of minutes.

'What's a propensity?' I ask.

Georgie looks up, sees my book and says, 'Read the whole sentence.'

'And your defect is a propensity to hate everybody.'

'It's Elizabeth talking to Darcy isn't it?'

'Yeah.'

'It means like a preference or a tendency to hate everybody.'

'Ok.'

I read on a bit.

'She's having a right go at him.'

'She's great isn't she?'

'I really like her but he's a right plonker.'

'You'd better read on,' says Georgie.

I light the gas under the carrots and read a bit more until they boil then I drain the potatoes and mash them with milk and butter. I take the pies out of the oven and put them on plates with the mash, drain the carrots and put them on the side. Georgie puts the HP sauce on the table and we tuck in.

16

Soho's throbbing nicely as me and Lizzie walk down Wardour Street towards the Flamingo. The girls are standing at the doors of strip clubs inviting any likely looking punters inside to see the show, and their minders are hanging around nearby smoking fags and looking moody. We pass a group of Jamaicans standing outside the entrance to the St Moritz Club and catch the sound of soul music and the smell of grass. A group of mods come towards us in their Ben Sherman shirts and mohair suits, pilled up and nattering at one another. Lizzie bumps into a stripper she knows who's on her way from one club to another. While they stop to talk I walk on a bit and have a look through the door of Le Macabre, a coffee bar on the corner of Meard Street. The walls and the tables and chairs are all black. The tables are long and shaped like coffins, with candles lighting the glum faces of the beatniks sitting round them with their long hair and beards. There's a platform at one end and a bloke with blond hair down to his shoulders and wearing a black cape is reciting some poetry with a girl in black jeans and a polo neck sweater beside him playing a guitar. From what I can hear of the poem it seems to be about death and I'm quite relieved when Lizzie says goodbye to her friend and we move on.

Further along the pavement there's a row going on between two men among a group of drinkers outside the pub on the corner. One of them's older with a moon face and a pot belly. His pint's splashing on the pavement as he shouts abuse at a young, good looking bloke in a dark grey suit who's smoking a cigar and snarling back at him. As we make a detour round them, the fat one chucks his pint in the young bloke's face and tries to grab him round the neck. They roll onto the pavement and thrash about a bit while the rest of the group from the pub have a laugh at them. Finally, a couple of them pull the men apart and stand them up. As we walk away Lizzie says, 'That fat one's a painter.'

'I wouldn't want him doing my living room,' I say.

'An artist, silly.'

'Piss artist.'

'The other one's his boyfriend. They're always at it.'

We get to the Flamingo, push through the crowd around the door and go down the stairs to the

171

basement. It's six bob to get in and Lizzie gives the bloke a quid, gets the change and asks what time Zoot Money's on. The bloke says it should be about midnight.

We walk in to a wall of smoke, sweat and dancing bodies. It's mostly black men and white girls and a few groups of mods standing by the walls. We push through the crowd until we can see the stage at the far end. There's a young bloke in a grey suit with short blond hair blowing a really gutsy blues harmonica and the band behind him are well away. He sings a couple of verses about some evil woman who's given him the runaround and the organ player swoops in with a solo that gets me and Lizzie dancing in among the crowd. Then the organ's swapping breaks with the guitar and the harmonica's in there as well, and they build it up to a great finish before going straight into a fast rocker. We're jiving and twisting and giving it all sorts until the song finishes and a bloke comes to the mic and asks for a big hand for Chris Farlowe and The Thunderbirds.

While the roadies are shifting the gear around on the stage a couple of black men come up to us and say they like the way we dance. They've got American accents and Lizzie asks them where they're from. They say they're from Texas but they've come from the American Air Force base at Greenham Common in Berkshire. There's no R & B down that way and that's why they come up for the all-nighters at the weekend. We ask them if they fly planes and they tell us they're bomber pilots. They're telling us about the different types and how big and heavy they are when another black guy, who's been laughing and grinning behind them, butts in and says they just repair trucks and stuff and they couldn't fly a kite between them. They start joshing and pushing each other around and we slip away through the crowd.

We find a quiet corner and watch the band wander onto the stage and plug in guitars and switch on amps. The guitar player diddles around a bit and the sax players are firing off a few notes, until the drummer clicks four times with his sticks and Zoot Money runs on, grabs the mic off the stand and powers into Sweet Little Rock and Roller. He's shaking himself about and leaping up and down and the crowd whoop it up. The dancing's wild and me and Lizzie are out there jiving up a storm and there's nothing but the music.

After they've nearly rocked the roof off, Zoot sits down at the organ and leads the band into a slow one and I want to do a smooch with Lizzie but we're in the wrong club for it so we move off to the side and let the straight couples get a good feel of cach other. While we're leaning against the wall a mod comes up to me.

'Any pills at all?'

I look at Lizzie and she shakes her head. 'No thanks sunshine.'

'I'll do you a dozen dubes for a quid. You won't get cheaper. I've got blues, bombers, green and whites...'

'We're all right thanks,' I say.

As he wanders off Lizzie says, 'Fancy a drink at the Huntsman?'

'Yeah go on,' I say.

As we're moving through the crowd to the door

173

a scuffle breaks out in front of us. There's an older Jamaican bloke smacking a dark haired girl in a black dress. He knocks her down and as he goes to kick her a couple of men pull him off and hustle him away through the crowd. Lizzie goes to the girl and helps her up. She seems to be all right and Lizzie has a few words with her and takes her off to the exit. She's slim and willowy with a lovely face and a great figure and I feel jealous for a second as I see Lizzie put her arm round her, even though I know it's daft considering I'm never bothered by what she does for a living. There's a load of people jamming the doorway and when I get up the stairs and into the street the girl's getting into a taxi and Lizzie's closing the door for her. The taxi drives off.

'Who was that?' I ask.

'She's a showgirl from Murray's.'

'Why did he set about her?'

'She's knocking off some politician and he wants to put the black on him and she won't play.'

'Sounds dodgy.'

'She's not been in town for long.'

'Needs protection.'

'You volunteering?'

'I've got enough problems.'

We walk round the corner into Peter Street. The Huntsman's behind a grey doorway with peeling paint, next to a tailor's shop. Lizzie rings the bell and the door's opened by a woman in a man's pinstriped suit, stiff collar and a club tie. Her hair is short and swept back in a Tony Curtis. She looks us over and then she nods and stands back to let us pass. We go along a passageway to the back of the building and down a flight of stairs to the basement. The room's bathed in a low pink light and there's a photograph of Marlene Dietrich in the top hat and tails on the wall, next to one of Edith Piaf, looking tortured. Paul Anka's singing Tonight My Love on the jukebox and clinging couples are moving slowly round the floor. I follow Lizzie to the bar at the far end and we order whisky from a tall blond boy in a pair of Bermuda shorts and nothing else except a gold chain round his neck. I turn round, look at the dancers and spot the sales assistant from Perry's Uniforms smooching with a big muscly bloke with a shaved head. He sees me, gives me a smile and a wave and when the song finishes he peels himself off Charles Atlas, comes over and leans on the bar next to us.

'You should be in your school uniform.'

'I'll lock you in a trunk,' I say.

'Promises, promises.'

I introduce him to Lizzie and he tells us his name's Aubrey. He asks me what I thought of Miss Stewart at the shop and he gossips on about how mean she is to everyone and how he reckons she's a muff diver only she won't admit it, and she beats up her husband instead and bullies everyone who works for her while she's arse-licking the posh customers. He asks me if Georgie's my little sister and says how much he liked her. As he's blathering on, muscle man comes up behind him, gets him in a head lock, drags him back on the dance floor and starts feeling him up. We finish our drinks, move onto the floor and dance while the Everly Brothers dream, dream, dream. The music gets slow and smoochy again and we're in a clinch and kissing

175

and when we glide over near the bottom of the stairs I notice the woman in the pinstripe suit run in and dart over behind the bar. Two men in grey macs and fedoras come down the stairs and have a look over the dance floor before walking to the bar. They're taken into a back room by the pin-striped lady.

'The Dirty Squad come for a taste,' Lizzie says.

'Slimy bastards,' I say.

'Did you know Gerry Mann got done for men dancing together at his club?'

'Wasn't he bunging the plod?'

'He was but some professor or some such fol-lowed his son to the club one night, and when the kid told him to get stuffed he marched into Bow Street, got hold of an inspector and kicked up a fuss about clubs that encourage gross indecency, so they had to take Gerry to court.'

'What happened?'

'The prosecution said that plain clothes police had entered the club and witnessed men dancing with each other. Gerry's brief said they were danc-ing the Madison in which people of the same sex have to form a line.'

'Did it work?'

'He got two years.'

'Bad luck.'

'He does all right inside, does Gerry.'

I look over towards the bar and see the topless barman being summoned into the back room by the pinstriped woman.

The Pretty Police coming into the club have taken the shine off the evening and I want to get out. Lizzie looks at her watch and puts an arm round me.

'Home James?'

Up in the street Aubrey and his tough guy boy-friend are arguing hammer and tongs in a doorway over the road. Aubrey's pirouetting about on the pavement, waving his arms and slinging insults at muscle man, who's standing in the doorway with his arms folded and his feet apart, saying nothing. We slink away before he sees us, turn the corner into Wardour Street and hail a cab.

17

I get Georgie's new school uniform out of the wardrobe and lay the blazer, blouse and skirt out on the bed for her. We went and put some fresh flowers on our Jack's grave this morning and then we had a walk on Hampstead Heath before lunch at the Two Blues in Heath Street. She didn't say much except to name some of the birds we saw on the Heath, and now she's at the bookshelf deciding what books she's taking with her. I've told her that there'll be a library with all sorts of books but she says she wants to have some of her own there. I get her school shoes out of the bottom of her wardrobe, decide they could do with a clean and take them into the kitchen. I'm wondering if I should have bought her new ones to go with the new uniform but once I've polished them and buffed them up a bit they look good enough, and she's got her sandals for the summer as well.

When I go back to her bedroom she's already got her skirt on and she's buttoning up her white blouse. I tie her tie for her and help her on with her blazer. She looks at herself in the mirror then she turns to me, looking a bit forlorn.

'Do I look all right?'

'You look lovely,' I say.

Even though it's Sunday we've decided on the weekday uniform rather than the cloak and the boater for her to arrive in. I tried to ring Miss Simpkins to check but there was no reply.

I pick up the books she's chosen to take with her and put them in the tuck box along with the sweets and biscuits and fruit that I've got for her. I remember her toothbrush and go into the bathroom to get it. While I'm there I unscrew the bath panel with a nail file and take out five tenners. I go back into Georgie's room and she's sitting on the bed reading. I look at my watch, see that it's past three o'clock.

'It's time to go.'

She stands up and puts the book in the tuck box and I shut it, lock the padlock and give her the key and the money. She looks at the notes and puts them in her purse.

'At least I'll be rich.'

'You'll be fine.'

She looks down at the floor. I can see how frightened she is and I want to go to her but I decide we ought to get moving.

'Miss Simpkins said there's another new girl arriving today and she's in the same class as you and the same house as well so you won't be the only one.'

Georgie nods and I go into the hall and wait while she unlocks the front door. She opens it and as I follow her into the corridor Lizzie comes out of her flat.

'I was just coming to say goodbye.'

She gathers Georgie into her arms and says, 'I can't believe you're leaving us!'

'I'm only going to school,' says Georgie.

'Well when am I going to see you?'

'It's the end of term in six weeks.'

'Can we come and visit?'

'I don't know.'

'Well you be sure to write to us.'

Georgie nods and I can see she's about to cry.

'We've got to go or we'll miss that train,' I say.

Lizzie gives her a kiss and says, 'You take care now my love.'

We get to Victoria in good time for the train. I park beside the Victoria Palace Theatre and we walk past a poster for the show that's on there called Rose Marie. There's a photograph of a curly haired girl in a dirndl skirt singing a song to what I think are a bunch of boy scouts but which Georgie tells me are Canadian Mounties. I wish I was taking her to see the show instead of sending her off on a train to I don't know what. I remind myself that it's for her own good and to keep her safe and away from the people I've got myself caught up with. She'll get a good education and be able to mix with anyone and do what she wants in her life.

We cross the road at the traffic lights, go into the station and a porter takes the tuck box and puts it on his trolley. I look up at the big board and see that the train to Dover stops at Leavenden Halt and it's the first station out of London. I leave Georgie with the porter while I go to the booking hall and buy one single and one return ticket. As we approach the platform I can see a large group of Leavenden schoolgirls and I'm glad to see that they're not wearing cloaks and straw boaters. I tip the porter a shilling, tell him to put the tuck box in the guard's van and we walk along the platform to where the girls are waiting. The grown-ups with them are nearly all women. Most of them look too old to be their mothers so I guess that they're nannies. They sit on benches while the girls stand in groups talking and laughing and I can hear by their voices how posh they are. A couple of the girls turn round and look at us when we get near them and then turn back to their friends.

We go to a bench and one of the women smiles at us as we sit down. I want to say something to her but I can't think what. A few minutes later the train puffs in and stops with a squeal of metal on metal. Doors are opening and there's a crackly announcement over the speakers that I can't understand except for the word 'Dover.' The girls are saying goodbye to their nannies and getting on the train. Georgie and I follow them, move along the corridor and go into a compartment with four girls about the same age as Georgie. The girls stop speaking and look at us as we sit down. The doors bang shut, the guard blows his whistle and the train huffs and puffs away from the platform. We pick up speed as we go through a tunnel and then we're going past the backs of factories and then we're on a bridge and the Thames is stretching out to the left and the right of us and the sun is glinting on the water. The girls are still looking at us and the one sitting opposite, who looks about the same age as Georgie with her hair in plaits says, 'Are you new?' Georgie nods and the girl says, 'Which house are you in?'

'Richmond,' says Georgie.

'Witchy Wainright,' says another girl and the others laugh.

'That's your housemistress,' says the girl with the plaits.

'Watch out for her broomstick,' says the girl sitting next to her. 'She flies over the dorm on it every night. She boiled a girl in her cauldron once when she caught her out of bed.'

The girls find this hilarious and Georgie does her best to smile. After they fall silent and look out of the window at passing south London, I ask the one with the plaits if she's in Richmond House herself and she indicates the other girls and says, 'We're all in Edenbridge. We beat Richmond at lacs last term.'

'Is that lacrosse?' I ask.

'Yes,' she says and looks at me as if I'm from another planet. One of the other girls giggles.

'Are you in the team?' I ask.

'I'm cover point,' she says.

'Do you all play?'

The others all nod with varying degrees of enthusiasm. The girl in the plaits asks Georgie if she plays lacrosse. Georgie shakes her head.

'What do you play?' asks the girl.

'I've done netball,' says Georgie.

A girl sitting by the window imitates the way Georgie says netball and the one girl next to her giggles.

The girl with the plaits sees them laughing, turns to Georgie, and says, 'We don't have netball but lacs is really easy to learn.'

Georgie nods and looks down at her hands in her lap.

'We were told there's another new girl arriving today. Do you know if she's on the train?' I ask.

The girl with the plaits shakes her head. 'I didn't see anyone.' She looks round at the others, who also shake their heads. 'She might be coming by car.'

The train starts to slow down and the girls stand up and move into the corridor. We follow them out of the compartment and while we wait behind them for the train to pull into the station the girl who was sat by the window turns round and looks at Georgie, then turns to her friend and whispers something to her which makes her laugh.

When the train stops and the doors are opened we move forward. I reach for Georgie's hand but she pulls it away. On the platform the girl with the plaits turns to us.

'We go in a coach now. Have you got anything in the guard's van?'

'Only her tuck box.'

'You'd better tell one of the porters to get it.' She points to a couple of men in overalls who are wheeling trolleys towards the guard's van.

'Will you make sure Georgina gets on the coach please?' I ask.

'Yes,' she says.

'What's your name love?'

'Annabelle.'

I can see the porters have started unloading luggage from the guard's van and I turn to Georgie. 'I'd better get along there before your tuck box goes to Dover.'

'Bye then,' she says.

I want to give her a hug but I know it'll only embarrass her. 'Write to me soon eh?'

'Yeah.'

I leg it to the guard's van and get there just as the guard's shutting the door. He opens it up again and I point at the tuck box on top of a packing case at the back. The guard swings it over and one of the porters puts it on a trolley. I spot Georgie's trunk under a pile of suitcases on the other trolley as the porters push them both off along the platform.

The guard shuts the door, stands away from the train, blows his whistle and waves his arm towards the driver. He steps onto the train and closes his door as the engine snorts and puffs smoke and the train moves slowly along the rails and out of the station.

I look to see if Georgie's still there but all the girls have gone.

I go to the ticket office and ask for the next train to London. The man tells me it's due in fifteen minutes. I go through to the other platform and sit on a bench. A sudden gust of cold wind makes me shiver. I pull my coat round me and turn up the collar.

It's nearly eight o'clock by the time I get back to

the flat. I pour myself a whisky, sit at the kitchen table and wonder if Georgie's going to be all right. Annabelle seemed like a nice girl and the sort that would look out for her while she finds her feet. I'm only sorry she's not in the same house as her. I decide to phone Miss Simpkins the next day and find out if the girls are allowed to phone home at all and if so when. I finish my drink, go into the bedroom and look in the wardrobe for something to wear for the Glendale. My eye rests on a lurex cocktail dress with a blue and silver leaf pattern and a slash neckline which looks about right. I take off the trouser suit I wore for the school trip, slip on the dress, a pair of nylons and the Enrico Coveri stilettos. I sit at the dressing table, put on some more make-up and brush my hair. I put on my black velvet coat, with my purse in one pocket and my knuckleduster in the other.

Dennis is behind the desk in the foyer. Even from a distance I can see his face is still bruised. I go over to him.

'How are you Dennis?'

'Not so bad miss.'

'I'm sorry you got a slap.'

'I've had worse.'

He looks at my cleavage and says, 'Going out on the town miss?'

'Wish I was,' I say as I button my coat and open the glass door.

18

I turn left off Regent Street, swing a right into Kingly Street, park at the end and walk along Beak Street to the Glendale. The bouncers wave me through this time and I go downstairs into the club. It's a bit before nine so I go to the bar and order a whisky. The club's quiet and there are only a few punters at the tables with girls drinking champagne. The punters can only buy drinks by the bottle once they're at a table and the girls have to order champagne. The rest of the girls are standing at the end of the bar gossiping and laughing while the house band trudge through The Shadow of your Smile. I can see that the pianist's reading a book he's got leaning on the music stand while he plays. There's a sound of high-pitched voices and four Japanese men in dark suits come down the stairs into the club. A group of girls who've been sitting at the bar go over and greet them and then take them to a table in an alcove at the far end of the room. The cigarette girl walks over to them with her tray and her fishnet tights and the band wake up a bit and swing into Blueberry Hill.

As I finish my drink I see Nick come down the stairs carrying a briefcase. He sees me, comes over and sits on the stool next to mine. He points at my drink.

'Scotch?'

'Thanks,' I say.

He asks the barman for two whiskies. 'Did your sister get to school all right?'

'We got the train earlier.'

'Good.'

'They told me there was another new girl arriving today but I didn't see her.'

'Yes. The Nigerian Minister of State's daughter. She may have travelled by car.'

'Nigerian Minister of State?'

'For Naval Affairs. He's just arrived.'

While I'm trying to take this in Nick picks up his drink and says, 'Shall we go through?'

We walk past the dance floor and through the padded door behind the bandstand. Greta is sitting on one of the plush sofas smoking a cigarette. Felix Bielsky's standing at the bar talking to a tall bloke in a dark suit that I've seen around Notting Hill. He sees us come in and waves the tall bloke away.

'Good evening to you. Ah, I see you have drinks already. Please to come this way.'

He leads us into the office that Greta took me into last time with the curtained window that looks into the club. She comes in behind us and shuts the door. Nick sits at the desk and Bielsky puts a chair in front of it for me, then he sits next to Greta on a leather sofa that's against the wall. Nick opens his briefcase, takes out a passport and some blue files and puts them on the desk. He looks through them and gives me the passport. I open it and see that I'm Caroline Ward from Basildon like the funny little man said. He picks up one of the blue files, has a quick look inside and hands it to me. On the top of the first page it says, 3rd Submarine Squadron Faslane. HMS Narwhal. Then there's stuff about the weight of it and the engine and that. As I'm reading Nick says, 'The Narwhal is a submarine of the Porpoise class and the information that the Russians want is the radar, detection and armament specifications, which are on the last two pages.'

I turn over and have a look but it's just columns of words and figures that mean nothing to me. 'The file you have in front of you contains false information and that file will be given to Olga Petrova to pass to her GRU contact, in the knowledge that it is false. The specifications therein are misleading and will cause the Russians to be detected immediately if they try to attack a Porpoise submarine on the basis of that information.'

He picks up another blue file and points at it.

'Olga will also be given access to this file, which she will believe contains the correct specifications. She'll be provided with an opportunity to steal it, just before she leaves for Berlin. It will be a counterfeit as well, of course, but she will think it is genuine.'

He hands the file to me.

'If you look at the bottom line on the last page of that file, you will see that it says FM sonar (QLA) and then some data. If you now look at the same line on the last page of the counterfeit document, you will see that it says FM sonar (JK/QC). This is how you will be able to tell the difference between the counterfeit and the real thing. If Olga takes the file with (QLA) on the last page to the drop it means she's a double

187

agent betraying us to the Russians and you are to kill her once she has delivered it.'

As I'm comparing the two files I hear someone shouting and a crash coming from the club. Bielsky goes out of the door and closes it behind him. Greta goes to the door, switches off the light and then opens the curtains of the window that looks into the club. I look through the window and see the bouncers dragging one of the Japanese businessmen off an older man who's lying on the floor with blood on his face. The bouncers hustle the Japanese man across the dance floor and up the stairs. A couple of girls help the older man up and onto a chair. One of them wipes the blood off his face and the other pours him a glass of champagne. The other one pulls a chair up next to his and puts her arm round him. The bandleader goes to the microphone, announces the cabaret, counts in the band and a line of shimmying girls in feathery costumes and silk tights sashay out from behind the padded door and go into a high-kicking routine on the dance floor. The rest of the punters turn their attention from the fight to the girls, knock back more drink and watch the show.

I catch sight of Olga coming down the stairs. She's wearing a black taffeta dress and she has to twist and turn to get her bulk between the tables as she walks towards the bar. Greta closes the curtains and switches on the light. Nick and I sit down and Bielsky comes back in.

'Everything all right Feliks?' asks Nick.

Bielsky nods. 'Just a scuffle.'

'What happened?' asks Nick.

'The older one worked on the Burma railway,'

says Bielsky as he sits down.

Greta says to Nick, 'She is here. You want her?'

Nick turns to me.

'Is everything clear?'

'I reckon,' I say and pass the files back to him. Nick nods to Greta and she leaves.

We wait in silence until the door opens and Greta walks in followed by Olga. She sits down next to me and I see how ugly she is up close. Her eyebrows meet in the middle and her face is as fat as the rest of her. Her mouth is wide and droopy at the corners and her dark brown eyes are hooded and half closed as if she's dead bored and about to fall asleep. Her black hair is thick and matted and looks like a guardsman's busby that's been sat on by an elephant.

'Olga, this is Rina, who I've told you about, and who you will be taking to Berlin with you. Her cover name is Caroline Ward.'

If she remembers me from seeing me outside Lizzie's she doesn't show any sign of it. She gives me a blank stare and I shake a hand that's as crusty as sandpaper. Nick picks up one of the blue files and passes it to her.

'This is a copy of what you will take to Malikov. You make contact via the usual letter box and then wait for the drop.'

Olga opens the file. While she's looking at the contents Nick says, 'Rina will go to the drop with you.'

Olga looks up from the file, glances at me and says, 'Is dangerous.'

'She's there to be trained, as you know,' says Nick.

Olga looks at me again, raises her eyebrow and says, 'For honey trap maybe?'

'As an agent,' says Nick.

'What if there is trouble?'

'She can handle herself.'

Olga snorts and looks at me as if I'm nothing. Greta says something in what I guess is Russian and Olga grunts back at her. Greta replies with an edge in her voice. I catch the name Budanov, who I chucked out of the window of the Dorchester, and now Olga's looking at me a bit differently.

Nick takes the file from Olga, gathers up the remaining files on the desk and puts them in his briefcase. He looks at Olga and says, 'The original file will be available for you to collect from Broadway in one hour. Go to the basement and a records clerk will meet you.'

Olga nods. Nick takes another folder out of the briefcase and hands it to me.

'You are a fashion designer recently graduated from the Royal College of Art. You are on your way to Dresden for a meeting with the Breuninger fashion department with a view to joining their team of young designers. You are stopping in Berlin to visit the Pergamon Museum. You will find a selection of your designs, your degree and curriculum vitae in that folder, which you will take with you.'

He turns to Olga.

'Your cover remains as usual.'

While I'm wondering what she's going as, Nick closes the briefcase, stands up and says, 'You will travel together on Lufthansa flight LH2468 leaving Heathrow at 0940 hours tomorrow. Cars will collect you from your homes at 0630 and you will be given tickets and deutschmarks then.'

Bielsky crosses to the door and opens it for Nick, who nods to him, flicks a quick look at me and leaves. Olga stands, turns to look at me and her mouth lifts very slightly at the corners as she says, 'Tomorrow.'

'Tomorrow,' I reply and give her a smile. Just because she's a grumpy cow I'm buggered if I'm going to be one. She goes to the door and Bielksy opens it wide for her, then follows her out. I don't want to be seen leaving with her or Nick so I stay seated and open the folder Nick gave me. I see that Caroline Ward's got a Diploma in Art and Design and she's also trained as a milliner at a company in Bond Street. As I'm looking at the drawings of dresses and hats and handbags Greta says, 'How do you feel?'

'I'm not sure,' I say.

She gets up off the sofa, stands beside me and puts a hand on my shoulder. 'Would you like a drink?'

'Thanks,' I say.

She opens a drawer of a metal filing cabinet. 'Whisky, gin, vodka?'

'Whisky, thanks.'

She pours whisky and vodka, replaces the bottles in the cabinet and brings the glasses to the sofa. I leave the folder on the chair, sit beside her and we sip our drinks. She looks at me with her soft kind eyes, puts her hand on my shoulder and I feel myself relaxing. She's looking as elegant as she did when I met her, in a long dark red dress with a short black shoulder cape. She's wearing a simple string of pearls and her eye shadow and mascara are just enough to set off her blue-grey eyes. She smiles.

'She is not the monster she seems.'

'I've met friendlier women.'

Greta laughs softly and takes a drink.

'They did a horrible thing to her.'

'Nick told me about the Olympics.'

'Now she is angry and afraid.'

'And getting her revenge.'

'Yes.'

We sit in silence for a bit and I can feel her eyes on me and I'm wondering why I feel close to this old lady who I barely know and why I'm feeling that I don't want to leave. She strokes her hand down my arm.

'Have you been to Berlin before?'

'I've never been anywhere abroad.'

'Do not worry. It will be interesting for you.'

'I suppose so.'

'Olga knows it well and will keep you safe.'

Listening to her deep purry voice, I suddenly feel tired and like I want to lie down beside her and sleep for a month. She sees my eyelids drooping.

'It is nearly midnight. You leave early in the morning. Perhaps it is time for home and bed?'

She picks up her stick, helps me up off the sofa and we leave the office and go into the cocktail bar. Bielsky's at the bar talking to a tall man in a grey fedora who's nodding at what he says and writing in a notebook. Greta opens the padded door for me and holds my hand in hers.

'You take care Rina.'

I squeeze her hand and turn and walk through the club. On the dance floor the girls are swinging their hips and gliding slowly back and forth in a line behind a girl who's standing on her head and doing the splits.

I park in Hall Road and walk round the corner. I open the glass front door and see Dennis asleep behind the porter's desk. I take the lift to our floor, walk along to Lizzie's door and knock quietly. There's no response so I cross the corridor and let myself into the flat. I hang my coat up and I'm just about to open Georgie's door to check that she's asleep when I remember where she is. I hope she's sleeping in her dormitory and not lying awake and missing her own bed. I feel wrong going away like this when she's just left home. I'll try to phone Miss Simpkins from the airport and ask if I can talk to her.

I go into my bedroom, find the piece of paper with the Leavendon number on it and put it in my handbag. I suddenly feel the need for music and I put Miles Davis's Kind of Blue on the Dansette, lie on the bed and let Miles caress me with those soft licks. When he slides into the second track I turn on my side and notice the cover file Nick gave me leaning against the wardrobe. I reach for it and open it.

Caroline Ward from Basildon is a talented girl. The dress designs are stylish and sexy with some really high hemlines and I like the faces she's drawn on the models that seem to say that if you don't like it you can get stuffed. She's worked for

Dior and Balenciaga in London and Paris and as I read through what she's done I'm wishing I could have passed exams and that and gone to college and done fashion like her. Then I remember it's all baloney and she doesn't exist and I shut the folder and lie down again with the music.

I'm almost falling asleep when I remember I've got to pack for an early start in the morning. I take my small suitcase off the top of the wardrobe, throw in a couple of skirts and blouses, two dresses, a pair of low-heeled court shoes and a thick cashmere sweater in case it's cold. I take my Smith and Wesson and some spare rounds out of the wardrobe, wrap it in some underwear, put it in the bottom of the case and check that my flick knife's inside the strap of my handbag. I go to the bathroom, take four hundred quid from behind the bath and put it behind the lining of the case. I decide to travel in my ski pants, suede jacket and boots. I put my make-up bag out to remind me to pack it in the morning.

I take my clothes off and slip into bed. I open *Pride and Prejudice,* join Elizabeth and her friends in front of the fire at Netherfield and agree with Miss Bingley when she declares that there is no enjoyment like reading.

19

Dennis rings me to tell me the car's arrived. I say I'll be down in a minute, drain my cup of Nescafé, pick up my suitcase in the hall and open the front door. I lock up, go across to Lizzie's and knock. When there's no response I head for the lift, press the button and wait. The doors open and there's Lizzie, looking as knackered as I've ever seen her. She almost trips on the carpet as she gets out of the lift. She sees my suitcase.

'Is that car outside for you?'

'I reckon.'

'Berlin?'

'Yeah.'

'Fuck.'

'I know.'

She puts her arms round me. 'When are you back?'

'Who knows.'

We kiss and she nuzzles my ear. 'You come back to me soon, lovely girl.'

Just as I feel my legs going weak, a door opens behind me, someone coughs and we separate in time for the nasty gent from next door to walk pointedly between us and get into the lift. He puts his bowler hat on, clutches his briefcase and stares straight ahead as the doors close on him. Lizzie and I giggle and snog a bit more until the lift comes back and I hop in and wave her goodbye.

After the lift makes a soft landing on the ground floor Dennis comes out from behind his desk, opens the glass door for me and I step out into a grey drizzle of rain. A black Morris Cowley is parked along the service road and the driver's smoking a cigarette in the front seat. He sees me coming, gets out, opens the back door of the car for me and puts my suitcase in the boot. I settle into the seat and try to calm the fluttering in my stomach at the thought of flying in an aeroplane. The driver gets into the car, passes me a small folder with my passport, ticket and some deutschmarks inside and pulls the car out onto Edgware Road. As we drive round Marble Arch, he says, 'Which building?'

'What?' I say

'At Heathrow. Which building do you want?'

'I don't know.'

'It'll say on your ticket.'

I open the ticket and look at it. 'Building One, Europa, it says.'

He nods and accelerates down Park Lane.

We go through Knightsbridge and Hammersmith and along the A4 to Heathrow. The driver stops outside Building One, takes my suitcase out of the boot and I go through the revolving door. I've no idea what to do or where to go so I stand under the big board which says departures and look down the list for a flight to Berlin. I see my one that leaves at nine-forty and I'm looking around for someone to ask where I should go when I see Olga billowing out of the revolving door in a dark red cloak with the hood up; and I thought spies were supposed to look inconspicuous. I walk towards her and she sees me, nods and puts down her suitcase.

'Good. You are here,' she says.

'Morning,' I say.

'You have ticket?'

'Yes.'

She looks at the board, picks up her suitcase and leads me towards a row of desks. We join a queue in front of the one that has a sign saying Berlin above it and she stands with her back to me. When we get to the front of the queue I watch while she gets given her boarding pass and her suitcase wobbles away along the moving belt. I hand my passport and ticket to the bored looking bloke in the uniform. He has a look at them, ticks something off on a list, gives me my boarding pass and I say goodbye to my suitcase. I follow Olga through a door and along a corridor past different lounges with gate numbers on signs outside them. We get to the one that says Berlin with our flight number and sit down among the other passengers. There's various announcements coming over the speakers, first in English then in other languages, and I can see different planes through the glass wall of the building; some stand waiting and others are moving along or being towed. I feel a twinge of fear as I see one taking off in the distance. I look at Olga and smile but she turns away and lights up a fag. I can see from the clock that we've got nearly an hour to wait. I see a row of payphones on the wall opposite the lounge and I tell Olga I'm going to make a call. She nods and draws on her fag.

I dial the number for Dorothea Simpkins at

Leavendon and after a couple of rings the secretary picks up. I push a shilling into the slot, say my name and ask for Miss Simpkins. There's a pause and I'm just about to repeat myself when she comes on the line.

'I'm glad you called Miss Walker.'

'Is everything all right?'

'I have been trying to telephone you.'

'Why?'

'I'm afraid there's been an incident.'

'What?'

'Involving your sister.'

'What's happened?'

'She has assaulted a pupil.'

My stomach turns over and I have to lean against the wall to steady myself. 'What happened?'

'Georgina hit another girl in the dormitory and she has been taken to Tonbridge Cottage Hospital with severe facial bruising.'

'Is she going to be all right?'

'That remains to be seen. In the meantime, I must tell you that we cannot tolerate violent behaviour such as this and I must ask you to remove her from the school immediately.'

'I can't.'

'May I ask why?'

'I'm just about to get on a plane and go abroad.'

'Is there a relative who could come and collect her?'

'No.'

'When do you return?'

'I'm not sure.'

'Really Miss Walker, this simply will not do. The

injured girl's parents are on their way from Scotland to visit their daughter in hospital and I understand that they are considering criminal charges.'

'Let me speak to Georgina.'

'If you cannot arrange for her to be removed immediately I shall place the matter in the hands of the local police.'

'Let me speak to her and I'll see what I can do.'

'Hold the line.'

I can hear her telling someone to go and get 'the Walker girl' and I wish I was there so I could give Dorothea Simpkins a clip as well. After a bit Georgie picks up the phone and I can hear her breathing. I ask her what's occurred and at first she won't speak but after I've told her it's all right and I'm not angry, she replies,

'This one girl kept calling me guttersnipe and she got the others to as well and when we went to bed she took my blazer and put it in the toilet and pulled the chain and the others were all laughing and calling me guttersnipe as well so I hit her.'

'Was it the girl on the train who was sat by the window?'

'Yeah.'

I can hear her starting to cry. 'I understand why you've done it.'

'They was all at me,' she says, through her tears.

'I know. It's all right.'

'They've said I've got to leave.'

'Is that what you want?'

She's silent for a moment.

'That Annabelle was nice to me. She said she

199

would show me things today. We were going to meet in the tuck room after lunch.'

I can tell she wants to stay and try and make a go of it in spite of what's happened and I feel proud of her. 'I'm going to try and sort this but if I can't you might have to leave and it'll be Lizzie who comes for you. I've got to go away for a bit and you'll have to stay with her until I get back.'

'Where are you going?'

'Germany.'

'Why?'

'I'll tell you after I get home.'

'When's that?'

'Soon.'

I can hear her starting to cry again and I push my elbow against the sharp corner of the phone box until I get a pain up into my shoulder.

'Try not to worry, you've just had a ruck with an idiot who was looking for a slap.'

She sniffs and says, 'Ok.'

I put the phone down and I can see from the clock that there's still some time before the flight leaves. I go to Olga and ask her if she has a phone number for Nick Boulter. She says she hasn't so I get some more change from her and dial Lizzie's number. I tell her the situation and when she's done slagging off the upper classes I get a number for Nick from her and tell her she might have to collect Georgie and look after her for a bit. She says she'll be delighted. I tell her I'll try and call her later and we say goodbye.

I dial Nick's number and just when I think I've missed him he picks up. 'Boulter.'

'I'm at the airport.'

He's silent for a moment then he says, 'Do not identify yourself.'

'I've just heard from the school. She's had a fight with a girl who was picking on her and put her in hospital. They want to kick her out but you're going to stop them. She stays at the school or I don't do the business. I'll call you tonight.'

I hold the receiver up so that he can hear the voice over the speakers telling us to board Flight LH 915 to Berlin. I put the receiver back to my ear and Nick says, 'Get on the plane.'

I sit by the window and try to move clear of Olga who's bulging out of the seat next to me. Various passengers consider taking the aisle seat on the other side of her and then decide against it and move on towards the back of the plane. Finally, just as the cabin doors are shut, a wizened little old man slips in next to her and opens a German newspaper. The engines roar suddenly and my stomach lifts as the plane moves forward. Olga turns to me.

'You not fly before?'

I shake my head and she reaches into the folds of her cape and produces a flask. As an air steward passes and checks our seat belts she hides it again and when he's gone she hands it to me. I unscrew the top and smell whisky. I take a long pull, feel the warmth as it goes down and think about poor Georgie. I can only hope that Nick or Sir Robert will be able to fix it so that she stays at the school and it'll all blow over and she can settle in. It was good to hear that Annabelle is being friendly. I hand the flask back to Olga and she takes a swallow and puts it back inside her cape. She covers my hand with hers.

'Don't be frightened.'

The plane comes to a halt on the runway and then a moment later the engines roar really loud but we're still stopped and the plane's shaking and so am I and then we're pulling forward really fast and I'm pressed back in my seat. It's getting faster and faster and then we lift up into the air and the engines whine; all at once I let go and I feel like everything's all right and I'm not scared any more. Olga looks at me and smiles. I smile back and she takes her hand off mine.

I sit forward and look out of the window at the tiny houses and the roads and the fields and such and I think how many little people down there are living their little lives with all their worries and their excitements and how small and silly it all seems from up in the sky. I bet if you were up in space or on the moon the whole world would look tiny and not important at all.

There's a dinging sound from above me and Olga and the wizened old man undo their seat belts. There's nothing but clouds to look at out of the window so I undo my belt and sit back in my seat. Olga closes her eyes and after a bit her breathing gets heavier and her head starts lolling sideways towards the wizened old man who's deep in his newspaper and doesn't seem to notice. I close my eyes and my mind goes back to Georgie. I thought that getting her away from my life and all the aggravation would keep her safe but I suppose there's just as much to hurt you in different ways wherever you go. I'm glad Georgie dotted that girl. She'll get respect for it and the others will leave her alone. I reckon fear works just as well with any kind of people.

I doze off for a bit and when I wake the steward and the stewardess are pushing a trolley down the aisle and handing out trays of food and drinks. I can smell bacon and coffee and suddenly I'm really hungry. I look out of the window and see the clouds have parted and there's green fields and little towns and villages looking all neat and tidy far below in the sunshine. The trolley gets to our row and the wizened old man looks up from his paper, sees Olga's head an inch away from him and jumps up in fright. Olga jerks upright and lets out an enormous burp. Heads turn to look at us and the steward says something to her in German. Olga takes a deep breath, waves a hand, says something I don't understand and the steward laughs and passes a cup of coffee to the wizened old man. The stewardess offers him a tray of food but he shakes his head and goes back to his newspaper. She gives the tray to Olga instead and as she leans over with mine our eyes meet and we share a brief smile. The steward gives us coffee and I bite into the best sausage I've ever tasted.

20

We walk out of Tegel Airport and get into an old Mercedes taxi from the rank. Olga gives him an address and I hear her say what sounds like Hotel Castle. I ask her if that's where we're staying and how far away it is. She tells me it's the Hotel Castell, it's about twenty minutes away and we are staying there. The car moves off and we're driving through a well kept park before we get into wide tree-lined streets and then into what looks like the centre of the city, although there's still trees along the busy roads. There are quite a few army trucks and jeeps going about and I'm tempted to ask Olga about what goes on here but it seems like she doesn't want to talk or get friendly and I'm thinking that it's probably best to keep it that way, in case I have to kill her.

The cab pulls up in a quiet street with trees on each side. The hotel's a drab, grey, flat fronted building with an arched door. We get out of the taxi and take the cases out of the boot. Olga pays the driver and we go into the dimly lit foyer of the hotel. The walls are a dirty brown colour and there are two moth-eaten wing backed armchairs beside a small round table. We go to the reception desk in the corner where a grey haired woman is bent over a book that she's writing in.

Olga says something and the old woman looks up and just about manages a smile as she closes the book and reaches for another from the shelf behind her. Olga gives our names and the old dear writes us down in the book and hands us each a key. I tell Olga to ask her if I can phone London from here and after they've discussed it for a bit Olga says there's no phone except the one in reception but that I can do it from there.

We go up the narrow staircase onto the second floor landing and walk along the dark corridor. A door opens and a maid in a grey dress and apron, who looks no more than fifteen, comes out of a room holding a bucket and mop. She glances at us then she stands back to let us pass and looks at the floor. Olga stops in front of a door near the end of the corridor and hands me a key. As I go to unlock the door she nods towards the room next door.

'I am there. Five minutes, you come.'

I let myself into the room and put down my suitcase. I cross to the window, open the curtain and note the windowsill and the drainpipe that's within reach to the left. The room is small with just enough room for a single bed, a narrow wardrobe and an old armchair like the ones in the foyer downstairs. There's a washbasin in one corner, with a mirror above it and a picture of a bowl of fruit on the wall opposite the window. I put my case on the bed, take out my clothes and hang them in the wardrobe. I unwrap my gun, weigh it in my hand and wonder if I want to use it on this one.

It's difficult to carry without it being seen, makes a lot of noise and marks you out as the shooter unless you get rid of it right away. I decide that a blade or bare hands are probably better for this job and I slip the gun under the mattress. I put my underwear on the shelf in the wardrobe, lay Miss Austen on the table by the bed and go next door.

Olga's door's open so I knock and go in. She's kneeling on the floor twiddling the dial on a transistor radio that's balanced on top of her suitcase. She turns to me.

'Close door and come.'

I do as she says and she points at the radio's aerial. 'Move around please.'

I point the aerial towards the window and the crackling from the speaker turns into what sounds like German speech. 'Good,' says Olga.

She turns the dial, finds another station where a woman, who sounds like she's got her mouth full, is talking in some other language. She turns down the volume, stands up and looks at her watch.

'Ok. First lesson. You sit down please.'

She points to the bed and after I sit she turns up the radio, takes a notebook and a pen out of her suitcase, and sits next to me.

'In few moments she on radio will say weather forecast for local. At end she say name of next record she will play. According to name of singer we know where to make meet from decoding.'

While I'm wondering what she's on about she opens the notebook and shows me a page with four columns of letters next to each other. The woman on the radio is still talking away and Olga's listening and then there's a bit of a jingle and she says something else and then Sinatra swings into My Funny Valentine.

Olga writes Frank Sinatra on the page opposite

the columns of letters and then she moves closer to me on the bed.

'Now I show you how to decode this.'

She points at F in the first column of letters and then at the letter opposite in the second column which is a C, then she points at the C in the third column and then writes down the letter opposite it in the fourth column which is an S, then she does the same thing with each of the other letters of Frank Sinatra. When she's finished she shows me the notebook where she's written Spinnennetz B. I ask her what it means and she says it's a bar called the Spider's Web. At that moment Frank starts singing I've Got You Under My Skin and I get a flash of watching her through the mirror at Lizzie's getting her end away with those insects and I move a little way away from her along the bed. She looks at me.

'You understand to decode?'

'I think I've got it,' I say.

'Ok. Now we wait for time of meet to come.'

Sure enough the next song is Elvis singing One Night With You. Olga snaps the notebook shut and says, 'Ok, now we have time and place for drop. One in the morning at Spinnennetz Bar.'

'Do you know where it is?

'Is nearby, across Ku'damm.'

Olga turns off the radio, goes to the window, stretches her arms up above her head and gives a great yawn. She turns round to me and says, 'I sleep now.'

'Ok,' I say as I get up off the bed. Olga takes her cloak off and throws it over the armchair. She unbuttons her blouse, pulls it over her head and

I get a sight of her massive shoulders and arms, all ripply with muscle. As I head for the door she says, 'You like to have dinner then maybe go to cabaret before meet?'

'Why not,' I say and slip out through the door before she can take her bra off.

I go into my room and lie on the bed. I try to relax and drift off but I keep thinking of what's coming and how I'm going to get a sight of the file Olga's passing to the Russians to see if it's fake or genuine, and how I'm going to take care of her if it turns out she's working for them. I get up and check that I've got the piece of paper with the different letters on the bottom of the last page of the file, which say whether it's counterfeit or kosher. I take it from among Caroline Ward's designs, fold it up and put it in my pants.

As I walk past the window I can see into the building opposite. There's a man and a woman sitting on a sofa on the floor below. They're talking but she's got her back to me and I can only see her auburn hair. He's dark haired and handsome in a white shirt and tie. As I'm watching and wondering what they're saying the woman leans forward and starts pointing her finger at the man. He gets up and he's shouting at her and waving his fist and then she's up as well and they're having a right go at each other. The man grabs a jacket off a chair and he's off out of the door and the woman picks up a cup off the mantlepiece, flings it at the door and it smashes. She sits herself down in a chair in front of the fire and folds her arms. She doesn't look like she's crying or anything so I reckon she's told him what for and feels good about it. I wonder if that's the end of it or whether he'll come creeping back later and they'll kiss and make up.

I'm feeling tired now and it's too early to phone Nick, so I lie on the bed and close my eyes. The mattress is really hard and lumpy but in a bit I relax and I'm seeing the view out of the window of the plane again and the tiny houses and roads, and I think how all this aggravation that we have in our lives is only tiny and small as well and doesn't really matter at all.

I'm woken by a banging noise and I sit up and can't think where I am and I start to breathe quickly. I see my suitcase on the floor and I remember I'm in Berlin and someone's knocking on the door. I unlock it and open up and Olga is there in her cloak holding a towel and a bar of soap. I can see a large leathery thigh where the cloak has parted below her waist.

'I take bath. You want?'

Not being quite sure what she has in mind I shake my head and say, 'I'm all right thanks.'

'We leave in one half hour. Ok?'

'Ok.'

She stomps off along the corridor and I go back into the room and look at the time. My watch says it's gone six o'clock and I decide to phone Nick. I take some deutschmarks out of my purse, find his phone number and head downstairs.

The old lady's behind the desk and at first I think she's writing in her book again but when I get close I see that she's asleep with her head resting on her folded arms. I cough a couple of times and she wakes, sits up straight, says something to me in German and smiles. I ask her if she speaks English and she smiles again and says, 'A little bit, I think.'

I tell her I want to phone London and show her the number. She pulls an old candlestick phone towards her across the desk, takes the earpiece off the side and dials a short number. She waits a bit and then says some stuff in German and spells out the number. It sounds like she's spitting the numbers out as if they don't taste nice. She waits for a minute and then puts the phone on the counter and passes me the earpiece. I pull the phone towards me.

'Hello.'

'Do not identify yourself.'

'What's happened?'

'Fortunately the cheekbone is not broken and the girl, although in severe shock and quite distressed, is expected to make a full recovery.'

'Serves her fucking right.'

'The girl's parents have been persuaded not to pursue the matter.'

'Can she stay at school?'

'Your sister's case has been considered by the headmistress and it has been decided that she will enter a probationary period for the remainder of the term. If another serious breach of the rules occurs she will be expelled. I trust that is satisfactory.'

'It'll do.'

'Your sister has been told of the decision and appears to accept it.'

'Ok.'

'Our arrangements remain?'

'Yes.'

I hang up the earpiece, take a couple of slow breaths and I feel relieved that she's safe, at least for now. I pass the phone back to the old lady, offer her five deutschmarks and she takes the note and gives me three coins in change. I thank her and go back upstairs.

I have a wash at the basin, put on some make-up and brush my hair. I look at the clothes I've brought and decide on a loose skirt and a silk blouse which will be just about smart enough for a club but easier to move in than a tight dress, in case there's any rough stuff I put on my court shoes which have a low heel and a solid enough toe. I pick up my suede jacket and go and knock on Olga's door.

She's wedged herself into a dark red taffeta dress with long sleeves that must have the strongest stitching in the world. The material rasps against her thighs and her armpits as she walks to the bed and picks up an evening bag. Her hair is plastered down with lacquer and she's wearing red lipstick and black eyeliner. The whole effect is grotesque but when she turns towards me and stands for a moment, it's clear she's expecting a compliment.

'You look lovely,' I say.

She looks relieved. 'You also.'

She takes a light jacket out of the wardrobe and puts it on. I'm wondering where the file can be. It's too big to be in the evening bag so it must be under the dress somewhere. I open the door for her and we go down the stairs to the foyer. The old lady is either writing or asleep and she doesn't look up as we walk past her.

The street is quite busy and as people hurry

211

past us I catch bits of German and see different fashions and colours in the clothes and I really notice it being foreign and not like London. When we get to the corner and turn onto a much wider street with trees along each side of it and bright lights from bars and restaurants, Olga says, 'This is Kurfürstendamm, called Ku'damm for shorter. Famous street.'

We walk on for a bit then she stops outside a restaurant and looks at the menu by the door.

Through the window I can see white table-cloths and waiters in aprons.

'We go here,' she says as she pushes open the door.

A waiter approaches us, takes us to the back of the restaurant and seats us. At the next table an elegantly dressed older couple are sipping soup and ignoring each other. The man has a droopy moustache and wears a monocle. The woman has steely grey hair and a prim look about her and she raises her napkin and dabs her lips between each mouthful. She looks round at us and when she sees Olga she becomes very still and goes rather pale. She dabs her lips again, looks down at her soup and pushes it aside. I try not to smile and pick up the menu. It's all in German of course so I lay it down again. Olga looks at me over the top of her menu.

'Stew or sausage?'

'I'll have the same as you,' I say.

'Beer?'

I nod and she waves to the waiter and gives him the order. The prim lady is still staring.

Olga takes a look at her and turns to me. 'You

think she wants me?'

'I reckon if you played your cards right,' I laugh.

Olga turns and winks at the woman. She drops her napkin, stands up, nearly knocking her chair over and hurries towards a door with a drawing of a lady in a big hat on it. Her companion glances up briefly, adjusts his monocle and continues sipping.

The stew is thick and heavy with beans, chunks of meat and two dumplings. Olga leans over her bowl and shovels it in as if she's going all out to win an eating contest. I manage about half of mine in the time it takes her to finish and when I sit back and indicate that I've had enough she reaches for my plate, wolfs the contents, gulps down her beer and calls the waiter. While she's talking to him the prim lady comes out of the cloakroom, edges towards the table and sits with her back to us. The waiter toddles off and comes straight back with a plate of cakes and pastries and two more beers. Olga offers the plate to me and when I shake my head she makes short work of two apple tarts and a pile of whipped cream. She finishes her beer, burps twice, and looks at her wristwatch.

'You want to go club?'

21

Out on the street, Olga puts two fingers in her mouth, whistles at a passing taxi and the driver swerves to the kerb and stops. We get in and she gives him a name. As we move off she groans, rubs her back and says, 'Mattress so damn hard.'

'Mine was really lumpy,' I say.

'Stuffed with hair from concentration camps.'

'What?'

'From shaving heads of Jewish women in Ravensbrück.'

'Really?'

'Oh yes. By order of SS man, Oswald Pohl.'

'What happened to him?'

'Hanged.'

'Good.'

'Hid in Bavaria after war but Americans found him.'

Olga looks out of the window and keeps rubbing her back then her hand moves over the seat and finds mine. I don't pull it away as I need to keep her sweet. I'm looking up at the moon through the trees and thinking about the evil that went on in the concentration camps when she squeezes my hand and says, 'Maybe we go to different kind of club?'

The way she's looking sideways at me gives me a good idea of what kind of club she's thinking about.

'If you like,' I say.

She speaks to the driver and he nods and we go on along the Ku'damm with jostling cars and tooting horns and then turn off and drive along quieter streets for a bit until the taxi turns into a backstreet and stops. Olga pays the driver and we get out, walk along the street, turn into an alley-way and stop outside a door with a sign next to it that says Aquarium Club.

A bearded man in a sheath dress and a blond wig opens the door when Olga knocks and after she talks to him and hands him some notes he stands back to let us in. We walk along a dark corridor and Olga gives some coins to a dark haired boy of about fifteen who is sitting on a stool in the shadows at the far end. The boy hangs our jackets up on some hooks in the corner and I follow Olga down the stairs.

The room's dark and the air's heavy with cigarette smoke. There's a chandelier hanging from the ceiling but most of the bulbs are gone and the lights on the walls only give a dirty glow to the peeling paintwork. Through the gloom I make out a naked man and woman on a dimly lit stage at the far end of the room and as my eyes adjust I can see that the man is giving her one. She's lying on her back on an iron bed and he's on top of her and she's stretching her arms out and moaning. He goes at her like that for a bit then he turns her over and gets into her from behind. She's up on all fours and trying to look like she's carried away with ecstasy but just looks bored and pissed off.

Olga finds a table near the back of the room and I sit facing away from the stage. A man in a rubber dress and fishnet tights wobbles up to the table carrying a tray. Olga orders whisky and I do the same.

'We have bottle?' asks Olga.

I want something to take my mind off the cabaret so I nod in agreement. I look round at the next table and there's a man in a tutu and ballet shoes with a clown mask, beside a young girl with close cropped blond hair who looks like she's naked until I spot the sequins on her body stocking. Looking at the other punters, who are mostly men in various kinds of dresses and a few butch women in men's suits, I wonder why the floor show is so tame. I hear a few people clapping and look round and see the couple on the stage give a quick bow and walk off.

The whisky arrives and I pour a drink for us both and down mine in one. Olga does the same and pours us another. She nods towards the stage.

'You like show?'

I shrug. 'Not much.'

'Better later, I think.'

A fat bloke with a bald head and sunglasses in a blue silk dressing gown with mules on his feet comes up to Olga and starts talking to her in German. She replies to him and he pulls a chair up beside her. When he raises his long cigarette holder to his lips I see that he's got a small whip tied to his wrist. He slips his arm round Olga's neck and starts mouthing something into her ear which makes her laugh so I turn away and let them get on with it.

The next act up on the stage is two women. The older one's wearing an old-fashioned gold coloured crinoline dress with a crown on her head and the young one's in a leather jerkin and tights with a pageboy haircut. Some plonky old-fashioned music starts and the Queen calls the page to her and makes her kneel on the floor in front of her. As the Queen lifts up her dress and the page reaches for the waistband of her long silk knickers, I feel a poke in the shoulder. I turn round and Olga and the gent in the dressing gown are standing behind me. Olga bends close to my ear and says, 'Come.'

She turns and walks through the tables after the blue dressing gown to a door at the side of the room. I follow her and the man through the door into a long room with a row of three or four beds down one side, with curtains round them and lights inside. There's moaning and groaning coming from the first one as we walk past and a slapping sound from the next one. The one at the end of the room is empty and as we get to it Olga's escort slips off his dressing gown and dives onto the bed. Just as I'm about to make my excuses Olga closes the curtains on him and turns to me.

'Take file from drawers!' she hisses.

She turns her back to me, bends over, lifts her dress over her head and I see the file sticking out of the top of her knickers. I reach across her massive arse, pull the file out, slide it up under my blouse and into the waistband of my skirt. She sees me do it, puts her arm round me and whispers in my ear, 'You make good spy.'

She points at the tent and says, 'You want?'

'I'll see you back at the table,' I say as I slip out

of her grasp and walk away. I only hope the bed's strong.

I go past the other beds, keeping my eyes front and go back into the club. On the stage, the Queen's lying on the floor with the crinoline over her head. Her knickers are off and the page is doing her duty between her legs.

I'm tempted to sit down and watch the show but I think better of it and look round for the ladies' room. I see a couple of likely looking doors in the far corner and make for them. As I'm weaving through the tables I feel someone walking behind me. When I get into the corner of the room I turn and it's the girl in the body stocking. She looks no more than seventeen and she's slim and elfin but she looks strong, like a ballet dancer. I stand back to let her go past me. As she does so one of the doors opens and two very drunk men lurch out and push her against me. She puts her hands on my hips to steady herself and stares into me with eyes that are such a deep crystal blue that for a moment I feel myself letting go and wanting her, but I come to my senses just in time and gently push her away. She seems about to speak, but then she lowers her head, turns back into the club and she's gone.

I go into a cubicle, lock the door and lean my back against it. When my head clears I take the piece of paper out of my pants to remind myself what I'm after and I remember that I have to look at the bottom line on the last page of the file and see which letters are in brackets after it says FM sonar. If it's JK/QC in the brackets, then Olga thinks it's the file with the false information about the submarine that she's passing to the Russians and she's ok. If it says QLA in the brackets, then it's the genuine stuff and I've got to kill her. I open the file, turn to the last page, look at the bottom line and see QLA.

I rip the file up as small as I can and try to flush it, but it won't go down. I take the pieces out, open a bin that's next to the toilet and shove them in among a bunch of old sanitary towels. I come out of the cubicle, wash my hands and feel for the blade in my suspenders. I take it out and put it in the back of my waistband. I'm thinking that it's best if I do Olga in the street and leave her there, which is a risk but I don't have much choice. I don't want to kill her because I've come to quite like her, but she's a traitor after all and she did kill Lordy, who was a nice old boy even if he was an old pervert, and he got Georgie into Leavendon which was good of him.

I go back into the club and see her coming out of the room with the beds. She's alone and she's been quick and I wonder if she's suffocated the man in the mask. She sees me and points to the exit door. As she walks past me she says, 'We go to drop. You have the file?'

I nod and follow her. The club's filling up now and people are crowded round the bar at the back. There's a fast-talking comic on the stage who's getting some laughs and being heckled. As we're going through the crowd round the exit door I feel a hand on my arse and another going between my legs. I turn and see a grinning red-faced man. There's a big laugh from the audience so I catch him a sharp one below his ribcage with my elbow. He groans and doubles over while I nip up the stairs behind Olga and out into the alleyway.

It's dark and quiet and that little bit of action has got me going. I take out the blade and drop back a pace or two behind Olga. I look round and see there's nobody in sight. As I'm about to trip her up to get her on the deck where I can do the business, there's the blast of a siren and a police car skids to a stop at the end of the alley. Another car pulls up behind it and Olga grabs me and pushes me into a doorway. Four German police get out of each car, take their guns out and hurry past us to the club. One of them bangs hard on the door. The man in the blond wig opens it and they push him aside and file in. I can hear screams and shouts as we hurry to the end of the alley and into the street.

We get to the main road and stop a passing cab. Olga gives the driver the name of the Spider's Web and says something else to him. He takes off fast, weaves around the cars in front and then turns off into a quiet street. Olga puts her hand on mine.

'Thank you for waiting.'

'That's ok,' I say.

'When you look like me you take every chance you get.'

I laugh and for a moment I feel sorry for what I've got to do. Then I remember what she did to Lordy and remind myself that she's well in the game.

The traffic's thicker now and there are more people on the street. We go on down the Ku'damm and then the taxi does a left turn and then a right into a street with a concrete wall on each side. I hear the roar of an engine and then a pair of blinding lights are coming fast towards us. The car's filled with light. The driver shouts and wrenches the wheel over. There's a loud bang and the car smashes against the wall. I'm thrown against Olga, our heads crunch together and I pass out.

I feel a thump in the back, then another. I'm being pulled about and pressed against hard edges and I can't move my arms. My eyelids are rubbing against something. I hear the noise of an engine and I know that I'm sliding about in the boot of a car that's stopping and starting. I'm blindfolded, my hands and feet are tied and my head hurts. The sound of engines tells me we're in the city and then the car speeds up and the bumps get smoother and we're on a fast road. I feel around with my feet, find that I'm alone and wonder what happened to Olga. I squirm around and try to feel a sharp edge or a tool I can use to get free but there's nothing. I twist my wrists back and forth against the ropes but they won't give.

I lie on my side and brace my legs against something solid. After a while I start bumping about again and then the car stops and I hear doors open and close. The boot lid squeaks, I feel a blast of cold air and an arm goes round my back and another under my knees. I'm lifted up and carried for a short way and then I hear a door being unlocked and creaking open, then footsteps on a hard floor and I'm sat on a chair. A rope is tied round my waist and the blindfold's removed. I look up and see that I'm in a big wooden barn with three men standing in front of me. The one in the middle is very tall and big and broad with it. He stands with his feet apart and his hands behind his back. I recognise the shape of the big round head on his shoulders. One of the other men turns on a light and I'm looking at Heinz's leering face.

He takes a step towards me and waves pieces of the bloodstained pages of the file that I dumped at the club in front of my face.

'You need your glasses to see secrets you want to give to Russian filth?'

He tosses the paper on the floor and walks round behind me breathing heavily and talking in German. He comes in front of me again and leans his horrible red face into mine.

'You work for fucking aristocrat fucking Boulter helping Russian bastards who destroyed Fatherland. You and fucking Russian bitch animal. I kill you both slow and painful like the vermin that you are!'

He steps away and says something to the other two men who open the door and leave. He kicks the wall and looks at me.

'He make me work for him. Tell me it is against communist bastards but all the time he cheat me and make me help them. Twisted scum like him soon find out what happens to those against Germany.'

There are squeals and grunts outside and then the doors swing open and Olga bursts in head first with the two Germans hanging on to her arms and trying to control her as she thrashes about between them. Heinz strides over to her, gets her in a head lock and between the three of them they force her onto a chair next to me. While Heinz sits on her lap, one of the men takes over the strangle-hold, and the other one finds a rope to tie her onto the chair. She seems to quieten down but when Heinz gets off her and they let go of her she rears up and catches him under the chin with her head. He staggers a bit then he swings round and fetches her a haymaker to the side of her head that knocks her out. She falls backwards onto the floor and the chair smashes underneath her. As she rears up again, Heinz takes a revolver out of his belt and shoots her twice in the head.

He walks away and leans against the wall rubbing his chin. The two other men look at him as if they're waiting for him to say something. He waves them away and they go and stand by the doors. He looks at me and after some time his mouth widens into his leering grin. He reaches inside his coat, pulls out a long blade and walks over to where Olga's lying. He kneels down, takes hold of her hair, lifts her head up and starts slicing at her neck with the knife. When he gets to the bone, he puts the knife down, takes hold of her hair with one hand and her belt with the other. He stands up and lifts her slowly off the floor like a weightlifter lifting a bar bell. When he's got her up level with his chest, he drops down onto one knee, smashes her neck down onto the other knee and snaps the bone. He lays her down on the floor and starts cutting through the cartilage and the remaining flesh. One of the guards slithers down the wall and passes out.

Heinz gets the head free, picks it up by the hair,

223

comes towards me and dangles it inches from my face.

'You want to kiss your girlfriend goodbye?'

As Olga's face swings in front of me, dripping blood, I strain against the ropes with everything I have to get the pain.

He drops the head on the floor, walks round behind me, grabs hold of my hair and I get a sharp pain in my neck as he jerks my head back. A moment later I feel his lips and his hot whisper in my ear.

'She so fuck ugly she only good for burning but you are nice little kitten for me to play with, eh?'

I feel the blade against my neck and then he starts untying the ropes round my wrists. He calls to the guard who is still standing and he unties my ankles. When he's done, Heinz comes in front of me and kicks Olga's head aside. The guard stands back and points his AK at me. Heinz leans close to me, grinning.

'First we see what you got, then I decide which part of you I take first. Hand, foot, or tit maybe?'

He grabs my collar, pulls me to my feet and shoves me into the middle of the room. I weigh my chances of rushing the guard before Heinz can reach me but decide that short of him having a stroke at the crucial moment, it can't be done. All I can do is try to buy time and hope for an opening. I step back, slip my jacket slowly off my shoulders, let it fall to the floor and start undoing the buttons of my blouse. Heinz chuckles, picks up Olga's head and sits in the chair I was tied to.

When I'm naked, Heinz says something to the guard who passed out and is now sitting against the wall. The guard gets up, comes towards me undoing his flies, and pushes me against the wall. As he leans into me and tries to force my legs apart I ram my knee up into his balls and feel his nose splinter as I nut him. The guard falls. Heinz lunges at me but I dodge sideways and dive at the guard with the AK. As I get hold of the barrel a weight lands on me from behind, knocks me to the ground and everything goes black.

I come round as I'm being dragged across the floor. There are hands round my neck and they're squeezing tighter and Heinz is mumbling some German. I'm going out again but then there's the sound of an engine. The hands loosen and I'm let go. Heinz is shouting something and I raise my head and see the guard turning off the light and opening the doors. As he goes outside a pair of headlights flare. He fires two shots and a machine gun opens up. The guard screams and falls backwards through the door. Heinz throws himself on the floor as a hail of bullets rip into the wall behind us. The doors open wide, headlights flood the room and I make out a small crouching figure silhouetted in the doorway. The driver gets out of the car, comes into the barn and turns on the lights. It's the girl from the club with the cropped hair and I nearly cry out with joy when I see Greta in the doorway holding an AK47.

She smiles at me. 'You are safe now.'

She walks forward, pointing the AK at Heinz's head. She says something in German and he gets up off the floor and puts his hands in the air. The girl helps me up, sits me on the chair and gathers up my clothes. She sees Olga's head on the floor, looks round and sees the body. She gives me my clothes, picks up the head, takes it to where Olga lies and places it beside her.

In the silence, an owl gives a long hoot, as if in mourning for Olga, and some distant night bird squawks a faint response. Greta indicates the guard with the smashed nose, who is lying in a corner holding his crotch. The girl goes to him, takes a revolver out of her belt and motions him to stand next to Heinz. He gets painfully to his feet, makes his way over and stands swaying next to his boss.

I've finished putting on my clothes and I'm squeezing my feet into my boots when Heinz gives an almighty roar, picks up the guard, swings him at Greta's head and knocks her to the ground. As I dive for the AK, Heinz jumps over Greta and charges headlong out of the door and into the night. The girl runs to the door and fires a couple of shots after him but he's gone.

I go to Greta to see if she's hurt but she's already getting to her feet. She shrugs off my attempt to help her, picks up the AK and goes to the door. She stands beside the girl and looks out into the darkness. She turns to me.

'It is no matter. We get him next time.'

She walks slowly to the guard lying on the floor and puts a single shot in his head.

I look at the neat little figure with the quiet determination who's saved my life and I want to thank her but suddenly I'm swaying, and feeling myself falling, then there are arms round me and it goes dark.

Greta and the girl help me up off the floor and

take me across the yard to their car. After Greta's opened the back door for me, the girl takes two petrol cans out of the boot and gives one to Greta. I get into the back seat and watch them walk to the barn, open the cans and pour the contents along the bottom of the walls. They come back to the car and Greta gets into the driving seat. She starts the engine and swings the car round in a tight circle until we're facing the road. I hear a crackling noise behind us and I turn and see flames leaping up the walls of the building. The girl gets into the front seat and slams the door. Greta puts the car in gear, we roar away and there's a great woomph from behind us as the roof goes up. I turn and look at the great pillar of flame until it disappears behind a line of fir trees. As we reach the main road, Greta pats the girl on the shoulder and says, 'This is Silke. She is my granddaughter.'

22

We're in my room at the hotel. Greta's in the armchair, I'm sitting on the bed and Silke is cross-legged on the floor beside her. The body stocking's now covered by a pair of tight jeans and a sweater. We're drinking brandy from china cups and Greta's been telling me how Silke's father died in the gas chambers along with her brother, and that Silke's mother, who was Greta's daughter, died in the camp while giving birth to her. She and Greta were able to survive in the camp because Greta had been a jeweller and the SS used her to value the gold and silver they took from prisoners before they gassed them. She would tell them what was worth keeping and what should be melted down.

She tells me about how they lived in the camp, how brutal the guards were and how they often had to eat rats and mice to survive.

I'm sickened by what I'm hearing but when I say I can't believe that the Nazis could have been so cruel Greta just shrugs.

'There are thousands of Nazis like Heinz and his cronies still living in Germany with false papers, and even working in the government and the German army. Idiots like him think they can recreate the glorious days of the Third Reich. The Americans released hundreds of officers and SS men from internment when they realised that they needed the intelligence that Nazis like General Gehlen and his men had collected on the Russians during the war. They had microfilmed it and hidden it before they surrendered. They traded it for their freedom and now they spy for the US.'

I'm amazed at what she's saying and thinking how little people know of what goes on in the world. I reckon most people think that the Nazis were all hanged or banged up for life after the war for the atrocities they committed, and now she's saying that there are loads of them walking round free as air because of what they've got on the Russians.

I take a drink of my brandy and look across to the window. I see that dawn's breaking and it makes me want to get back to what's happening now.

'How did you find us?' I ask.

'We were closing on Heinz just as he captured you.'

'You were after him?'

'Of course.'

'Why?'

'It is what we do.'

I can see from the way she's looking at me that she won't say any more on the subject. I pour us another brandy and ask, 'How do you think Heinz found me and Olga?'

'He followed you from London.'

'Thinking that we're Nick's agents?'

'Yes.'

'And you were following him?'

She nods.

'Was he in the club?' I ask.

'He sent one of his men in.'

I remember a young bloke that could have been one of them leaning on the wall near us when Silke and me were in the dark corner. 'Is it true that Nick's a traitor?'

'Oh yes,' says Greta.

'So why did he want me to get rid of Olga? Why not let her give the true submarine secrets to the Russians?'

'Because he made her kill Lord Duncaid after he found out that the lord was about to expose him as a traitor.'

'Nick told her Lordy was bent?'

'Yes. So she kills him because she hates Russians. Then Nick realises he must have her killed as well, in case she finds out that he was lying to her. It would tell her that he is the real traitor.'

'But I checked the file and Olga was going to pass the genuine secrets over.'

'No. That file was fake. Nick switched files at Broadway later.'

'How do you know?'

'We have man in files office.'

My head's starting to swim with all this but I trust Greta even more now she's saved my life.

I'm sorry Olga's dead, since she was going against the Russians after all, but at least it wasn't me who killed her. I'm wondering if Nick will want me gone the same way as Olga in case I've rumbled him as well. As if she's read my mind, Greta looks at me and says, 'You are in danger.'

Silke looks up at me and I feel a tingle as I meet her eyes. I breathe out slowly, look at Greta and say, 'From Nick?'

'Oh yes,' she says.

'What if I grass him?'

'You have no proof.'

'So I kill him.'

'That is no good,' says Greta.

'He can't get me if he's dead.'

'And if there are others?'

She's looking steadily at me and I know she's right. If he's got company they'll be up to speed with me and Olga and the plans, and they'll have me killed as soon as I've done him.

'So what do I do?'

She pours another shot of brandy and offers the bottle to me. I shake my head. She takes a sip.

'I go to London and tell him you are killed. You stay here in Berlin and we look after you.'

I sit back on the bed and look at the two of

them. The wise old lady with the wrinkled face and the knowing look in her eyes, who's seen more cruelty and suffering in her life than anyone ever should; and the beautiful young girl who was born in hell. I know that Greta's all I've got against Nick and whoever he may have behind him, but I know I'm not going to do as she says. I won't be beaten by a bunch of upper class cunts who think they're better than people like me. She's looking at me as if she's waiting for an answer so I swallow the rest of my brandy.

'Is there a convent near here?'

We've left Greta sleeping at the hotel and Silke's driving along a wide street that's nearly empty of traffic at this time of the morning. I reckon we've got just enough time before dawn breaks to get what I need. I can see a big arch up ahead that's lit up with floodlights. As we pass it, she tells me it's the Brandenburg Gate and swings the car to the right. We drive down a tree-lined street for a while and after we cross a wide square she points to a tall building on the left and pulls into a side street just beyond it.

I tell Silke to stay in the car while I have a look round but she says she wants to come with me, so we walk along the pavement and into a courtyard. There are tall brick buildings on two sides of it with arched stained glass windows with saints and adoring women staring up at them. We go round the back of the building and I find a door that I could open if I had my picks, but all I've got is a blade. Silke points to a drainpipe and some sash windows above that look easy enough.

Before I can stop her she's climbed up the pipe like a cat, walked along a ledge, and is sitting on a second floor windowsill, beckoning me to join her. I climb up, get beside her and see that the window opens onto a landing. I slide the blade between the casements, push the catch aside and lift the window.

Silke slips through and I join her on the landing and close the window behind me. The doors in the corridor are shut, and all seems quiet, so I close the window and follow Silke down the stairs.

We've almost reached the basement when a door opens above us and we freeze against the wall. Footsteps recede along the corridor and another door opens and closes. We wait a moment, then we go down the stairs. I switch on the torch and see what I'm looking for – two laundry baskets standing beside an open door.

We enter the laundry and I head for a clothes rail next to three ironing boards in the corner. I find a black robe that looks about the right length, take it off the rail and hold it against me, while Silke opens cupboards and drawers until she finds veils and starched white hats. The first one she tries on me fits, so we bundle up the gear and head for a door that's between two sinks at the back of the room. As we're pulling back the bolts on the door, a bell starts dinging somewhere and there's the sound of doors opening and closing and people moving around above. We shut the door behind us, walk round to the front of the building, go across the courtyard and into the street.

We drive back to the hotel, go up to Greta's room and find her still sleeping in the armchair.

Silke lies on the bed and seems to fall asleep instantly. I want to go and lie down beside her but I think better of it. I put the nun's habit in the wardrobe, take a towel from the rail by the basin and head for the bathroom.

The hot water geyser on the wall gurgles and rumbles when I turn on the tap, then it fires up and hot water gushes into the bath. I go to the mirror and look at the side of my neck where Heinz cut me. It's a couple of inches long but it's closed up and has stopped bleeding. Polo neck sweaters or a choker for a couple of weeks and a dab of foundation to cover the scar after that should do it.

I take my clothes off, sink into the lovely warmth and massage my wrists and ankles where the ropes have left marks. I lie back, close my eyes and think about what's gone on. I realise that Greta must have sent Silke into the club after she saw Heinz's man go in, then they must have followed us, stayed out of sight while Heinz and his men took us inside, and then moved in when they heard the shots that killed Olga. I let myself drift off and get dreamy and woozy and think of home and Lizzie until the water starts to get chilly. I get out, dry myself, pick up my clothes and go to my room.

Tegel airport is busy and I get a few looks in my nun's habit as we walk towards the ticket desk. Greta helped me get the wimple and the veil right this morning and with a pair of horn rimmed glasses to complete the effect, I reckon I'll be ok if

233

Nick's got anyone looking out for me at Heathrow. I'm wishing Greta was going to be in London with her good advice and her contacts in the spy trade, but she's staying in Berlin to continue her pursuit of Heinz.

At the desk, I'm lucky to get booked on a flight that leaves in a couple of hours. Silke buys the ticket for me and we head towards the queue for departures. She's changed her jeans and sweater for a pencil skirt, a linen jacket and heels. She walks on ahead of me and I see how gracefully she moves. As we near the departures gate she glances back and sees me watching her. She turns and engages me with those beautiful eyes.

'There is time before the flight. Would you like to have coffee?'

'Sure,' I say.

We go across the entrance hall to a cafe and the young waiter, who's been watching us approach, walks forward eagerly and pulls out a chair for me. We sit down, Silke orders coffee for us and the waiter nods and looks at her legs. She shifts on her chair, pulls her skirt down and he looks embarrassed and toddles off to the counter. We share a smile.

'Good job you aren't wearing what you had on in the club last night.'

She laughs and says, 'You are right.'

'Do you go there much?'

She shakes her head.

'Never before. I only went for my grandmother.'

'You work with her a lot?'

'Of course.'

She turns her head and stares across the entrance hall. I look at her delicate profile. She seems somehow fragile and yet strong at the same time. She turns to me.

'I would be dead but for her.'

'Where did she take you after the camp?'

She leans forward and speaks quietly. 'I was very young and don't remember much but I know that after the camp was liberated and burned we were put in a house nearby, then Feliks stole a car and took us to Berlin and we hid in sewers while he robbed money from Gestapo and then took us to Copenhagen. We are there for one year, then Feliks goes to London and grandmother and me come to Berlin, and I have governess who lives with us. Grandmother is sometimes with us, sometimes in London, sometimes South America where she is searching for ex-guards and SS like your man Heinz. Also Russians who did bad things when they invaded.'

'Does she kill them when she finds them?'

'Only if she does not have enough proof or witnesses to report them to the authorities for trial for war crimes.'

'And you helped her?'

'Sometimes.'

I'm about to ask her what Greta put her up to and hoping she didn't use her for bait when there's an announcement over the speakers. Silke listens.

'That is the call for your flight. You must go.'

She puts some coins on the table, I pick up my suitcase and we walk towards the departure gate. When we get there she hands me the ticket, we say goodbye and I look into those incredible blue eyes. She holds my hand.

'I hope I see you again.'

Before I can reply she turns and walks away.

I watch her all the way to the main doors then I go through passport control and customs without any problem. When I get to the lounge I think about phoning the school to find out how Georgie is but decide to leave it until tomorrow. I find myself a seat and catch up with Elizabeth Bennet instead.

After a while the flight's called and I join the queue and try not to get nervous. When I get on the plane I get a window seat so I can look down from the sky again. As the plane rolls forward to the runway and the stewardess gives us the life jacket routine I start to feel scared and I grip the arms of the seat. When the engines rev up and the pilot lets the brakes go and I'm pushed back in my seat with the acceleration I get a rush of fear. Once we lift off the runway and rise up through the clouds I feel myself calming down and when the sun appears above the white carpet of clouds I take a few deep breaths and I feel good.

23

I'm in a phone box on the corner of Maida Vale and Clifton Road, dialling Lizzie's number. I'm looking at a white builder's van parked across the road from the flats. The man in the driving seat is pretending to read a newspaper while he watches the building. Judging by his lily white hands he

hasn't done a day's hard work in his life and I
reckon he could well be one of Nick's mob waiting to see if I'm home again.

After a few rings Lizzie answers and I push
threepence into the slot.

'I'm calling you about the repair that you wanted
to the refrigerator you bought from us recently.'

She's silent for a moment, until the penny
drops. 'Er, yes. What about it?'

'I could have one of our men over to you this
morning, if that would be convenient?'

'Yes, I'll be here.'

'He's finishing a job in Heath Street in Hampstead at the moment, so he could be with you in
an hour or so.'

Another pause.

'Could he have a look at my Kenwood mixer
while he's here?'

'I expect he can, but that will be a separate job.'

'That's ok, as long as he can fix it.'

'I'll tell him about it when he phones in.'

'I'll expect him in an hour then.'

'Ok, goodbye.'

Knowing that I've got to be at Kenwood House
on Hampstead Heath in an hour to meet Lizzie,
I walk along Clifton Road to the cab rank on
Warwick Avenue. I tell the driver to take me to
the entrance to Kensington Gardens on Bayswater Road, at the top of Queensway. The driver
looks at me in the mirror as we drive and I know
he wants to ask me what it's like being a nun so I
close my eyes and clasp my hands together on my
lap. When we get to the park gate I pay the fare,
walk to the ladies' toilets that are just inside the

park, and wait. When a large lady in a straw hat goes through the entrance and down the steps, I follow close behind her and keep her between me and the attendant as I slip into a cubicle. I put my suitcase on the lavatory seat and take off my wimple and habit. I open the case, look through the clothes and put on a grey pleated skirt, a cherry-red polo neck, and my short linen jacket. I put the horn rimmed glasses back on, roll the wimple and the veil up inside the habit and put it under my arm.

I walk into the park and dump the habit in the first bin that I see, then I go across Bayswater Road and along Queensway to Whiteleys, remembering when me and my mate Clare used to nick stuff from there when we bunked off school together. I go up the curving staircase to ladies' clothes on the first floor and buy myself a beret. I find a changing room, put my hair up under the beret and pull it down until it almost meets the top of the glasses, for maximum cover. I go down to the street, walk along Porchester Gardens to Leinster Square and spot an anonymous looking hotel called the Parkway on the far side. I go across the square, walk up the front steps and into the foyer. There's no one at the desk, so I ring the bell and wait.

A grey haired bloke in a baggy suit with dandruff on the collar comes out of a room at the back and goes behind the desk. I tell him I want a room, give him the name of Alice Crawford and pay a ten shilling deposit. He gives me the key to a room on the first floor and offers to carry my suitcase up for me. I tell him not to bother, pick up the case, and make for the stairs. When I notice the payphone in the corner of the lobby I turn back and ask him for change. When he obliges, I climb the stairs to the room, put my case on the bed and go back down to the lobby. I'm just about to dial the school to check on Georgie when I remember how quickly Nick was able to get Georgie's sentence commuted after she put that girl in hospital. I decide not to call in case Dorothea Simpkins has a hotline to Nick and tells him I've been in touch from a British phone. I decide to ask Lizzie to try and find out if she's ok instead. I put the phone down and go up to the room.

The cab drops me on Hampstead Lane and I go through the gate onto the heath and walk along the path through the trees to Kenwood House. The late afternoon sun warms me as I round the corner and go past the front of the house. A group of Japanese come out of the main door chattering away as they walk past me. I see Lizzie sitting on a bench in front of the building at the far end. As I get near her she glances at me and looks away again. I stop in front of her, take off the glasses and she smiles.

'I told you to jack in your line of work and get yourself a proper job years ago, but I never thought you'd start repairing fridges.'

'They tell me I've got the figure for it,' I say.

'I'll have a look later and let you know'

I sit down beside her and we have a quick hug. She takes a thermos flask out of her handbag, pours a drink and hands it to me.

I put the glasses back on as a park keeper walks past us with a rubbish sack and a stick with a spike on the end. Lizzie clocks the horn-rims.

'Who's after you?'

'Take your pick,' I say, taking a sip of whisky.

'How was Berlin?'

'Complicated.'

'Was Olga working for the Russians?'

I shake my head and finish my whisky. Lizzie pours me another and I tell her everything that happened in Berlin. When I've finished, she shakes her head.

'You'll have to deal with Nick sharpish before he finds you.'

'I know.'

'What will you do?'

'I might take a trip to Ringwood.'

'What for?'

'I'm thinking that if I can get evidence of the Marquess doing his party tricks with dead girls, I can get him to serve Nick up as a traitor. That way, anyone who might be in bed with Nick won't know I'm involved and won't be coming after me.'

'Sounds good.'

'Can I get a favour?'

'As long as it doesn't involve dead bodies.'

'Can you phone the school for me and make sure Georgie's ok?'

'Of course I can. How's she been getting on?'

'She smacked a kid for calling her common and put her in hospital.'

'That's my girl.'

'They were going to kick her out but Nick got involved and they put her on probation.'

'So you don't want to phone yourself in case he rumbles that you're here.'

'Right.'

We have another drink and watch some little kids playing with a toy aeroplane near where their mother sits on a rug, unpacking a picnic. The breeze is puckering the surface of the lake and whispering in the trees. People are strolling about or sitting on the grass near the water and I feel peaceful and calm, like I could sit here forever in the warm sun. I slide my hand into Lizzie's and she squeezes it gently. After I move a little closer to her, she says, 'Where are you staying?'

'Hotel in Bayswater.'

'Mmmm,' she says, as she strokes the back of my hand.

'Come and have a look, if you like?'

'Thought you'd never ask.'

The park keeper's heading our way again so we get up and walk past the front of Kenwood House, through the trees to the gate and hail a cab on Spaniards Lane.

It's gone five o'clock when we get to the hotel. The foyer's empty so we go to the payphone in the corner and I dial the school, give the receiver to Lizzie and tell her to ask for Dorothea Simpkins and see if she can talk to Georgie. When Lizzie gets through to Dorothea she goes a bit posh and says that she's calling on behalf of Georgina Walker's sister, who's abroad, and that she's gathered that there was an unfortunate incident a few days ago and she's concerned about Georgina's welfare. Could she please have a word with her? In the silence that follows Lizzie gives me a thumbs

241

up, then she thanks Dorothea, puts her hand over the mouthpiece and says, 'She's going to try and find her.'

While we're waiting, the grey haired man who checked me in comes out of the door at the back, gives us a look, goes behind the reception desk, opens a ledger on the desk and peers down at it. He scratches his head, releasing a fall of dandruff, closes the book and bumbles off again just as Lizzie says hello to Georgie and asks her how she is. She listens for a moment, then she tells her there's someone to speak to her and passes me the phone.

'Are you ok?'

'Not bad.'

'Is the girl you had the ruck with back yet?'

'Tomorrow.'

'Be careful.'

'They've moved me to a different house.'

'That's good.'

'It's the one Annabelle's in.'

'Oh, that's lovely.'

'We've got an exeat this weekend and she's invited me to her house to stay.'

'That's nice of her.'

'She's got a pony.'

'That'll be fun then.'

'Yeah.'

'How are your lessons.'

'Ok.'

I hear a voice in the background.

'It's tea time. I've got to go,' Georgie says.

Before I can say goodbye, she puts the phone down. I feel a surge of relief, knowing that she's all right, at least for now. I put the receiver back.

'How is she?' Lizzie asks.

'Pretty good, I reckon.'

As we climb the stairs I tell Lizzie about Georgie's weekend with Annabelle and the pony. When we get into the room, I lock the door, take off my hat and glasses, slip off my jacket and fold myself into Lizzie's arms.

When I wake up, it's dark outside. I turn on the bedside light, look at my watch and see that it's seven o'clock. I've slept since Lizzie went home more than twelve hours ago. Before she left she gave me the phone number of a photographer called Dom that she knows in Wimbledon, who deals in cameras and can tell me about what I need for the Ringwood job. She said she'd tell him to expect a call from Angela. It's too early to phone him so I have a wash, get dressed in what I was wearing yesterday, put on the glasses and go downstairs in search of breakfast. The old boy's been replaced by a small, neat looking woman with her hair in a bun, who gives me a bright smile. I ask her if I can have breakfast in my room and she tells me that I can and gives me a menu. I ask for scrambled eggs, toast and coffee, and she nods and scuttles off through the door behind her. I go back to the room, lie on the bed, open my book and enjoy Elizabeth telling Darcy where to stick his marriage proposal.

After I've eaten, I go downstairs to the pay-phone and dial the photographer's number. A bloke answers, and when I say I'm Lizzie's friend Angela, he asks me when I want to come over. I say as soon as possible and he tells me he'll be free in about an hour, if I can get there. I tell him I can and get the address from him.

Back in the room, I take my Smith and Wesson out of the suitcase and consider whether to hide it somewhere, or take it with me. I change into my ski pants and slide it into the back of the waistband. I put money and lock picks in my pockets, put on my hat and glasses and go downstairs. The lady wishes me a good day and I walk down the steps and along the pavement. A cab comes round the corner and pulls up a short distance away. A young couple get out and I wait while the man pays the driver and hear their American accents as they pick up their cases and walk away. I give the driver the address and settle into the back seat. I take out my compact, look at my face in the mirror, dab some powder onto my cheeks and put on some lipstick. Just as I'm about to close the compact I catch the reflection of a white van that looks familiar in the mirror. The van follows us as we turn onto Bayswater Road and when we stop at the traffic lights at Notting Hill Gate and it pulls up close behind us. I can see a pair of hands on the wheel that could well have been the ones I saw holding the newspaper outside my flat yesterday morning.

As we get to the roundabout just before Shepherd's Bush Green, I rummage round in my handbag, then I lean forward to speak to the driver.

'I'm awfully sorry mate, but I've come out without my purse. I must have left it on the dressing table. Would you mind if we went back so I can get it?'

'That's all right love,' he says, as he steers the cab round the roundabout and back the way we've just come. Back on Bayswater Road, I look in the compact mirror again and the white van is three cars behind us.

When we get to Leinster Square, the driver asks me where I want him to stop. I tell him to go to the far corner. When he stops the cab the meter's showing one and ninepence. I step out of the cab, give the driver half a crown, tell him I've changed my mind and walk round the corner into Garway Road just as the white van pulls into the square. I go down the first set of basement steps and stand where I can just see the road. While I'm waiting to see if the van's still on me, I'm thinking that if Nick knows I'm in town, the sooner I get to Ringwood and try and sort this mess out the better.

After five minutes there's no white van so I reckon I'm all right. I come up the steps and see a narrow road opposite. I walk along it and into a yard with garages. There's no one about so I go to the garage at the far end, pick the mortice lock and open one of the doors. There's a grey Standard Ten inside and a workbench with packing cases and some sacks underneath it. I go in and lock the door behind me. The Standard's doors are locked so I take a long screwdriver off the bench and put a pair of pliers in my back pocket. I slide the screwdriver blade in between the top of the window and the door frame and force the window down far enough to reach inside and get hold of the handle. I open the door, get in the driving seat and use the screwdriver to prise off the panel

245

under the ignition keyhole. I find the two red wires, cut them both with the pliers, strip the ends and twist them together. I get hold of the two brown wires, cut and strip them, then I touch one to the other and the engine fires up first time. I look along the bench for some tape and get lucky again. I tape up the bare ends of the wires, put the tools under the seat and unlock the garage door. I drive the car out, lock up again and pull out onto Garway Road.

When I get to Shepherd's Bush Green I stop at the Shell station, fill up the tank, buy an A–Z street map and look up the photographer's address in Wimbledon.

24

I finally find Clarence Road after searching the maze of suburban streets with the map in one hand and the other hand on the steering wheel. I park outside number twenty-three, next to a red Messerschmitt bubble car, which looks a bit out of place among the Hillman Minxes and the Ford Anglias. I walk up the path to the front door of a semidetached house with fresh white pebble-dash and a neat privet hedge round a square of lawn. I ring the bell and after a couple of minutes the door's opened by a short man of about fifty, with a bald head, glasses and a neat moustache. He's wearing a yellow short-sleeved pullover and a bow tie. He looks me up and down.

'You've come about the camera?'

'That's right,' I say.

He holds his hand out and says, 'Nice to meet you. I'm Dom.'

'Angela,' I say, and shake his hand.

He stands back to let me in and points to a door on the right.

'Do you mind waiting in there, while I finish a session in the studio?'

'That's ok,' I say, and walk past him into a living room with a beige leather three-piece suite, a glass coffee table and a TV set in the corner.

'Won't be long,' he says as he closes the door.

My eye is caught by a figure in a photograph above the mantlepiece. As I get close to it I see that it's Dom, wearing a pointy green hat with a bell on the top, grinning from ear to ear and waving, surrounded by a large crowd of garden gnomes. Below the picture, the mantlepiece is crowded with miniature gnomes, fishing, pushing wheelbarrows, sleeping, laughing and generally having a good time. A few of them at the back of the crowd are naked and looking a bit dodgy.

There's a big one in a policeman's uniform in the corner behind the TV, having a good laugh, and in the opposite corner a washerwoman type with a big bosom and her sleeves rolled up, is standing next to a mangle.

As I'm looking round for any more jolly little folk, there's a bump and a squeal from above, and then the sound of high-pitched voices. The noise gets louder and louder and there are more bumps, and then the patter of feet on the stairs. When the front door slams shut, I go to the window and see three dwarves striding along the path. Two are male and one is female. The lady has a bit of sash cord tied to her ankle and she's buttoning up her blouse as she walks. One of the men is hopping along with one leg in a pair of trousers and struggling to get the other leg in. When they get to the Messcherschmitt, one of the men opens the top and jumps over the side, into the driving seat, and starts the engine. The woman climbs into the back, unties the sash cord and throws it into the gutter. The other man finally gets his trousers on, hops in beside her, and lets the top down. The engine gives a great whine, the driver lets the clutch in, and the bubble car shoots off up the street.

I sit on the sofa, and while I'm telling myself that I shouldn't be surprised by anything that any friend of Lizzie's is up to, Dom puts his head round the door.

'Shall we look at cameras?'

I follow him along the hall, through the kitchen, and down some steps into a basement room.

Dom switches on the light and opens a cabinet on the wall that has three shelves full of different cameras.

'Lizzie said you wanted to photograph covertly in low light.'

'That's right,' I say.

He takes a small camera off the shelf that's got a tube coming out of the side with a small metal box on the end.

'This is known as a button camera. This one was actually captured from a KGB spy. The idea is that the camera is worn inside a coat, from which a button has been removed, leaving a small hole in the fabric.' He points to a round disc on the front of the camera. 'The button, here, which protrudes slightly from the front of the coat, hides a lens which screws onto this subminiature camera. This flexible tube runs into a pocket. You simply place your hand in your coat pocket and squeeze the lever at the end of the tube. Strings then pull open the doors on the centre of the button, and a snapshot is taken at the same time. It is important to wear a loose coat so that no bulge is visible.'

He passes the camera to me and I can feel how light it is.

'If you don't need to hide the camera of course there is the Minox B subminiature which is very good in low light with a shutter speed as slow as half a second.' He picks up a small silver metal camera about four inches long. 'With an ultra-sensitive film you'll get a far better image with this, although you do have to hold it up to the eye.'

He pulls the ends of the camera, extending it by a couple of inches.

'I should be able to do that,' I say.

'Oh well, in that case, this is the chap for you.'

He hands it to me. 'And I can develop and print for you of course.'

The rather eager look on his face, as he says this, makes me think about what kind of complications could occur if someone else sees the pictures. 'Is there an instant camera that I could use?'

'Well, yes there is,' he says, looking slightly disappointed as he reaches to the top shelf. 'This is the Polaroid Highlander. It will do the job, with or without the flash, but you won't get the same definition and as you can see, it is considerably larger.'

'Do I get the pictures right away?' I ask.

He opens the camera and slides the lens forward then he turns it round, points to a button on the back of the camera and says, 'You simply take the picture, wait sixty seconds, lift this flap on the back and there's your photograph.'

'That's the one for me,' I say.

'Very well. It will cost you one hundred pounds and no one will know you got it from me.'

'Ok,' I say.

'Would you like me to show you how to use it?'

'I would.'

He closes the camera, opens the flap on the back, takes a small packet off a shelf behind him and shows me how to load the film. He opens the camera again, slides the lens forward, pulls an eyepiece out of the side, and then a square metal frame in front of it.

'This is the viewfinder.' He points to a button under the lens. 'And this is the shutterbutton.' He hands me the camera. I press the button and hear it click.

'I need it to be silent.'

'Ah, well, you'll want a blimp.'

'A what?'

'A sound blimp.'

He goes to the corner of the room, picks up a small leather briefcase and stands it on the table. He flicks a catch by the handle and the back of the case drops down and opens like a book. I can see wads of foam rubber inside. He pulls a square piece of leather out from the front of the case, leaving a hole about two inches wide in the centre and a smaller hole to the side of it. He takes the camera from me and wedges it into the foam. He takes a step back, lifts the briefcase up and I can see the lens through the hole in the middle, and his eye looking at me through the other one. He holds it still for a moment.

'Hear anything?'

'No,' I say.

'This will cancel sixty per cent of shutter noise and the Polaroid's pretty quiet anyway.'

He shows me how to slide the leather piece that covers the holes in the front back in place and snaps the briefcase shut. He hands it to me.

'And it's a discreet way to carry the camera.'

I try a few shots, and after a couple of attempts I've learnt how to use the thing and managed to convince him that I'm not up for any nude test shots of me, or him, or both of us, so that he can show me the time delay feature. I give him a ton for the camera, add a score for the briefcase, and follow him upstairs. When we get to the kitchen he tries his luck again and asks me if I'd like to come back another time to pose for what he calls some 'tasteful boudoir shots,' but I'm saved by the doorbell.

'That'll be my next session,' he says, as he goes to the front door and opens it to a middle-aged couple. They are both very fat and the lady is holding a Pekinese dog in her arms. Dom greets them and they walk into the hall. The man turns and looks me up and down.

'Is this the taxidermist?'

I squeeze past the woman with the dog, and walk up the path to the car.

Lizzie told me that Ringwood Hall is near a village called Kintbury in Berkshire. I stop at a garage on the A4, buy a road map, a torch, and a Cornish pasty. I sit in the car munching the pasty and look for Kintbury on the map. When I find it, I put the edge of the pasty against the scale at the bottom of the map and measure the distance to be about sixty miles. My watch tells me it's nearly midnight so I reckon I'll get there sometime after one o'clock. I put the map on the seat next to me, pull out onto the road and wind the Standard up until it's bowling along comfortably at about sixty-five miles an hour. I turn on the radio but I can't find Luxembourg or any decent music, only some bloke going on about politics on one station, and a woman talking about how to knit woolly gloves on another. I'm tuning in to some orchestra music with a violin and thinking of how Georgie would like it when a black car pulls alongside and I see a gun barrel pointing at me.

I slam on the brakes and put my head down as a bullet shatters the windscreen. I feel a blast of cold air and pebbles of glass pummel my head and shoulders. The car skids sideways and I look up and see the rear end of the black car in front of me. The shooter is leaning out of the nearside window and taking aim. I take my foot off the brake, shove it into third, floor the accelerator, pull out to try and get past him on the outside but he swings out and blocks me. I brake again, get in behind him and take out the Smith and

Wesson. I pull up close to him, swing the car left and take a shot at the head behind the gun poking out of the passenger window. I miss him but he disappears and the black car accelerates. I pull back and shoot for the tyres. When the car lurches to the left and slows, I know I've got one. The car lurches right, the shooter leans out again and it's the ginger haired bloke I last saw in Catford. He fires one at me, and a bullet rips into the roof of the car. I give him a couple back, pull out, overtake and watch them in the mirror as they limp to the side of the road and stop. Nick's boys are not giving up.

I slow down until the blast of cold air coming through the hole where the windscreen used to be is bearable, and drive for a couple of miles until I see a sign for a place called Pedworth. I turn off and stop the car at a bend in the road. I get out, take off my beret, shake the granules of glass off it and brush myself down. I lean against the car, take a few deep breaths and look up at the new silver moon as it comes out from behind a cloud. There's no way back now. If I run from this mob, I'll be running forever until they kill me.

I start the car and drive on slowly until I see the few streetlights of a small village ahead. I pull off the road onto a cart track, bump along it for a bit and turn the car in behind a small barn so that it's hidden from the road. I get out and walk back to the road and into the village. I pass a pub called the Lord Nelson and walk on down the main street, past the village shop, until I see a Ford Anglia parked up beside the village church which is a good distance from any houses. I pick up a sharp stone, walk past the car, smash the driver's window and slip round behind the church. When I don't hear anything, I go back to the car, open the door, and use my knife to get at the ignition wiring. The Anglia starts up first time and I check the fuel gauge and see that the tank's half full. I drive back to the cart track where I left the Standard, pick up the briefcase and the road map and try to work out how to get to Kintbury and Ringwood Hall.

25

I make good time along the A4 and only get lost once on the country roads before I find myself approaching Ringwood. It's almost two o'clock when I get to the back lane that runs behind the estate. I get to the wooden gates, pull the Anglia onto the track opposite that leads into the woods and drive along to where I hid my car last time. I take the briefcase off the back seat, lock the door of the Anglia, and make my way back to the road.

I decide not to open the gates, in case there might be someone about, and walk alongside the stone wall until I find a place where there are gaps between the stones that I can use as footholds.

After a couple of tries, I make it to the top of the wall, slide down the other side and land on a bed of leaves. I stay still for a moment and listen to the faint sounds of night creatures among the trees, then I make my way slowly through the woods to the back of the house. I can see the outline of the battlements in the moonlight, like so many fists raised against the sky. Everything seems quiet when I get there so I go to the back door of the old brick building, pick the mortice lock, and walk between the rows of beautiful old touring cars. I reach the trapdoor at the far end that covers the stairs to the basement, where the old sinner got up to his tricks before. I put my pick in the keyhole but find it's not locked.

I raise the trap a couple of inches, put my ear close to the gap and listen. After a few minutes I've heard nothing so I slowly raise the trap, edge down the stairs, and lower it again. I wait at the bottom of the stairs in the darkness and check for any sounds. I take the torch out of my pocket, cover the end with my hand, turn it on and bleed out just enough light to see where I'm going. I move along the corridor, past the door to the room where I hid under the bed.

At the very end I find an alcove and another set of steps curving downwards. I creep down a couple of steps and I can see a faint glow of light which gets brighter as I move slowly down. As I get to the fifth step there's the sound of a door opening down below. I switch off the torch, nip back up the stairs, open the first door I come to and get behind it. I hear footsteps on the stairs and a light goes on in the corridor. I ease the door open just enough to see the back of Symmonds the butler, in his tailcoat and pinstripes, walking towards the stairs and holding a bunch of keys. I wait until the light goes off and I hear the trap open and close. I open the door, turn on the torch and go down the curving stairs to another passageway that's a bit narrower than the one above.

There are two doors leading off it, one halfway along on the left and another at the far end. I listen at the first door and try the handle. I make short work of the lock, slowly open the door and the light of the torch falls on a wooden coffin. I feel round the door frame and find a light switch. I turn it on and see that the coffin is of a highly polished dark wood with a picture of a woman with a halo on the top of it. It's resting on red and purple silk drapes that curve up the walls behind it.

There's a figure in a black hooded robe kneeling in front of it, holding a child in its arms.

I'm starting to feel sick and a bit faint as I try not to imagine what might be inside the coffin but I remind myself why I'm here and move forward to take a closer look at the kneeling figure.

I'm relieved to see that the child in its arms is made of plaster and the figure is also made of some solid material and has never breathed. The picture on the coffin lid is of a young girl in a black robe with a long sad face and delicate hands held in prayer. The smell that emanates from the coffin as I ease the lid up is anything but delicate, and the young girl lying inside has been dead for some time. I stand back, open up the briefcase and take the camera out. I push the camera lens forward and pull the eyepiece out of the side and the metal frame in front of it. I look through the viewfinder and take a shot of the coffin and the girl. I wait for a minute like he told me then I open the flap on the back and there's the photo. I take it out, close the flap, step back and take another one of the whole scene with the kneeling figure.

I close the lid of the coffin, switch off the light, go into the corridor and sit on the steps. I open the flap and take out the second picture which has come out well too, even though these ones are no use without the old creeper doing his nasties. I go along to the passageway and put my ear to the door at the far end. When I hear nothing, I do the lock, open the door, shine the torch round and find a light switch.

There's a naked girl at the far end of the room. She's standing on a round shell, like one you'd see on the seashore, only much bigger. She's got a great long mane of thick brown hair and she's holding the end of it to cover herself below the waist with one hand, and she's got the other hand across her breasts. The girl's face is familiar. I'm sure I know her from somewhere. I walk towards her and recognise Julie, the young tom I sent off to Bournemouth. I go behind her and see that her skin has been sewn onto a wooden frame at the back of her, which is suspended on a line from the ceiling. Her skin has some kind of glaze on it which makes it look as if it's alive, but it's cold and clammy to the touch and when I try to move one of her arms it springs back to where it was when I let go of it. I look at those dark eyes that were so full of tears when I put her on the train, and I can see some fine metal clips on her eyelids that are keeping them open. I want to cut her down, pull that wig off her, wrap her in furs and take her off and bury her somewhere well away from these revolting monsters who could do this to a young girl.

As I turn away I notice a slide projector, sitting next to a record player on a table beside the door. I walk over to it, press a switch on the side, and suddenly Julie's come alive, in a ghostly kind of way, and she's floating on a lake, under a big sky, with a woman next to her giving her a flowing robe to cover herself. There's a winged angel, with a girl on his back, flying towards her on the other side.

I switch off the projector, look around for somewhere to hide myself and see a row of wooden packing cases in the corner. I kill the light, turn on the torch, go behind, the packing cases and stack them up so that I'm hidden, with a small window for the camera. I put the briefcase in position, open it and take out the leather flap that covers the holes in the front. I look through the viewfinder and adjust the camera until I've got a good shot of the room. I sit on the floor and pull my knees up under my chin. At least it's warm in this basement. I'm hoping I'm going to get some action tonight, but if I have to wait I will. At least Nick's lads won't be able to get at me here. I'm hoping Symmonds being in earlier means that he was preparing the scene for His Lordship.

I close my eyes, lean my head on the wall behind, and try to lose the image of that poor girl.

I'm looking back and wondering if she'd have been better off taking her chances in London and whether I did wrong by getting her away, but then I tell myself that I only did what I thought was best at the time and that's all you can ever do. There's a rustling sound near me, something skitters across the floor and then it goes quiet again. I relax and let the silence wrap itself round me. Just as I'm drifting off I hear the sound of footsteps outside in the corridor. I get up and kneel behind the camera.

The door opens, the lights go on, and the butler comes in carrying a bag and a feather duster. He puts the bag down, approaches Julie and flicks the duster over her. He opens the bag, takes out what looks like a postcard, stands back, looks at the card, then at Julie, and adjusts the hair round her face and then lower down, where she's holding it in front of herself. He stands back and has another look, then he opens the bag and takes out a hair dryer and an extension lead. He plugs the lead into a socket on the wall, turns on the hair dryer and wafts it up and down her body. I look through the viewfinder and see Symmonds go to the wall, unplug the hairdryer and put it in the bag. He switches on the projector, has another look at the postcard, adjusts the dial on the front of the projector and puts the postcard in his pocket, then he turns to a telephone on the wall, picks up the receiver, gives a handle on the side a couple of turns, and waits a moment.

'The Botticelli is ready, My Lord.'

He puts the receiver back, picks up the bag and the feather duster, opens the door and closes it behind him. Moments later, I hear a rustling in the silence and I see a rat scampering towards Julie. It stops in front of the shell, gets up on its back legs and puts its front paws on the edge. It's twitching its nose about and sniffing the air when a thud from above makes it freeze and then scoot off into a corner.

There's a shuffling sound in the corridor, then the door opens slowly and the Marquess, wearing a red silk dressing gown and slippers, comes in and stands looking at the scene in front of him. He smiles, shuts the door behind him and pads towards Julie, mouthing something that I can't hear. He kneels down in front of her and starts wringing his hands as if he's begging her for something, then he leans forward, grips the rim of the shell and starts licking her feet. He licks his way up to her ankles, then her knees and her thighs. When he gets to where she's covering herself with her hair, he pulls back and has a long conversation with her, that involves a lot of hand wringing and nodding, then he takes hold of her wrists, pulls her hands and the hair away and pushes his face in between her legs.

I take a picture at the crucial moment of entry, and while he's burrowing in there like a truffle pig I open the flap and take the photo out. I look at it and see that it's only a silhouette and his face is hidden anyway. I need a shot that identifies him and I need to get closer. I pocket the photo, look up and see that he's now standing in the shell with her, fondling her tits and licking her neck. I get a shot of him as he kisses her on the lips, take it out and see that he's better lit and you can see his face. After a bit more snogging, that I have to turn away from, he steps out of the shell, goes to the door and knocks on it. Moments later Symmonds opens it and comes in. The Marquess raises a finger towards Julie and Symmonds walks round behind her, unfastens the line from the ceiling, that's holding her up, and carries her to a chaise longue that's against the wall, close to where I'm hidden. He lays her down on the chaise longue, turns on the light and goes to the record player next to the projector. He cranks the handle on the side, lowers the arm onto the turntable and a string orchestra strikes up a waltz. Symmonds looks to the Marquess, who gives him a nod, and then leaves.

The Marquess approaches Julie and stands in front of her. He makes a low bow, bends down, puts an arm round her waist, lifts her up and holds her against him. As her head rolls back, he puts a hand on the back of her neck, lifts her head and leans it on his shoulder. He takes her hand in his, tightens his grip on her waist, and waltzes her round the room with his head resting against hers and a dreamy smile on his face. As they come past the edge of the packing cases I click the shutter and hope for the best. They circle the room a few times, and I take out the photo. As I look at it and see that it's just a blur, the music stops.

The Marquess cradles Julie's head in his hands and kisses her, then he carries her back to the chaise longue, lays her down on it and kneels down in front of her. There's more mumbling that I can't make out and then he stands up and his dressing gown drops to the floor. I know this is my chance for a picture that will clinch it. He lowers himself on top of Julie and I manage to angle the briefcase so that the camera's in position, and get a good shot of him as he moves back and forth on top of her. When I move the briefcase to try and get a better angle, one of the packing cases creaks. The Marquess stops, looks up and sees the camera through the gap in the packing cases. He screams, leaps to his feet, runs to the door, wrenches it open and Symmonds appears. The Marquess points at the packing cases and Symmonds comes towards me. When he gets close I shut the briefcase, step out from behind the packing cases, and take out my gun.

Symmonds freezes. The Marquess crouches down by the door, puts his hands up to his face and whimpers something. I tell Symmonds to give me the keys and he takes them out of his pocket and holds them out to me. I take the keys from him, walk past him to the door, keeping the gun on him and wait while the Marquess scurries out of my way. I shut the door, lock it behind me, open the briefcase and the flap on the camera and have a look at the picture of the Marquess on top of Julie. I've got him in profile and perfectly in focus. Julie's naked body is quite clear underneath him and with her head hanging at the angle I've caught it, and her mouth gaping open, she's clearly dead. I put it in my back pocket with the others, walk along the corridor and up the stairs to the trapdoor.

I lift the trap, climb out, lock up, and make my way among the old cars to the door at the far end. I'm just about to put the pick in the lock when the door swings open, a big fist smashes into my face, and I hit the floor.

26

I come to lying on my back on a damp mud floor. It's pitch dark and I've got a crashing headache. I put a hand to my face and I can feel that my cheekbone is tender and swollen but it doesn't feel broken. There's a bruise on the back of my head where I must have hit the deck. I try to move my arms and legs and they seem to be working ok, so I get up on all fours and stand up slowly. My head swims and I stagger against a wall of rough stone and sit down on the floor again. When my head clears enough I get up and feel my way along the wall until I come to a corner. I move along for what feels like about ten feet until I get to the next corner and then I come to a solid wooden door, with a round iron handle and a keyhole.

I sit down again, check my pockets and come up empty. I don't expect to find the blade that was strapped to my ankle but I check anyway. I lean back against the wall and massage my temples to try and ease the headache. I crawl back along the wall to the door, feel for the keyhole, and put my eye to it but I can't see a thing. I feel around among the muck and stones on the floor until I find a bit of twisted metal with a sharp point. I straighten it out a bit, work it into the keyhole and come up against something solid, which must be a key, put in from the outside. I work on trying to dislodge it for a bit, but I can't move it, so I sit back down against the wall. I'm wondering why I've been locked up instead of killed like the rest of the girls. I know it means someone's going to come and get me and all I've got against them is a bit of twisted metal.

I look up and see a small, faint patch of light, high up on the wall above, that could be an opening or a window. I stand up and feel my way round the walls to see if there's any chance of a foothold to climb up on. I get to the far corner and find an old crumbling chimney piece that's at an angle to the wall where the stones are pitted and irregular. I put the twist of metal in my belt, feel for gaps in the stones with my feet and start to climb up. I slip and fall a couple of times, but on the third try I manage to keep climbing until I feel a ledge above me. I get both hands onto it, pull myself up, rest on my elbows and take a short breather. I reach up with one hand and feel a solid iron spike sticking out of the wall. I grab it, pull myself up, turn round and sit on the ledge.

When I've got my breath back, I look up and see where the patch of light's coming from. It's a square opening in the opposite wall, with two iron bars across it, directly above the door. I reckon I'll just be tall enough to see through it if the ledge goes all the way round and I can reach it. I take hold of the metal spike again and pull myself up until I'm standing on the ledge with my back to the wall. I put my hands out to the side to get what grip I can and move my feet along the ledge. When I reach the corner I put a foot out to see if the ledge goes on along the next wall but feel nothing and almost fall, but when I steady myself and reach a bit further with my foot I find the ledge starts again, after a short gap, where it's probably fallen away. I step across the gap and make it as far as the hole in the wall. I turn round to face it, grip the lower of the iron bars, rise up on tiptoe and take a look. The brick building is a couple of hundred yards away through some trees. I can see the stable block next to it, the courtyard and the house beyond. Dawn's breaking and I can hear a horse neighing in the stables and birds singing in the trees. As I'm pulling on the iron bars to see if they'll give way, I hear the key turning in the lock below me.

I turn round as the door opens slowly and I'm looking down on a large bald head and a pair of wide shoulders that I last saw in a barn in Germany. Heinz takes a step forward, switches on a torch and flicks the beam round the walls. I jump off the ledge and land with both feet on top of his head. He goes down face first and I hit the ground beside him and grab the torch off the floor. As he turns over and tries to get up, I shine the torch in his face, take the metal spike out of my belt and slice it across his throat, but he pulls back and I miss the artery and only gouge his flesh. As he clutches the wound and curses, I stand up, kick him hard under the chin, and he falls back and rolls onto his stomach. I jump on his head with both feet and crush his face into the dirt. I step off him and roll him over. As I raise the metal spike to plunge it into his eye, he rears up, grabs me round the waist, and hurls me against the wall. I black out.

The grey above me looks like the sky, until I turn my head and see the real sky through a car window. I can hear bangs in the distance, like guns being fired. I try to move but my feet and hands are tied. I'm lying on the back seat of a car that isn't moving and every bit of me hurts. I raise my head and try to make out where I am, but all I can see are trees all around. As I try to sit up, I hear footsteps approaching. I lie down again and close my eyes. A door opens, and the car rolls as someone gets in. I feel breath on my face for a moment. When the car rolls again I open my eyes and see the back of Heinz in the driver's seat. He starts the engine and the car moves off.

As we gather speed, I arch my back slowly and look at the distance between me and that massive head. I press my feet against the door and slowly move myself along the seat until my head is against the other door. I take a deep breath, turn onto my back, pull my knees up to my chest, jackknife up off the back seat and kick with all my strength at Heinz's head. The windscreen shatters, the car lurches off the road, rolls down a bank and smacks against something solid. I bounce off the roof, land face down on the front seat, and I'm out again.

When I come to, I wriggle onto my back, sit up, and can't believe my luck. Heinz has gone clean through the windscreen. His head's on the bonnet and there's blood pumping from his neck, where it's been slashed by the frame of the windscreen. I lie back against the door for a moment, then I swing my legs up onto the frame where the windscreen was and scrape the rope that's round my ankles against the broken glass left in the gully. After what seems like ages, the rope gives way and I'm able to swivel round, kick open the car door and get out. I walk round the wrecked car, looking for something to cut the rope on my wrists, and find a sharp edge of metal where the front wing's been torn off, which does the job. I go and have a look at Heinz, feel for a pulse in his neck, and find that he's good and dead.

I lean on the bonnet of the car and wonder what I should do. I can see the house through the trees and I want to finish what I started, but without the photographs I've got nothing. I look down at Heinz's horrible head, and think what terrible things he's done to those girls, and all for an old devil who ought to be bleeding to death alongside him. I decide to search him before I go, just in case he's got the photos on him. I feel in his jacket pockets but there's only a packet of fags and a lighter. I push him over so that he's lying along the seat. As I'm leaning forward to get at his back pocket, a voice behind me says, 'You looking for these?'

I turn and see the man with the shotgun who stopped me in these woods before. He's holding his gun in one hand and the photographs in the other. He gives me a slow smile and as I look into his dark eyes, I feel my legs giving way underneath me.

I can hear a crackling noise in the distance and there are streaks of light dancing on the ceiling. I turn my head and the man with the dark eyes is sitting beside a roaring log fire. His shotgun is leaning against the wall beside him, underneath a stag's head. There's a white teapot and two cups on a table, and he's giving me that same smile that made me pass out before. He lifts the teapot.

'Cup of tea?'

I sit up slowly on the sofa I've been asleep on and nod my head. He pours tea and offers up the milk jug. I nod again and he adds milk and brings the cup and the sugar bowl to me. I take two spoonfuls, stir them in, and he puts the bowl back on the table, pours himself a cup, and sits down beside the fire. I take a sip, and then another one and suddenly I just want to stay drinking tea with this nice man in front of his lovely warm fire and never move again.

After a while he says, 'I'm glad you're back.'

I'm not sure how to reply, so I just nod.

'It's got to be stopped,' he says.

'How long have you known?' I ask.

'Too long.'

'Why haven't you done something?'

'No one would have believed me and they would have got me out of the way. A footman found out a while back and they drowned him in the moat.'

'Who knows about it now?'

'Only His Lordship, the butler and that big German bastard.'

He looks into the fire as if he's thinking about something. It sounds like he doesn't know about Nick Boulter's connection and the Marquess covering for him in return for the girls. It's probably best to keep it that way.

'Where is that big German bastard?' I ask.

'In the ground.'

'And the car?'

'Gone.'

I look out of the window, see that it's dark. 'What time is it?'

'Gone midnight.'

'Have I been asleep all day?'

'Didn't seem right to wake you.'

I can't believe that I've slept so long. 'Where are the photographs?' I ask.

He stands and takes a key out of his pocket. He picks up a clock off the mantlepiece, opens the back of it and takes out the photographs. He looks at them for a moment, shakes his head, hands them to me, and says, 'It's got to be stopped.'

'Where did you find these?'

'The big man's pocket.'

I pass two photographs back to him. 'Hang on to those for insurance.'

He puts them inside the clock and places it back on the mantlepiece.

'Which way is the house?' I ask.

He leads me to his front door, opens it and points off to the right. 'Take that path under the chestnut tree, go on over the rise, and you'll see the house.'

He takes my blade out of his pocket and gives it to me, then he looks me in the eye and shakes my hand. I walk along the path towards the chestnut tree.

27

The full moon gives me plenty of light to see my way along the path through the woods. The back of the house is mostly dark apart from a few lights on in the upper rooms. I'm going to try and find the Viscount, tell him the score, show him the pictures and hope he's bent enough to grass his mate Nick Boulter for a spy. In exchange, I'll keep his old man's nasty tricks out of the papers and uphold the family honour. I just need to be careful they don't drop me in the moat, but if I don't risk it, Nick and his mob will get me anyway so I haven't got much choice but to have a go.

I walk slowly along the side of the stable block, keeping close to the wall, and stop at the corner. The kitchen windows on the other side of the courtyard are dark and so are the ones above on the first floor. All I can hear is the odd snuffle and rustle from the stables, and there's no one about, so I move along to where the courtyard narrows, go across to the house and try the handle of the kitchen door. It's locked and I've got nothing to work it so I try the windows on each side. The third one along is unlocked and the casement slides up easily. I climb through, stand in the big sink on the other side and close the window behind me. I drop onto the floor, walk round the big wooden table and ease open the door.

There's a faint glow of light from the end of the corridor and I walk towards it as quietly as I can while I try to remember the route me and Lizzie took when we were here before. I spot what looks like the staircase that Nick brought us down from the room we slept in, which I remember was on the first floor, and I reckon I should be able to find the Viscount's room from there. As I put my foot on the first step, the back door opens, a light goes on behind me, and I hear a girl laughing. I go up the stairs and round the corner as another girl tells her to be quiet. A light goes on above me and the two girls are coming up the stairs behind me, talking in low voices. I keep going up, past the floor our room was on, until they peel off on the third floor landing. I wait until I hear a door open and close, then I go back down the stairs. As I turn the corner onto the landing, I bump straight into one of them.

'Oops!' she says, dropping her bag. She bends down to pick it up. As she straightens up I see that it's Mary, the girl who brought me and Lizzie breakfast. She looks at me for a moment, then she recognises me.

'Oh,' she says, looking flustered.

'Hello Mary,' I say.

She goes to walk past me but I put a hand on her arm.

'I'm just off to bed,' she says.

'Can I talk to you a minute?' I ask.

'I've got to be up early.'

'I want to show you something.'

'What?'

I hold the picture of the Marquess lying on top

271

of Julie in front of her. She looks at it and her eyes widen. I show her the others one by one and see the look of horror on her face. She leans back against the wall, looks at me, and says, 'That's terrible. How could he...'

'I know.'

'How could he do that?'

As she starts crying, a door opens and a man's voice says, 'Be quiet or bugger off out of it!'

I take Mary's arm. 'Where's your room, love?'

I follow her up to the top landing, along a corridor, through a door at the end and into a bare room with a narrow bed on each side and a small chest of drawers. She sits down on one of the beds and she's crying and shaking. I sit beside her and put an arm round her. She dabs at her eyes with a hanky.

'How could they do that to Julie?'

'You knew her?'

'She was a scullery maid.'

'Since when?'

'She'd just started, a bit more than a week ago. They put her in here, with me. I was showing her the ropes and that. She was ever so nice. They told me she'd been sacked for thieving.'

So Julie did get herself a job and try to make a better life for herself and this is what she got.

'Is the Viscount here now?' I ask.

'Yes.'

'Can you take me to his room?'

'What for?'

'I'm going to show him the pictures and get him to stop it.'

'He won't do it.'

'Why not?'

'He's scared of his father.'

'How come?'

'Because he can disinherit him any time he likes, and he hasn't got a pot to piss in.'

There's a hard edge to Mary's voice. She isn't the meek little creature who brought the hot water to me and Lizzie.

'I'll take you to his mother.'

'His mother?'

'She's the one.'

'Are you sure?'

'She's frightened of no one. Come on.'

She opens the door and strides off with such purpose that I follow her along the corridor and down the stairs. After a couple more stairs and corridors we stop outside Lady Northrup's door.

Mary puts her finger to her lips, opens the door quietly, and we go into the room. There's the sound of gentle snoring coming from the four-poster bed. A shaft of moonlight, coming through a gap in the curtains, plays on the outline of a sleeping figure. Mary motions me to stay by the door, walks round to the far side of the bed and sits on the edge. Lady Northrup stirs, slides a hand onto Mary's knee and says, 'Hello, naughty girl.'

As she lifts the blankets invitingly, Mary says, 'There's someone here.'

'Mmmm?'

'To speak to you.'

Mary turns on a lamp by the bed and Lady Northrup is suddenly up on one elbow and looking at me.

'What the fuck is this?' she says.

'You have to listen to her!'

'This is an outrage! Get out both of you!'

She gets out of bed, grabs her dressing gown off a chair and reaches for a bell pull by the mantlepiece. Mary gets to it first and pulls it out of her way. Lady Northrup takes a swing at her.

'You impertinent little bitch!'

I flick a light switch by the door and the chandelier fires up. I hold the first photograph out in front of me and walk towards Lady Northrup. She snorts in anger, then she snatches the photograph from me and studies it. After a moment she sits down on the bed and lowers her head over the picture. After staring at it for a moment, she looks up at me.

'Where did you get this?'

'I took it myself.'

'Where?'

'In that building out the back with the old motors.'

'When?'

'Last night.'

I hand her the rest of the photographs. She looks at each one in turn, then she hangs her head, leans forward with her elbows on her knees, and gives a long sigh.

After a few moments, a clock on the mantlepiece makes a quiet little ding. Lady Northrup sits up straight and pulls her shoulders back. Her face seems to narrow as she purses her lips and fixes me with a stern look.

'Who are you?'

'Does it matter?'

'Are you alone?'

'Yes.'

'I suppose you want money.'

'No.'

'What then?'

'Do you know Nicholas Boulter?'

'I do.'

'He works for MI6, but he's spying for the Russians. Your husband knows full well that he's a spy, and he can prove it, but he won't. Nick Boulter's supplying him with dead girls to fuck provided he keeps it dark. If you get Boulter arrested and charged with high treason, those photographs, and the ones like them that I've hidden somewhere else, will be given to you. They're Polaroid shots, so there are no copies or negatives. Once you get rid of the girls' bodies and the artworks and the bits and pieces out there, there'll be no more evidence of your old man's twisted doings.'

'And you just want Boulter charged with treason?'

'Yes.'

'Your patriotism does you credit.'

'It's not that simple.'

'Oh?'

'Boulter knows I've rumbled him and he's out to kill me.'

'I see.'

Lady Northrup glances at the photographs again. She turns to Mary.

'Go and find Symmonds and tell him to bring His Lordship here immediately.'

Mary bobs a curtsy and leaves. Lady Northrup goes to her dressing table and sits down. She picks up a powder puff and dusts it over her face. She applies a pencil to her eyebrows and dabs her lips with a tissue. She surveys the result in mirror and then crosses to a cabinet in the corner and picks up a bottle.

'Will you have a drink?'

'Whisky, thanks.'

She pours two large ones, hands one to me, waves me towards a chaise longue in front of the fireplace and sits opposite me in an armchair. We both take a good drink.

'Who else knows about this?' she asks.

'Only Mary, and your man Symmonds. The man who supplied the girls is dead.'

'There's been more than one girl?'

'Oh yes.'

She looks away, lowers her head, and grips the arm of the chair. After a moment she takes another drink.

'How do I know I can trust you?'

'You don't need to.'

'Why?'

'Like I said, once you've got the photographs, and the bodies are gone, there's no evidence.

'Any allegations from someone like me against a man like your husband will be laughed at.'

That seems to satisfy her and she drains her glass, goes back to the cabinet and pours another one. As she turns round and offers me the bottle, the door opens and the Marquess walks in in his dressing gown, followed by Symmonds. The Marquess sees me and turns pale as a ghost.

Symmonds bows his head and steps back.

Lady Northrup stands in front of her husband

and shows him a picture. As he opens his mouth to speak, she fetches him a smack across the face that sends him staggering, then she gives Symmonds a kick in the balls that has him doubled over and moaning in pain. She grabs the Marquess by the collar and throws him onto the chaise longue where he sits whimpering, his head in his hands. She turns to me.

'Kindly wait for me in my drawing room.'

I hold out my hand and she gives me the photographs. She looks at Mary and says, 'Make sure our guest has everything she needs.'

Mary opens a door at the back of the room and I follow her into a dressing room and through another door into a lounge, with a sofa and armchairs, and a writing desk in the corner, under a window. I go and look out over the moonlit parkland rolling away from the front of the house. I'm thinking how you can be born to all this and still be squalid and rotten and filthy, but if you're the gentry you've got a better chance of getting away with it. A deer scampers out from behind some trees and stops on the lawn as if it's listening for something, then it runs off into the woods. Mary comes and stands next to me.

'Muntjac,' she says.

I turn and look at her.

'A kind of little deer.'

'Oh,' I say.

We look out at the moonlit landscape. I can feel her arm touching mine. I take her hand. 'I know what it took for you to do that.'

She lowers her eyes. I can feel her starting to cry. I put a hand on her shoulder and she leans

277

into me.

'She was so lovely.'

I put my arms round her, gently rub her back. 'At least they can't hurt her any more.'

She gives way to her tears and I guide her to the sofa and sit down beside her. After a bit she stops crying and dries her eyes.

'We should go to the police. He ought to be put in prison for what he's done.'

'Let's wait and see what Her Ladyship says first.'

After a moment she nods. 'You done a good thing.'

'It's not over yet.'

'You don't think...?'

'We'll see.'

As I say it, the door opens and Lady Northrup strides in and sits in an armchair opposite.

She looks at us both for a moment before speaking.

'Mary, would you wait outside, until I call you?'

'Yes, my lady.'

Mary stands, curtsies, and leaves the room. Lady Northrup takes a couple of breaths and looks steadily at me.

'Your demands are to be met. Evidence will be presented to the police within the hour and Boulter will be arrested and charged with high treason. I shall receive a telephone call from the Commissioner of Police confirming the arrest, to which you can be party. How soon can you produce the remaining photographs?'

'Within the hour.'

'You will bring them here to me.'

'What about the bodies?'

'Arrangements are being made.'

'There's something else.'

'What?'

'Mary.'

'Yes. Since you ask, I propose to release her from my employment, give her the title to a cottage on our Northumberland estate, and a stipend which will see her comfortable for life, in return for her discretion and as a reward for the judgement she has shown in this regrettable matter. I trust that is satisfactory.'

'It'll do.'

'There is a bedroom next door to the left where you may like to wait until the Commissioner telephones. I shall send for you directly I receive his call.'

I nod and stand up to leave.

'Would you send Mary in please?'

28

I'm lying on the bed in the room next door wondering what can go wrong. I've unlocked the window and opened it and I reckon I can get out and down a drainpipe in case Lady N has second thoughts and decides to set the dogs on me. She's quite a piece of work and I wouldn't put it past her but she knows there are more photographs out there and she probably won't risk it.

There's a knock at the door. I slide off the bed and open it. Mary is there looking worried and confused. I pull her inside, close the door, sit next to her on the bed.

'What's wrong?'

'She's giving me a house.'

'I know, she told me.'

'I don't deserve it. It's not right.'

'Of course you do. You took a big risk and did the right thing and she respects you for that.'

She looks down at her hands in her lap. 'Do you think?'

'I know she does, and I do too. If it hadn't been for you I would have wasted my time with the Viscount and might well have ended up in a painting myself.'

I feel her tremble beside me. I put my arm round her and feel how thin and fragile she is. 'They're powerful, frightening people, and they've made you feel that they're better than you, but they're not. You've stood up for what's right and stopped more lovely girls like Julie being murdered to satisfy an evil old pervert. Her Ladyship's rewarding you for that and you should be proud of yourself and take what she's giving you.'

She seems to think about what I've said, then she looks at me and gives a little smile. 'I could have a dog.'

'Of course you could.'

'Will you come and see me?'

'I'd love to.'

I feel her relax and calm down and I'm wondering if it's safe for her to go to her room. I reckon Lady N's on the level, as I've still got the photographs.

'I'll be all right, if you want to go off to bed.'

She looks at the door and then at me. 'Can I stay with you?'

'Of course you can.'

I lay her gently back on the bed and put the quilt over her. I'm tempted to get in next to her but I reckon Her Ladyship might not be best pleased to find me in bed with her girlfriend. I sit in an armchair beside the fireplace, put a cushion behind my head, and close my eyes.

The head of the man with the shotgun is sticking out of the top of an enormous teapot, and he's looking at me and smiling his creepy smile while Symmonds pushes the teapot across a beach towards a lake where the Marquess is bobbing about in a rubber ring. Lady Northrup dives in and swims towards him and she hits him on the head and pushes him under the water. The teapot's floating towards her and she starts banging on the side of it and Symmonds is pulling me towards the water. I fall in and then I'm awake. I'm looking at Mary's face, and she's holding my arm and pointing at the door.

The door opens. Lady Northrup comes in and says, 'Go to your room Mary.'

Mary gives me a parting look and leaves. Lady Northrup turns on her heel and I follow her along the corridor and into her room. She goes to the bedside table, picks up the telephone receiver that's lying on the table and beckons me to stand beside her. She puts the receiver to her ear and angles it so that I can hear as well.

'Forgive me, Commissioner. Please continue.'

'As I was saying, Your Ladyship, Boulter is being held at Bow Street police station, having been

281

arrested and charged with high treason. He was located at an address in south London and a witness is being interviewed with a view to adding a charge of sodomy.'

'Indeed.'

'Apparently it was quite disgusting.'

'How unpleasant for the arresting officers.'

'Quite. It's normally the purview of the Vice Squad, who are inured to such things. However, the documents regarding Boulter that we have received from His Lordship's office will be more than sufficient to ensure a swift prosecution. I trust that is satisfactory.'

'Indeed it is Malcolm. Thank you for informing me. I apologise once more for disturbing you at such an ungodly hour, and I hope we shall see you at a shoot very soon.'

'I look forward to it Your Ladyship.'

'Goodbye.'

She puts the receiver down, turns to me, and I realise I've been pressed right up against her, while I've been trying to catch what's been said. As I back off, she snorts.

'I didn't know he was a queer.'

I give a slight nod of the head and wait while she lights a cigarette. I hear a cock crowing and I look past her to the window where dawn's breaking. She flicks ash.

'Are you satisfied?'

'Yes,' I say.

'Give me the photographs, and go and get the other ones. I will wait for you here.'

I walk along the corridor towards the kitchen. A man in a waistcoat and a white shirt comes towards me with an armful of riding boots. I stand back to let him pass and walk out of the back door. The sun's risen, the stables are open and a groom is leading out a beautiful brown horse with a flowing mane and white fur on its face and its ankles. I've never seen a horse so tall and I watch as he mounts up and trots off into a field beside the stables.

I head into the woods and up over the low hill towards shotgun man's cottage. I feel a great relief knowing that Nick's banged up in Bow Street. Ginger and his cronies will most likely desert him now, and scurry back into the woodwork.

Squirrels are scampering about and leaping up into the trees, and a little brown thing, like a long furry sausage with short legs and a white bib, runs across the path in front of me. The birds are giving it full volume and the sun is shining through the trees. I just want to keep walking on through the woods to a place where there are no spies or dead girls or posh people, and everything's nice and peaceful.

The man with the shotgun is standing under a tree beside his cottage. As I get near he walks to the front door, opens it, and stands aside to let me go in. The fire's still burning and I go and stand near it. As I'm warming my hands, I hear the door close.

'What happened?' the man asks.

'It's stopped.'

'You sure?'

'As soon as I give Her Ladyship those last two photographs.'

'Her Ladyship eh?'

I nod.

'You went to the top then.'

I nod towards the clock on the mantlepiece. 'I need those pictures I left with you.'

He smiles. 'I ain't stupid.'

He leans his shotgun against the wall by the door, walks to the corner of the room and takes a hunting knife out of his belt. He kneels down, prises up a short floorboard, takes out the photographs, replaces the board, and treads it into place. He turns and looks me hard in the eye.

'You sure it's done?'

'Yes.'

He's gone very still, his cold grey eyes are boring into me, and the firelight's glinting on the knife in his hand. Just as I'm wondering whether I can get to the shotgun before he can, his face breaks into a smile.

'You done good.'

He sheaths his knife, joins me by the fire and puts the photographs in my hand. He nods his head, goes to the door and opens it. As I go past him he says, 'I knew you was all right when I seen you first.'

As I near the stables I see horses being led out into the field and some coming back across the yard and round the side of the house. I weave my way round them, and in through the back door. The kitchen is busy, and there's a lovely smell of bacon wafting into the corridor. People are coming and going with trays and I'm amazed at the number of servants I pass as I make my way up to Lady Northrup's room. I knock on the door.

'Enter.'

I go in and she's standing by the drinks cabinet in a black jacket, a white shirt, riding breeches and shiny black boots. She's holding a top hat and a riding crop in one hand and a drink in the other.

'Good. You're here,' she says.

I take the photographs out of my back pocket and hand them to her. She looks at each of them, gives a snort, smacks her boot with the riding crop, and puts them in a drawer of the cabinet.

'I think that concludes our business?'

'I think it does.'

'May I offer you a car to take you somewhere?'

'No thanks, I've got one nearby.'

'In that case, I shall bid you goodbye.'

She puts her top hat on her head, strides to the door and opens it for me. I nod to her and walk fast along the corridor towards the back of the house. A couple of gents in riding clothes walk past me. I look over my shoulder as Lady Northrup comes out of her room, greets them, and walks with them towards the main staircase. As I turn into the next corridor I look out of the window and see a big crowd of huntsmen and women on horseback gathered in front of the house. They're chatting away to each other and there are footmen in uniform and maids moving among them with drinks on silver trays, and there's a pack of dogs milling about on the lawn. The Marquess is there on a beautiful white horse talking to a rider in a bright red jacket with a hunting horn in his hand. Symmonds is standing nearby with a tray. I see Her Ladyship come out of the front door and mount up. She takes a glass and greets a woman with red hair who says something that makes her laugh.

On the way down the stairs, I wonder if I should try and find Mary to make sure she's all right, but I decide that the sooner I'm away from here the better and make for the back door. The courtyard's empty, apart from a young lad sweeping up, and I head off towards the road to the back gate. As I come out from behind the stables I hear the sound of hunting horns and dogs barking, and all at once the whole hunt comes round the corner of the brick building and rumbles past really close in front of me. I step back behind the corner and watch the mass of horses, boots and top hats trundle by I can feel how exciting it must be to be part of it, as long as you don't happen to be a fox.

The last of the hunters go past and I'm just about to come out from behind the building when a group of girls on ponies come round the corner, following the hunt. I step back again, and I nearly fall over when I recognise Annabelle at the back of the group, and next to her, on a dappled grey pony is Georgie.

I watch her trotting away after the hunt and turning to talk to Annabelle as she goes. I'm just hoping she doesn't fall off, and I'm glad to see that when the hunters turn off to the right, along a track into the woods, the pony group slow down to a walk and keep straight on along the side of a field of grass. I wait until they're out of sight then I cross the yard and walk through the trees alongside the road to the back gate. As I walk I'm wondering if Annabelle is the Viscount's daughter. I can look it up in that book Lizzie's got that has all the toffs' names in when I get back. If she is his daughter, I hope she never finds out what her grandfather got up to of a night.

The Anglia's where I left it in the wood and I get in, put the wires together and fire it up. I back it up onto the road, point the front end at London and put my foot down. The sun's shining, Georgie's enjoying herself, and there'll be no more dead girls underneath the old cars.

I turn on the radio and twiddle the dial until I get Elvis giving me a bit of Jailhouse Rock.

It feels good to be back in the city as I muscle through the stroppy West London traffic. I dump the Anglia in a side street off Uxbridge Road, wipe it clean of prints and get a cab to Maida Vale. I tell him to drop me at the lights on Edgware Road. I find a call box and dial Tony Farina's number. I tell him that Heinz is gone and arrange to go and collect my wages. I walk the rest of the way to the flats, checking for any lurkers with ginger hair. All looks clear, so I go into the foyer. Dennis looks up from behind the desk.

'Morning miss,' he says, as he crosses to the lift. I can see he wants to ask me why I look as if I've been dragged through a hedge backwards, and I'm glad he thinks better of it.

'How are you Dennis?' I ask, as he presses the lift button.

'Right as rain now, thank you miss.'

The lift arrives, he opens the gate and I put a ten bob note in his hand to end the conversation, and step into the lift.

'Thanks very much miss,' he says, as he closes the gate behind me.

I get off at my floor, step onto the carpet, and feel glad to be home. I stop at Lizzie's door and knock softly. A moment later the door opens and she's there, beautiful as ever, in her silk dressing gown.

Her face lights up in a smile, she looks me up and down, pulls me to her and folds me in her arms. Without a word, she takes me to the bathroom, turns on the hot tap, stands me by the bath and slowly takes my clothes off, kissing me all over as she does so. By the time I'm undressed, and she's slipped off her dressing gown and her bra and pants, the bath's full. She turns the taps off, helps me into the water, and disappears out of door. Moments later she comes back with two glasses of whisky, hands one to me, and slips into the bath.

After the whisky and the warm water have soaked away the miles and the bruises, I tell her everything that went on at Ringwood. By the time I've finished the story the water's nearly cold, the whisky's finished, and her eyes are wide.

'Those people, eh?'

'I know,' I say.

'Do you think Georgie's all right down there?'

'Lady Northrup can't know she's connected with me, and I reckon she's straight up anyway.'

'Sounds like she is, the way she got Nick banged up in two minutes flat.'

'Right.'

'What about that old butler?'

'He just does what he's told.'

288

We get out of the bath and dry each other with big soft towels. The phone rings and Lizzie goes into the hall and answers it. She gives her number and then I hear her say, 'I'll be free in a couple of hours.' After a pause, she says, 'Ok, I'll expect you then.'

I hear the click as she puts the phone down. I drop my towel on a chair, go into the hall and follow her into the bedroom. We slide between the sheets, I melt into her dreamy softness and we make love.

A week later, I'm sitting with Lizzie in Derry and Toms roof garden in Kensington High Street, having a bit of lunch and a glass of wine after a shopping spree with the money I've been paid by Tony Farina. It's a lovely day and London's looking handsome in the sunshine.

I look round for the waitress to order some more wine and catch sight of the headline on a Daily Telegraph that's lying on the next table – 'Russian spy defects to Moscow.'

I pick it up, and read:

"A senior MI6 officer who was under arrest, awaiting trial for high treason, has escaped from Wormwood Scrubs Prison and is believed to have travelled to Moscow, where he is under the protection of the KGB. Sources have revealed that the British-born officer had been working as a double agent for some years prior to his recent arrest. A government enquiry has been launched to ascertain how he was able to betray his country for so long."

It then goes on about George Blake, the spy who got done last May and given forty-two years. I pass the paper over to Lizzie and she reads a bit and dumps it on the table.

'They've sprung him, haven't they?'

'You reckon?'

'There's no other way he could have got out of the Scrubs so quick.'

'It's because he would have taken too many down with him.'

'That's it.'

'So they get rid of him.'

'Easy as that.'

Lizzie's got a customer when we get back, so I go into my flat, dump the bags in the hall and put the kettle on. A letter I got from Georgie the other day is lying on the kitchen table. I pick it up and read again about how she's getting on much better at the school now. She tells me what a nice weekend she'd had at Annabelle's big house in the country, and how she'd been taught how to ride a pony, and that she and Annabelle and some other girls had followed the hunt when it set off, and then gone off for a hack. I feel relieved that she's settled in at the school, that she's got a good friend, and that she knows nothing about what went on that weekend.

I put down the letter and fill the teapot. I pick up the bags from the hall, go through to the bedroom and start to unpack the clothes that I've bought. The Daily Telegraph is in one of the Harrods bags. I throw it on the bed but it slips off onto the floor and falls open. I see something familiar, pick it up, and I'm looking at a picture of Ringwood. Underneath, it reads:

"A catastrophic fire has destroyed the motor museum at Ringwood Hall in Berkshire. The museum was housed in a building adjacent to the Hall and was home to a fine collection of classic cars and motorcycles belonging to the Marquess of Denby. The fire is said to have razed the building to the ground but left the Hall and other buildings undamaged. The cause of the fire remains unknown."

I chuck the paper on the bed and take a slinky black Dior dress out of its bag. I hold it up in front of me, smooth it into the curves of my body and look in the mirror.

The publishers hope that this book has given you enjoyable reading. Large Print Books are especially designed to be as easy to see and hold as possible. If you wish a complete list of our books please ask at your local library or write directly to:

Magna Large Print Books
Magna House, Long Preston,
Skipton, North Yorkshire.
BD23 4ND

This Large Print Book for the partially sighted, who cannot read normal print, is published under the auspices of

THE ULVERSCROFT FOUNDATION